THE SUBURBAN SEDUCCIÓN

A NOVEL

by

DEBRA MARES

A JUSTICIA HOUSE BOOK

This is a work of fiction. All the characters, organizations, and events portrayed in this novel are either products of the author's imagination or are used fictionally.

The Suburban Seducción

A JUSTICIA HOUSE BOOK
303 Broadway, Suite 104-103
Laguna Beach, California 92651

ISBN: 978-0-9850893-6-8

Book cover design by Debra Mares

Printed in the United States of America

for
Nana

ACKNOWLEDGEMENTS

Thank you to Rachael Cianfrani, for your keen sense of the criminal justice system, defense tactical insight and amazing sense of story, Terrie Barna for your editorial expertise, Dr. Joseph Cohen, for your medical and forensic brilliance, Kacey Sutton for your encouragement to get into the mind of a killer, Mel Berger and Kathleen Breaux, for your literary direction, Robert Garrett, for your loving support, Mom, Dad, Suzanne, Christina, Coochie, Lucinda, Christian, Olivia, David & WoMen Wonder Writers, for your familyhood.

Many murderers posses antisocial tendencies, which our criminal justice system can adequately address. But then there are those for which our system is ill-equipped. They are the kind raging inside, who hurt because they've been hurt. The Suburban Seducción is a glimpse into the world of a killer and those who work to serve justice by stopping him.

—DEBRA MARES, AUTHOR
THE SUBURBAN SEDUCCIÓN

THE SUBURBAN SEDUCCIÓN

1

FIRST KILL

Lloyd Gil thumbs through the book, *Who was Frida Kahlo: The Biography of a 20th Century Mexican Painter*, and places it down on the mahogany coffee table in front of him. He has been stalking and shadowing Annabelle Phillips for five long weeks. Today, he is going to murder the thirty-eight-year-old pregnant Tuckford County housewife in first degree fashion, strangling her with his own bare hands then assaulting her sexually, and no one will be able to figure out why. This is the most important part of avoiding detection as a killer.

Lloyd reclines back into Annabelle's plush, golden couch, resting his hands behind his head in a relaxing manner. His muscular arms are still sore from yesterday's workout, and she innocently gazes at him. She is falling for Lloyd's green eyes, light skin, and slender but toned body, which fills out his tailored, light grey, classic suit.

He watches her lose herself in his presence as she sizes him up and down. It is a little after two in the afternoon, and she still has forty minutes before her three-year-old child will be up from her nap in the next room.

Annabelle's husband left town on business five weeks ago around the same time she discovered she was pregnant and met Lloyd. And she craves adult attention, especially by a man as good-looking as Lloyd. He knows this and he has timed this perfectly. He has flirted, intrigued and built up his new customer Annabelle over the last five weeks after she met him at the local diner and hired him to design her home computer system. Her lust, cravings, and natural female desires will lead to her own demise. At least, that is what Lloyd Gil rationalizes in his sick and demented mind.

A portrait hangs above the fireplace mantle. It is of Annabelle and her husband. Her husband, who looks in his forties, is tan, athletic, and sports a five o'clock shadow. He is a manly man. His wavy, golden-brown hair makes him the all-American husband. He is the perfect man for Annabelle, or so she told herself before marrying him. He has a heart of gold and will do anything for her. They are a match made in heaven.

They have an active sex life, usually making love each morning. It was something Annabelle instituted early on in the marriage with her high sex drive. And her husband willingly complies, as he does with anything that makes her happy. The perfection of this life is what Lloyd resents the most.

In fact, every bit of it disgusts him, especially the fact she is three months pregnant. He managed to have Annabelle divulge many private details of her life in the brief weeks they became acquainted at Hal's Diner, where she waits tables.

He has a way with women, even those who are loyal to their husbands. He knows this housewife is in her sexual peak, and she is curious about things she can never explore with her husband. Men in the finer parts of South Tuckford County are traditional. And all this is fine with women like Annabelle, except when men like Lloyd come around.

She hasn't been moved by a man since her junior college days, where she developed a love for poetry and a curiosity in the lives of writers and political activists. Lloyd is the first person in years that she has come across who can hold a conversation on a Mexican painter, and she is completely mesmerized.

Lloyd knows how to play the game. After all, he knows everything he needs to know about Annabelle and how to pull off murdering her, which he has spent hours playing out in his mind and planning. Now, he just needs to find the right time, which usually comes after building an adequate rapport and level of confidence. This right time is thrusting upon them right about now.

The two sit side by side in her home, sipping sparkling water and discussing the bisexual adventures of Frida Kahlo in the 1900s. This type of intellectual stimulation is something women who had settled for less in life, fantasize about doing, but rarely have such opportunities. Lloyd knows this and he takes advantage of it to carry out his ultimate fantasy—murdering the young pregnant housewives of South Tuckford County.

Lloyd Gil concentrates intensely on Annabelle. He tries not to move his head too much, because he doesn't want his dark brown hairpiece to fall off, which he set firmly over his blond hair this morning. He pushes up his dark-rimmed glasses, pretending to refocus his sight.

He doesn't really wear glasses.

He fears any moment that Annabelle's child will awake or she will recognize him as a local resident who lives a couple blocks away near Canyon Base Lake. This disguise is a very big part of his facade. He carries with him the book, the intellectual conversation, his pen, and a journal. It is all a ploy.

At 2:20 p.m., he leans over to Annabelle as he sips from the his glass engorged with sparkling water. Lloyd whispers into her ear how young she looks, how he can't believe how well-educated she is, and how in awe he is of her knowledge about a Mexican painter. He stares at her and her beautiful, dyed blonde hair, which is curled and falling below her shoulders. He focuses in on her lips, still shining from the lip gloss she smoothed on earlier during their walk from the computer store to her house. He imagines biting on her lower lip.

He hears a subtle cry from the next room. Annabelle's child begins to stir.

His window of opportunity is closing.

The sound of the cry disturbs him immensely, and he decides at this moment that Annabelle and her unborn child will pay for his rage.

The rush of adrenaline intoxicates him. His heart beats harder and faster, raising his blood pressure.

He reaches over and grabs her neck—violently. She looks at him in disbelief and begins resisting—the worst kind of reaction at all.

"You shouldn't have rejected me. Did you hear me?" Lloyd threatens, squeezing her neck tightly and not letting go. She struggles tremendously until her oxygen depletes and she loses consciousness. He then turns his attention to her vaginal area, violating her with a flashlight.

He hears nothing but a swishing sound of water flooding his ears. It's the sound of rage.

Could he actually get away with the murder of a young, beautiful housewife? Lloyd is sure he can. After all, he has planned this murder and believes he can outsmart law enforcement. And oftentimes, killers like him do get away with murder.

2

FIRST SUBMISSION

Ten years later, Lloyd Gil contemplates continuing his terrifying streak only blocks away from where he killed Annabelle Phillips. Lloyd nestles his nose into Eva's neck. Her collarbone pokes into his eye as she begins reading from *Who Was Pablo Picasso?*

She and Lloyd had just met the day before at a local art store. Her soft and supple, cream-colored skin excites Lloyd wildly. He traces her collarbone with his pointer finger and then around the brown freckles spotting her neck, before moving to the large, raspberry-colored birthmark staining the whole left side of her face. Her voice is soothing and romantic as she reads to him in a child-like but sexual tone from the book Lloyd had gifted her the day before.

Eva was barely familiar with Pablo Picasso, a nineteenth century Spanish painter. After all, she was not very educated. Recently, she had begun taking local community college courses in psychology; but even in the short amount of time

Lloyd knew her, he realized she didn't have it in her to reach her goal in becoming a Marriage and Family Therapist. Her past debilitated her; she left home at eighteen after finally growing tired of all the beatings endured by her highly domineering mother through most of her childhood.

Eva wanted to trust again and she had decided she was going to do that starting with the next man she met. And it happened to be Lloyd. Since meeting yesterday, she had fantasized about the possibility of him making love to her. He had led her to believe he was single, available, and finally ready to settle down. None of this was true.

Lloyd looks straight into her eyes and tells her sternly to put the book down.

She complies. After all, she knew very well how to follow orders, being forced into submission for years, usually at night, in the basement after her mother's whiskey binges.

Eva doesn't fit the type of woman Lloyd has fantasized about murdering over the past ten years. She has straight, auburn-colored hair, not the blonde flowing and curly kind. She has freckles and a disturbing birthmark on her face, not the flawless picture-perfect kind of skin. She is physically strong, not thin and slight. She is simple and subdued, not overly stimulated by intellectual conversation. But most importantly, she is childless and cannot bear children.

Lloyd has fantasized about murdering those who were feeling the pressure of their biological clocks. After all, Lloyd wanted to possess everything that was not his, including a woman's fertility.

Lloyd begins to lose himself in Eva's soothing voice.

He straightens himself up, hearing a helicopter above the house. The roaring engines from cars speeding down the street follow. Eva turns on the television to a local station and watches her neighborhood project on the screen.

"Look! Do you think something happened right here?" asks Eva.

Lloyd freezes, pushes up his glasses, and takes a deep breath, in and out.

"Turn off the television," he demands.

Eva complies.

"Take me to your room," he says unexpectedly.

Eva complies, taking his hand and leading him past her bedroom to a back guest room that has a door leading outside.

"Take it off," says Lloyd aggressively, motioning at Eva's clothes.

Slowly, trepidatiously, and innocently, Eva complies. She removes her t-shirt, her cropped pants, her bra and underwear. She doesn't question him.

He begins moving towards her.

Eva looks at the door, pauses, looks at him, and begins to move desperately for the exit.

"WHAT ARE YOU DOING?" he screams.

He notices that his hand is shaking.

"DON'T REJECT ME, EVA!" Lloyd blurts out.

Within seconds, he pins her to the bed with his body, burying her face into a quilt. He wraps his hands firmly around her neck then releases them. He keeps doing this, knowing Eva is slightly going in and out of consciousness. He is stimulated by her heavy breathing patterns.

"Lloyd," whispers Eva, during one of his releases.

He hates hearing his name said like this.

He swings Eva around to face him, gripping the hair on the back of her head tightly and stares at the scar on the side of Eva's pelvis.

"It's from my surgery," she says calmly, reminding Lloyd of her hysterectomy she confided in him earlier.

Eva appears unaffected, unfrightened, and almost at ease.

"You don't have to do this," she starts.   "Touch me anywhere you want. Take me. Just don't kill me. I'm yours. I won't ever tell anyone. Just don't leave me."

Lloyd removes his pants and has his way with her for the next hour while helicopters and police cars race through the neighborhood. Eva submits herself entirely to him. In return, he spares her life.

3

FIRST RETURN

At Lloyd's insistence, Eva walks reluctantly hand-in-hand with him in her poncho and boots, to the corner of the block. She is both frightened but intrigued by Lloyd who violated her over the last hour. Ten years earlier Lloyd had walked this same path with Annabelle, but it feels like yesterday and he enjoys the memory of it all. Yellow crime scene tape stretches from Annabelle's house all the way down to the corner mailbox where they are standing.

A police car with an open door blocks the street from any cars that may try to enter. The car is unmanned.

Lloyd takes careful mental notes of everyone on scene. Lloyd is overly curious about what if anything had happened at the same house he murdered Annabelle at.

Investigator Marty Kaplan stands in the middle of the street facing Annabelle's home and then looks directly towards Lloyd and Eva.

"They're probably wondering if we live in the area or if we need to get back into our home," says Eva.

Marty Kaplan has been a Special Homicide Team detective in Tuckford County for twenty years. He is nearing retirement, but still has the get-'em attitude of a young and hungry detective. He was the same detective who worked Annabelle Phillip's unsolved murder. He's especially eager to solve the sex crimes he investigates and seemed even more so for the murder of a young, innocent, and beautiful woman like Annabelle.

A Ford pickup truck rounds the corner quickly before coming to a screeching halt.

A man in his forties, semi-tall, with tan skin and a slightly bearded face, jumps out of the truck. He has golden brown, wavy hair, which he begins running his hands through.

Lloyd recognizes him as the same man in the portrait inside Annabelle's house ten years ago. He has gained weight, grown a belly, and his clothes are wrinkled.

It's her husband.

The man makes his way desperately towards the investigator, leaping over the yellow crime scene tape.

Yells from the detectives startle everyone.

"STAND BACK!"

"STAY RIGHT WHERE YOU ARE!"

"GET BACK!"

A detective begins drawing his service weapon.

Investigator Kaplan motions for the detective to stop.

"Tim Phillips? Marty Kaplan," says Investigator Kaplan, identifying himself. "I need you to stand right where you are. This is a crime scene and we don't want the evidence tampered with," Kaplan yells in a firm voice.

Annabelle's husband falls to the ground on both knees and pulls the front of his long wavy hair, cupping his eyes with his palms. He begins weeping and jerking his body back and forth.

The cries coming from him are uncontrollable. He begins yelling out Annabelle's name.

"HAVE YOU FOUND THAT BASTARD? PLEASE TELL ME, TELL ME YOU FOUND HIM!" Tim yells uncontrollably.

Lloyd grunts a noise that sounds like a laugh, which he follows up with a coughing sound as if to cover it up.

Eva looks at him, startled.

"Who is that?" asks Eva quietly.

"Isn't it obvious? That's the dead lady's husband. He probably killed another woman," says Lloyd, loud enough for everyone to hear.

"What dead lady?" whispers Eva, curiously looking at Lloyd.

The husband looks back at Lloyd, glaring at him.

"Screw you. Get outta here. And don't laugh at a man who lost his wife!" yells Tim aggressively, still on his knees.

Marty moves toward Tim and places his hand on his upper back, patting him while he continues sobbing. Marty doesn't take his eyes off Lloyd, who stands staring back.

After a few moments, Marty begins to approach Lloyd.

"Shhhh. Just let me do the talking," says Lloyd quietly to Eva.

"What's your interest here?" asks Marty in a commanding voice.

"Just observing. It's not every day police are crawling around the neighborhood. Did he kill another woman?" says Lloyd coolly.

"We're investigating," says Marty.

"A new one or the old one?" Lloyd says sarcastically.

"I can't disclose that. Please respect the man and let us do our job," says Marty, walking away and glaring at Lloyd with undetermined suspicion.

"Shit," says Lloyd under his breath.

"Did he kill someone before?" asks Eva.

"Yeah, his wife," lies Lloyd.

"And now another one?"

"Who knows," Lloyd says worriedly.

Lloyd and Eva turn back to walk back towards her house.

4

FIRST HOME RUN

Lloyd turns the deadbolt unlocking the front door of his house.   Part of coming home causes his memory of murdering Annabelle a decade ago to subside. A part of Lloyd feels relieved and another part feels worried about seeing police combing through the old murder scene an hour ago. But overall, Lloyd enjoys this homicidal memory.

As he walks inside, his frustration sets in.

Janice used to be a pleasant sight for Lloyd to come home to, but that too has faded into the distant past.   Her long, dark brown hair and perky breasts were initially what attracted him to her.   And he tried to do the right thing by her and live the right way.   He got married, bought a house, and landed a good job in Tuckford County as a software account executive.   Early on in their marriage, he was faithful to Janice and missed her on his frequent business trips. Now, he views his travel as an opportunity to have casual one night stands and hire prostitutes who come to his hotel rooms.

The smell of a roasting chicken fills the room. If Janice knew for one moment what Lloyd had done in the past, she would leave him. Despite her naivety, she is not an enabler. But Lloyd likes that she isn't curious, and never questions his whereabouts, lateness, or intentions with her. As long as his sales revenue from Software Solutions, Inc. pays for her Range Rover, spa visits, and couture fashion, she asks no questions. She never has.

Lloyd cares for her, or at least that is what he tells himself. The truth is that he knows very little about caring for another person.

Janice was the first woman who made him feel important and saved him from a path of self-destruction shortly after killing Annabelle.

After greeting Janice with a kiss, Lloyd removes his necktie and walks into the living room.

Wedding pictures of the two and her family crowd the mantle, sitting in black frames perfectly situated based on height. Janice has a keen eye for decorating, something that matters tremendously to the housewives in Tuckford County.

The bamboo floors give the home a clean, rustic feel and nicely contrast the white walls splashed with black-framed animal sketch art. The home boasts a modern farm chic feel with throw rugs and blankets warming the rooms.

Lloyd makes it into his office and walks up to his standing desk, kicking off his shoes and signing into his desktop computer, where he surfs the Internet to the Tuckford Press website.

"Decade Old Case Reopened After New Clue Discovered" sprawls across the online news heading.

He begins to read the caption:

Canyon Base Police reopening possible homicide of 38-year-old woman Annabelle Phillips left for dead in the Orange Groves a decade ago. Police asking the public for new information. Call 800-233-3454 with information.

Lloyd becomes startled, feeling Janice's hand on his shoulder, not realizing she has crept up behind him.

"Just in time. The chicken is in the oven. We have forty-five minutes until dinner," says Janice provocatively as she unbuckles Lloyd's pants from behind.

"Don't ever do that again. You scared me," he snaps.

"Sorry darling, I thought you noticed me," she says sincerely. "What are you looking at?" she asks curiously.

"What do you do all day?" Lloyd asks rudely, suggesting his displeasure with the way she spends her time.

"Darling, calm down. I've been cooking for us. Earlier, I was over at Bloomingdale's returning some items, plus I wanted to pick up a gift for Mom. What's been going on?" she asks obligingly.

"Police are investigating an old murder," says Lloyd, pointing at the screen.

"Where did that happen?"

"I guess on the 4500 block of Wesley. She was killed at her home, dumped in the Orange Groves."

"That's around the block. Did they give any more details?" continues Janice.

"No," he says curtly.

"Well, let me look at the article, is there a photo of the house or anything?" she asks, looking at the screen.

"You don't need a photo. All the houses look the same around here. White picket fence, red door, suburban in the driveway," says Lloyd disgustedly.

Lloyd walks away from the computer towards their bedroom. Janice scans the article.

There is no mention of Annabelle being killed at her home in the article. This is the first slip-up Lloyd has made, ever, with Janice.

In his bedroom, Lloyd begins unbuttoning his dress shirt and studying his face in the closet sliding door mirror.

Lloyd is startled yet again.

"Sweetie, is that blood on the back of your shirt?" Janice asks calmly, but in a concerned tone.

Lloyd clenches his fists and looks up at Janice in the reflection of the mirror.

He regains his composure, noticing the blood had oozed from Eva's fingernail scratches during their brief struggle.

"Yes, darling," he starts, patiently. "A ceramic fell from a shelf at the office. It jabbed my back. I didn't realize it punctured me," he says coolly.

"Oh dear, I'll grab a towel," she replies, seemingly relieved.

"No need, sweetie. I'm going to jump in the shower," he says nonchalantly, walking past her into the bathroom and shutting the door behind him.

5

FIRST POSSIBILITY

Lloyd sits alone at Hal's Diner. The smell of grease, bacon, and potatoes suffocate him, seeping into his fine, Italian wool suit.

Disgusted by the dining fare, Lloyd thumbs through the *Tuckford Press*.

He stops at the local news page and reads.

Canyon Base Police canvass the area for clues in cold case murder of 38-year-old pregnant housewife Annabelle Phillips. She was last seen at a local software store shortly before her murder 10 years ago. Police asking the public for help. Call 800-233-3454 with information.

"Sir, can I get you some more coffee? Your egg white omelet should be ready any moment. You said you wanted spinach in there, right?" asks the waitress.

"Yes. And no, I don't need any more coffee. I'm fine for now," he says, reading the narrow, metal name tag attached to her shirt—C A N D Y.

The waitress' lips pucker up at Lloyd. Her skin is flawless and her apron is tied loosely around her waist so as not to restrict her slightly pregnant belly. Her sparkling diamond engagement band practically blinds Lloyd.

"What's a pretty lady with a diamond like that working in a place like this? All the grease in this place might messy up that beautiful hair," says Lloyd flirtatiously.

"Oh, darlin'. Aren't you the sweetest? Where'd you come from?" she asks rhetorically, blushing at Lloyd. "My fiancé owns this diner by the way," she says.

"How'd he get so lucky?" asks Lloyd playfully, removing a book from his satchel and placing it on the table.

The waitress' eyes light up as she studies the title.

"Twenty Love Poems and a Song of Despair. My aunt introduced me to Pablo Neruda when I was seventeen. God rest her soul. She's probably looking down at me right now wondering the same thing. What on earth *am* I doing in this diner? I can just hear her now, 'Follow your dreams Annabelle, get out of Killmore, and don't waste life unfulfilled,'" the waitress says reminiscently, placing her hand on Lloyd's book.

"So what are you waiting for?"

"We're *trying* to leave Killmore. Before this baby comes," she says, pointing at her stomach. "My fiancé is out right now looking at some commercial space in Frenton. We've had a hard time getting our business license out there," she continues.

"Frenton, huh?" says Lloyd before pausing to pretend like he's thinking.

"I've got a good friend on the City Council there," he continues.

"Really?" she says curiously, falling for Lloyd's fraudulent seduction.

"Are you visiting from there? Or do you live here in Killmore?"

"I'm just visiting."

"Well, there's not many fellows carrying around books like *that* in this area," she says, beginning to twirl her long, blonde hair.

Her bare knees brush one another as she stands, smiling at Lloyd.

"ONE SPINACH OMELET!" yells the cook from the kitchen.

"I was gonna say... I haven't seen you in here before," she says, walking away towards the kitchen.

Lloyd watches the waitress' hips sway back and forth as she moves towards the kitchen. He can't take his focus off her panty line, subtly showing through her pants pressed against her taut behind.

A young girl, about fourteen years old, rests back into the booth in front of Lloyd. The older man she has been sitting with makes his way towards the bathroom. His beige, stained shirt, half untucked from his pants, shows off part of his belly.

Lloyd looks away quickly. It's Annabelle Philip's husband.

The young girl begins smiling at Lloyd. Her blonde, flowing hair drapes below her shoulders. Lloyd smiles back, reluctantly. And she looks away.

She reaches up towards her shake and begins to slurp from the straw. When she finishes that, she licks her lips and looks up at Lloyd again.

He watches her intently, aroused. Her crystal blue eyes look familiar.

Her lips, skin, freckles, eyes, and mixture of innocence and seduction overwhelm Lloyd. The mole above her lip gives her a Cindy Crawford look, suggesting she's beyond her years. She bears a striking resemblance to Annabelle, which begins to intrigue Lloyd.

His sexual thoughts are interrupted when she begins waving at him childishly.

"Hi, there!" she says innocently.

Lloyd looks down, beginning to butter his toast, noticing the waitress walking back towards his table.

"I know you," says the young girl.

"No, you don't, sweetie," replies Lloyd calmly, watching the man exit the restroom.

"I swear you look familiar," she says insistently.

"You must be thinking of someone else," replies Lloyd surely.

The man returns to the booth, sliding back into his side, blocking Lloyd's view of the girl.

"Dad, doesn't this guy look familiar?" she says, motioning him towards Lloyd.

"Leave him alone, he's trying to eat his breakfast," he says sternly.

The man turns and looks back at Lloyd.

The two stare at each other for a brief moment.

"I'm sorry. She does this all the time," he says to Lloyd apologetically, not recognizing him.

"Canyon Base! That's where I've seen you! You live in that corner house by the lake!" the young woman says excitedly.

"Ah ha! You're one smart cookie. That's right," says Lloyd, defeated.

After setting down Lloyd's spinach omelet in front of him, the waitress removes a check from her pocket and softly places it on the end of his table.

"Well, I'm glad you're visiting *our* side of town. They do say we have the best shakes in all the county," says the waitress proudly, winking at the young girl.

Lloyd smiles nervously.

"And the most beautiful women in South Tuckford. I'd love to hear what interests you in this particular writer," says Lloyd, pointing at his book still resting on the table.

"And I'd love for you to tell me more about Frenton and your connection with City Council," she says, flirtingly.

"My shift is just about over," she continues quietly, blushing at Lloyd.

Lloyd smiles acceptingly, agreeing to meet her behind the restaurant in five minutes.

After leaving a twenty-dollar bill on top of the check, he walks off and glances at the young girl, who is waving both her hands at him, boasting to her dad how she was right about recognizing him. Her hair flips up and down. Lloyd focuses on her developed breasts, now bouncing in unison as he walks towards the back door.

6

PREPARATION WORK

Lloyd looks aimlessly through the aisles of Hardware Plus. For having been in this store multiple times, Lloyd can't seem to find anything he is looking for.

He scans the aisle.

White teapots, white dish towels, white bath mats, white dish plates.

Checkered coffee cups, checkered saucers, checkered handles on utensils.

The checkers remind him of the tablecloths at Hal's Diner, where he left two hours ago.

Red coffee makers, red sugar bowls, red waffle makers.

Everything is color-coded, matching and coordinated with all the items grouped together on each side of the aisle.

A young mom and her blonde son carefully select items from the purple paisley section.

Lloyd stops and watches her reach to a shelf high above her head. Her breasts fill out her soft yellow sweater. The waist of her white pants are filled out by a slight pregnancy bulge in her stomach area. She reaches and struggles for a small item.

Her son sits on the ground, beginning to open an item sealed in plastic.

"Dillon. We don't open these things," she scolds in a soft voice, barely disciplining the boy.

The woman continues to struggle, reaching for the item.

All this arouses Lloyd.

He focuses in on her stringed panty line, which is showing slightly through her white pants.

He begins to salivate before catching a concerned look from another store customer, who has been watching his amusement.

"Ma'am, can I help you get that down?" says Lloyd, trying to act normally.

The pregnant woman glances at Lloyd, smiling and releasing her heels to the ground, causing her engorged breasts to bounce.

Lloyd cannot remove his eyes from her chest.

They lock eyes and smile at one another as she rests her reaching arm.

"Thank you. I think I got it," she says smiling, as the item begins to fall from the shelf.

It hits her young son, who begins to cry loudly.

Lloyd returns a glare to the observing customer as the perky housewife bends down to console her son.

"I'll get out of your way," says Lloyd, noticing he's completely lost the woman's interest.

He spends the next ten minutes browsing the shelves, unable to find anything he's looking for.

"Sir, can I help you with something?" a woman's voice says from behind him.

"I'm looking for..." Lloyd starts, noticing the clerk's hair tied high in a ponytail. It's blonde and curly.

"I'm looking for tape and cords. Something to tie down a tarp on the back of my truck. I'm moving items," he says casually.

This is not true. Lloyd is not moving, but he loves how easy the story comes to him.

"Sure, it's on aisle nine. I'll take you there," she says.

Lloyd follows her, focusing on her behind, moving back and forth.

"We have duct tape in all kinds of colors and patterns. Cheetah, polka dots, a bunch of fun designs," she says happily.

"Our masking tape is just in this beige color," she says with disappointment, showing it to Lloyd.

"Then we have these bungee tie-downs that would probably work. Do you need a tarp?" she asks.

"That's probably a good idea. And if you have a metal box, that would be great. To put the small things in so they don't fly out when I'm on the freeway," he continues, elaborating the story.

"Oh, right. We have tool boxes and stuff like that on aisle four. Do you want me to show you?" she asks.

"No, I can find them. But thank you for your help," says Lloyd, picking up the solid grey duct tape.

"You don't want to dazzle it up?" she says, grabbing a roll of pink glittered masking tape.

Lloyd imagines the sparkling tape drawing attention to the bottom of Canyon Base Lake.

"The sparkling kind is for amateurs," says Lloyd.

"Or for young, cute blondes," she replies.

"In that case, I'll take five," he says.

7

FIRST CLUE

Lloyd lays his head in Eva's lap on her couch. She massages his head, trying to relieve the pounding headache he's had for the past two hours after leaving the hardware store.

The ruffled curtains on the rods pinned up on Eva's living room windows remind Lloyd of his mother's taste before she met his stepdad. Eva resembles his mother before she began buying into the classy suburbia lifestyle after meeting his stepfather. And this is what Lloyd likes most about Eva.

Lloyd was close to his mother growing up. But being conceived when his mom was only fifteen years old by a married and violent man who was much older than her, seemed to build a rage inside Lloyd that he never fully understand.

Lloyd's mother was punched and kicked so hard in the stomach when she was full term with Lloyd, in a last ditch attempt to abort him. Thankfully, the kick triggered her to pass out and be rushed to the hospital.

Lloyd never discussed what this was like for his mom, but at his wife Janice's urging, he had learned about it from his aunt. His biological father tortured his mother throughout her pregnancy and tried many times to abort Lloyd through violence.

When Lloyd's stepfather entered her life, she grasped at the opportunity to mold herself into a Tuckford County housewife and forget her traumatic past.

But Lloyd didn't mold as well. When his mom married, he began acting out, never having had a positive father figure in his life. He was possessive of his mom and wanted nothing to do with his new stepfather. And his mom couldn't risk this interrupting her new suburban life.

So she kicked Lloyd out of their family home the day after he turned eighteen. And Richard—his new stepbrother—took over his room.

Eva tickles Lloyd's face, circling around his lips, his nose, then up to his eyebrows. It was something his mom used to do when he was a boy. And he asked Eva to do the same to him.

Eva moves her finger down to his collarbone.

"Have you ever loved someone so much you would do anything for them?" she asks.

Lloyd thinks for a moment. A picture of his mom pops in his head. He erases it as quickly as it comes to mind.

"I can't say that I have," he replies unemotionally.

"It's this feeling that no matter what they did, you'd always be there for them," says Eva dreamingly.

"Really? And what does that feel like?"

"Just like this overwhelming sense of security. Like you'll never be alone. Because you know that person would always be there for you."

"Interesting."

Lloyd looks up at framed photos on Eva's bookshelf resting against the wall.

"Who's that girl?" asks Lloyd.

"That's my sister," she replies.

"Your *real* sister?"

"Yep. We were in our teens there. I haven't seen her in years. I used to feel that way about her. Where we'd protect each other no matter what when we were growing up," she says.

"What happened?"

"We grew apart. Our family grew apart."

"Sounds like mine," says Lloyd.

"Do you think families should stay together, Lloyd, no matter what?"

"Not families like ours. They never knew how to be a family. There's nothing to keep together. What happened to her?"

"She got into some bad things. I didn't want to be a part of it anymore. I know if I called her tomorrow, she'd be here for me. Like I'd be there for her. I just couldn't be around her anymore."

"Be around what?"

"She got into prostitution, other stuff like that. I worry about her."

"Have you ever tried that?" asks Lloyd.

"I almost did. Mainly to get close to her. That was one of the reasons I moved here. I wanted to get away from all that. I knew I could fall into it so easily. It's a different world."

"Don't you think it's an interesting one, though? A fascinating one. Where you can be in total control of your body? Sell it, use it."

"It's a sad world to me. Have you ever met a prostitute, Lloyd?"

He looks at the curtains, the framed photos, the cross on the other side of her wall.

"I have," he says.

"Have you used one?"

"I have."

"WHY?" asks Eva, dramatically,

"Eva, a single man like me who travels a lot and isn't in a committed relationship having regular sex, still needs to take care of himself. I'm a man. A lot of men use prostitutes. It's not a big deal."

"Why *are* you still single, Lloyd? You seem like you have everything going for you."

"It's hard for a man like me to commit."

"I wanna ask you something," says Eva, before pausing and looking directly at Lloyd.

"Why won't you spent the night with me?" she asks suspiciously.

He looks at her wall heater, the dust film on her coffee table, and the antique collectible ceramics crowding a shelf close to the ceiling.

"Sweetie, your house reminds me of the house I grew up in. After we lost it, life got really hard. I'll tell you more about it when we know each other better."

Lloyd searches Eva's face for any indication whether she believes him.

Eva reaches over to the backside of the couch and pulls up the Hardware Plus bag. "What is this for?" she asks, showing him the contents.

Lloyd focuses on the pink glittery duct tape and a silver flashlight.

"It's to seal up a broken window on the side of my house. I should get back home and repair it before the rain starts. The repair man can't get out there 'til next week."

8

COVERING TRACKS

Lloyd reclines back at home on his sitting chair with his legs propped up on his leather ottoman and his laptop resting on his legs. Two hours ago, he left Eva's house to supposedly repair the broken window. But there is no broken window.

He searches the words online, "depth of Canyon Base Lake."

Reviews on Canyon Base Lake pop up. Lloyd reads them.

Fishing is my favorite activity on Canyon Base Lake. But you have to release any bass that you catch.

Paddle boats are available for rent on the south end of the lake. Please respect local residents' privacy when parking in the area.

He reads the last review.

Maximum depth is about 30 feet. Not recommended for swimming due to murky conditions.

Lloyd's mother Loretta brought him to the lake as a young boy. She tried to do things that mothers were supposed to do. Raising Lloyd as a young single mother, even sometimes taking night classes, was hard on both of them. And Lloyd wasn't an easy one to raise.

Next he searches the words, "arson" and "car."

He reads from the search strings.

Suspected arsonist claimed his car was stolen before the fire was set.

In suspected vehicle arson, the ignition should be checked for damage.

An investigator should determine how the car arrived to the arson scene.

Next he searches "deceased" and "smell."

He reads the search strings.

Corpses begin to decompose immediately after death.

Unmistakably putrid odors emanate from a corpse.

In addition to smelling up an area, the gases will cause the body to bloat and eyes to bulge.

"Honey, would you mind grabbing the emergency kit from your trunk? I'm updating all the supplies in our kits. I've been working on the ones around the house all day and want to take a look at the ones in our cars," Janice says.

"Sure, I'll get it in a bit. I'm just relaxing right now," Lloyd replies, closing the cover to his laptop.

"Well, if you'd like to give me your keys, I can run out and get it right now," she says.

Lloyd tenses up as his mind drifts to the tool box, tarp and tape sitting in his trunk. He's been waiting for the perfect opportunity to use these items. But it hasn't come upon him just yet.

Lloyd turns to Janice.

"No sweetie, I'll get the emergency kit in a bit. I have some other things to bring in anyway," he says.

Lloyd searches a new string.

He keys in, "remove blood stains."

He reads the strings.

Blood stains are the most difficult type of stains to remove.

If a blood stain is attended to right away, it can be more easily removed. If it has time to settle into fabric or a piece of furniture, you're in for a real job that may require a professional removal service.

"Janice, do you have anything to clean blood?" he yells to the kitchen casually.

She walks out and stands in front of Lloyd.

"Yes, but what do you need it for?" she asks.

"Janice, I asked you if you had anything for the stain. And you're drilling me with questions. Do you think a man wants to come home to this?" he snaps back.

Janice stares right at Lloyd.

"Lloyd, what is going on with you? Is it something I'm doing? You've been so short with me lately. What is bothering you?"

Lloyd closes his laptop and motions her to come sit near him.

Janice sits on the couch armrest near him and waits for a response. Janice has been the stable force in their marriage. Since the start, she has held Lloyd accountable for every irrational fit of rage he has subjected her to. They hardly fight, because Lloyd has learned to take responsibility quickly and apologize for his actions. He never really feels bad about how he treats Janice or the mean things he says to her. He's never had the ability to feel remorse. But he has programmed his mind to fix issues when they are brought to his attention. He has made a habit out of apologizing and taking responsibility.

Lloyd takes a deep breath and and exhales.

"Sweetie, I'm sorry. I just, have been thinking about my mom lately. Her birthday just passed," he says convincingly.

She strokes Lloyd's hair back and looks at him fondly, accepting his apology.

"What would I do without you?" she says. "You know what I was thinking today?"

"Tell me," replies Lloyd.

"How wonderful it would be to hear little footsteps running around here. Maybe by next year would be great, don't you think?" she says.

"Darling, you know how I feel about this," Lloyd says, questioning why he continues to spare her life.

"Well, I know. There never will be a good time. But babies are so wonderful and it will complete our family. You know how much I've been wanting this..."

"Darling..." says Lloyd sternly, cutting Janice off.

Before he can continue, she interrupts him.

"Lloyd... I'm pregnant."

9

DOMINANT

Lloyd slumps down into his sitting chair and flips through channels on his big screen TV. He searches for any show which might help him forget the news he learned a few hours ago about Janice being pregnant.

The flicker from the remaining embers of the fireplace light up the room from time to time.

He mutes the television, listening to the silence of his home and the crackle from the fire.

Lloyd scrolls through the movie guide.

He reads down the list.

Spring Break 2012.

Lust, Lick, Loose.

Asian Dancers.

Last Call Girl.

Then he sees one that catches his attention.

The Dominant's Defense.

Lloyd selects it.

A tall woman dressed in leather invites Lloyd into her "dungeon" for some "sex play." Her dark eyes and long, dark hair captivates him.

"Come with me. I make one promise. I'll share all of my toys with you as long as you're a good boy," the dominatrix says provocatively, motioning with her finger to follow her into a room down a dark hallway of a home decorated like a castle.

The quality of the movie is shoddy, but Lloyd doesn't care much about these details.

Lloyd moves over to his leather couch and nestles into it, grabbing for a fuzzy, wool throw blanket. He mutes the sound, listening for any stirring from Janice.

He returns the volume, watching the dominatrix in a dark room, which has cave-like crevices and rock formations painted on the walls.

The dominatrix opens the door of a black iron, life-size, bird cage-looking contraption hanging from the center ceiling of the room. She climbs into it and seats herself on a small bench running lengthwise in the cage.

Crossing her legs, her high leather boots creep up her thighs. The subtlety entrances Lloyd.

Lloyd begins unzipping his pants and stroking himself repetitively.

Curious about this dominatrix, he fantasizes about submitting to her.

"All you have to do is follow my commands. When you don't, I'll punish you. But it's for your own good. We'll start with a little spanking, a light one. And go from there. Do you understand me?" the dark-haired domme asks firmly.

Lloyd shakes his head in agreement.

A man walks into the dungeon-like room.

"Enter," she says commandingly.

A scratching sound coming from the side of Lloyd's house startles him.

Lloyd pauses the TV sound.

Another noise near a window in the same general location confirms it's real.

Lloyd turns the television off, zipping back up his pants and walking to his front door. He looks through the side windows near the door, noticing a woman towards the street.

She's alone. Lloyd opens the door and the woman stops in her tracks.

"Can I help you?" he asks sternly.

She turns around to face Lloyd. It's Eva.

"Hi, neighbor," she says shyly.

"Eva," replies Lloyd surprisingly.

She's dressed in a skirt below her knees, wool stockings, a knitted cap, and a puffy jacket.

"What are you doing here?" he asks in a low voice.

"I just...came to say hi," she says, walking closer to Lloyd.

"How did you find my house?" he asks.

Lloyd glances outside the house. The vapor from his breath condenses in front of him.

"Are you with anyone?" he asks.

"Who would I be with, silly?" she says. "Do you live here alone?" she questions.

"Kind of," says Lloyd evasively.

"Can I come in?" she asks challengingly.

Lloyd studies the subtle freckles on the sides of her nose pressed against her cream skin. Her hair falling to both sides of her shoulders pops out of her wool cap. Her tongue licks her upper lip, then her lower lip. She begins tugging at her skirt. Lloyd feels his groin pulsating.

Lloyd snaps out of his sick fantasy of having his way with her at his home, in his living room, while his pregnant wife is sleeping in the next room.

"That's not a good idea," he says. "Not now, but maybe another time, okay?" Lloyd says curtly.

"Lloyd. I know about her. I just wanted to see for myself," she says.

Lloyd looks down, remembering he's missing his hairpiece and glasses, hoping Eva doesn't notice.

"Know about who?" he asks foolishly.

"Her. Janice," says Eva.

"Eva, it's not the way it looks. We're still living together, but it means nothing. We're over, I promise. I should have told you. Can we talk about this tomorrow? She's asleep right now. I'll explain everything to you tomorrow," says Lloyd desperately.

"Why is she still here then?" Eva asks.

"I can't just kick her out," replies Lloyd.

"Then why wouldn't you just stay with *me*?" challenges Eva.

"Eva," he says sternly. "We'll discuss this tomorrow," he continues aggressively.

"But..." starts Eva childishly.

"Eva," he says sternly.

"I..."

"You need to leave," he continues harshly.

"Lloyd," she pleads desperately.

"Now," he demands.

Eva leaves, submissively.

Struggling to calm his rage, reclining back into the couch, he returns to *The Dominant's Defense*.

The porn has run midway through. The brunette domme sits on top of the young man, rocking back and forth. She squeezes his neck at the same time. His breathing becomes labored.

"Red," he yells.

The scene cuts out and the credits roll.

10

ACT OF LOVE

Lloyd walks through downtown Canyon Base. He forces himself to do anything to take his mind off the conversation with Janice last night about her being pregnant. The small boutique shops are decorated with Christmas lights and garland. The stores pull Lloyd back to his adolescence.

The first time he paid attention to the details of Christmas were after his mom had kicked him out of the family home. Having no friends, except for a girlfriend whose parents distrusted him, he had nowhere to go. So he lived on the streets.

The streets were a place that felt like home to Lloyd, more so than the warmth of an abundant home, especially around the holidays. At the same time, he resented the tree-lined concrete, the storefronts, and the boutiques. The commercialism was all fake to him, especially when the homeless lay in sleeping bags right outside.

Loud music from outdoor speakers echoes through the streets. The Twelve Days of Christmas plays. Lloyd can't stand the hassle of the holiday, the madness of the shopping season, the decorations, and elaborate dinner parties. Lloyd wasn't looking forward to any of it.

The two turtle doves, three French hens, four calling birds, five golden rings, six geese a-laying, seven swans a-swimming, and eight maids a-milking. Lloyd can't stand any of it. It begins ringing loudly in his ears.

Songs like this one have religious undertones that Lloyd resents. Janice tried to involve Lloyd in the church at the beginning of their relationship. He made it very clear he wanted no part of it. The only time he agreed to go with her was around the holidays.

Lloyd passes by a boutique shop on Canyon Base Street for the fifth time today. A sign inside reads that handcrafted bracelets, with name engravings, beads, birthstones, and charms could be made as Christmas gifts or just to say, "I love you."

Lloyd studies each of the samples. Every year, he obligingly walks into town to find a gift for Janice.

He browses over the different bracelets in the display case.

Annabelle. Taurus charm. "Love" engraved on a silver plate.

Debbie. Virgo charm. "Hope" engraved on a gold plate.

Kate. Scorpio charm. "Live" engraved on a pearlized plate.

"Sir, can I help you with something?" a female voice says from behind him.

"Yes, I'd like to take two of these," he replies, pointing to a specific configuration.

Over the next hour, the bead lady weaves together two bracelets. Lloyd sits in silence watching her take her time to delicately create each one. When he wasn't watching her, he flipped through a book about the paintings of Diego Rivera, a Mexican painter.

From time to time, the bead lady glances up at him and shows him her progress.

He gushes at her each step and watches her delicate hands maneuver each of the charms he selected into a beautiful bracelet.

After making the first bracelet, she removes her camel-colored sweater. Her large breasts fill out her matching sweater tank and her long strand of pearls falls neatly against her chest. A large gold charm at the end of the necklace matching her gold hoop earrings rests between her breasts, drawing Lloyd's eyes down as she weaves the bracelet string in and out of each bead, carefully and deliberately with each maneuver.

"So, here they are. How do you think they look?" she asks, neatly stretching each one on a white cotton cloth, presenting them in the best possible way. She adjusts the lighting, smiling down at her work.

He studies each one. She eagerly awaits his reaction. After all, it wasn't often that a handsome man like Lloyd spent the entire hour in a store watching her honing her beading craft. He reads the charms on each of the bracelets he has selected.

Eva. Patience. Friend.

Janice. Love. Life.

"They look great. Thank you," Lloyd replies, pleased.

"Well, whoever these women are, they are certainly lucky to have you in their life," she says endearingly.

"Well, thank you. One's for my sister," he says, focusing on the clerk's neck and her long, blonde, flowing hair draping around it.

"And this is for my late wife. I'm a widow," he says, pointing to Janice's bracelet.

The word "widow" sounds so natural.

"I'm *so* sorry about your loss," she says sincerely.

"It was many years ago. To cancer. She's in a better place now," he says deceitfully. "You've done a wonderful job with this whole beading station. It's such a novel idea," continues Lloyd, changing the subject.

"Thank you. You're too kind," she says, blushing. "So I'd like to point something out," she says, perking up.

"What's that?" Lloyd asks, flirtatiously.

"Well, I'm just fascinated by the book you're reading. He's one of my favorite painters," she says.

Lloyd smiles, proud he got this right. He had passed by this store five times today, either on foot or observing from his car. He had carefully noticed the replica paintings she had of Frida Kahlo and Diego Rivera hanging on the walls of her shop.

"What a coincidence," he says, convincingly. "It looks like I'm your last customer," says Lloyd, noticing the empty store. "Let's grab a drink."

11

TROPHY

A couple hours after leaving the bead store, Lloyd sits on Eva's couch opposite her, hoping she doesn't notice the fingernail scratches on his forehead and down the side of his face. Lloyd's burst of anger when the bead store lady declined his invitation to a drink ended after a brief struggle. She offered up her gold earrings and promised not to call police. In exchange, he spared her and her fetus' life.

"Where'd you get those?" Eva asks, pointing at the scratches.

"Trimming some trees. The branches fell loose," he says easily. "Come closer to me, sweetie. Finish opening your gift."

Eva moves closer, obligingly sitting next to him as she opens the cover of a small white box.

"Lloyd, I can't accept these," she says, closing the box and grabbing the candy cane-colored paper scraps sitting on the coffee table. Attempting to rewrap the gift, she tugs the red shiny ribbon around the box and the paper.

"Really, I can't..." she pleads. "It's really thoughtful of you, but these are just... you can't afford these," she continues.

"Eva, look at me. I want you to have these," he insists. "You mean the world to me. You're all I have. Please accept them," he begs.

Lloyd takes the box from Eva, unwraps it, and removes the bead store lady's gold hoop earrings. One by one, he carefully pierces the posts into Eva's ears and clasps them. She remains still, fixing her eyes on her family photo with her sister, and says nothing, allowing Lloyd to have his way.

"It's just... are they real gold? Because I can't wear anything but genuine gold. Otherwise, I break out. I'm allergic to the fake stuff," she says.

"Yes, they're real. I made sure of that," says Lloyd confidently, handing her the box with the custom-made bracelet.

"Well, it's so nice of you. It's the first holiday gift I've ever received," she says gratefully, while unwrapping her second gift.

"I'm glad you like them," he says, pleased at her reaction.

"I'm embarrassed. I don't have anything for you. I wasn't expecting you..." says Eva, pausing while she pulls out the bracelet from the box and almost cries.

"That's not the point. You don't need to get me anything. Your friendship is plenty, Eva," says Lloyd, receiving Eva's undivided attention.

"I feel we have something, Eva, something special. I need you," he says convincingly.

"What do you mean, Lloyd?" she asks.

"It's just that when we are together, I feel more complete. You're my soulmate."

Eva looks at him, wanting to believe everything he is saying. Lloyd has an effect on her, telling her the things she has not heard from a man before.

Over the next hour, Lloyd reminds her of every reason they are good together—how they first met and how great it would be to spend the new year together, like a fresh start.

He apologizes for being aggressive and says he's learning to control his temper.

They recount their early childhoods and he listens while rubbing her hand as she recounts some of the abusive nights with her mom.

She rubs his back as he recounts nights as a teenager, sleeping in cars and sometimes on the street after his mom kicked him out of the house. He recounts the struggle it was to get back on his feet and build a life for himself.

They make love for the first time. Lloyd makes sure it feels different for Eva this time. He thrusts into her slowly and passionately kisses her neck. He keeps his eyes open and fixed on her, carefully making sure she climaxes over and over again. It wasn't the selfish way that Lloyd had sex with her the first time. It's different, but calculated and deliberate.

After they both climax, he spoons her from behind and drifts to sleep.

Eva grabs for one of the earrings and touches her ear, which is burning the side of her face, causing it to swell up. Her allergies have set in. Realizing the earrings are fake, not real like Lloyd initially led her to believe, Eva stays still and tries not to wake him; then she slowly removes the earrings, trying not to panic.

12

SUPPLIES

Lloyd parks his car behind Hardware Plus, in a discreet parking spot near the dumpsters. He calms his breathing, still replaying yesterday's assault of the bead store clerk in his mind and trying to reassure himself that he didn't leave his fake glasses behind in the store. He wonders if it was a mistake to give Eva the earrings he snatched from the clerk, then he quickly dismisses that concern, believing he won't be caught. He dashes from his car and heads inside the hardware store.

He knows exactly where to go inside the store. He sweeps up a tarp, duct tape—this time the cheetah color— and weights. He slides his items on the miniature conveyer belt at the register, smiling at the young, brunette cashier as she hits her total button and flirtingly says, "Twenty-eight dollars and fifty cents is your total, sir."

She tries not to stare at the scratches on his face.

Lloyd gives her cash and a half-believable explanation. "Can you believe a couple thieves did this to me, for my phone?" says Lloyd, pointing to his face.

"Oh my gosh, that happened to my friend. Were they guys with hoodies?" she asks, believing his story.

"Exactly. How did you know?"

"Like I said, it happened to my friend."

"People get desperate in the winter. As if I don't have enough things to worry about," says Lloyd, holding up the bag she just placed his items in and handed him. "I've got a roof leak," he says deceitfully.

"Everyone's been coming in for those things, and sandbags. Do you need any of those? They work better than the weights," she offers, helpfully.

"That's nice of you, sweetie, but I think this will cover it."

Within five minutes of leaving the hardware store, Lloyd pulls up to Eva's house and makes his way inside with his spare key.

Eva pulls up in her driveway behind his car within minutes.

The two sit at her dining room table.

Lloyd opens up the Tuckford Press to the local section and reads the headline, "Cold Case Killer Still At-Large." He slams the paper shut.

"Don't you want to read what they're saying about that old case?" Eva inquires.

"No, Eva. I don't want to read about that. I have no interest. And why would you think I do?" he asks accusingly.

"Well, you seemed to be interested in the case when we walked over there," she says.

"Well, since you seem to be interested in it as well, I'll just rely on you for the news. How does that sound?" he says sarcastically.

"Lloyd, where were you today?" she asks suspiciously.

"I ran some errands, finished some projects around the house, and had a bite to eat," he replies. "Why?" he questions.

"I thought I saw your car at the hardware store. In the back," she says accusingly.

"No, it must have been someone else's. I wasn't anywhere around here," he says deceptively.

"Hmmm. I could've sworn I saw you come out, too," she replies.

"No, Eva, that wasn't me," he says firmly.

The two make their way to the couch and Lloyd flips through the television channels. Eva sits next to him obligingly, stroking his leg.

Lloyd begins to kiss Eva's neck.

Eva moves away, unintentionally.

"Do you want to stay over?" she asks.

"I can't. I've got to go check on that window, make sure the rain's not getting in."

"Why don't you want me touching you?" asks Lloyd.

"I'm just... not in the mood. I'm about to start my... it's that time of month," replies Eva, looking at Lloyd and waiting for any kind of reaction to indicate whether he believes her.

"That doesn't matter to me," he says.

"I'm just not in the mood, Lloyd," she says, exasperated.

"Are you sure that's what it is, Eva?" he says, grabbing her neck.

"Lloyd, stop!" she says in frustration.

He looks at her with distrust, releasing her neck and making his way towards the front door.

"Can you lock the door behind you?" says Eva, relieved.

13

STRUGGLING

Lloyd stands at his office desk at home, holding the phone receiver up to his ear. Within thirty minutes of Janice leaving the house, Lloyd is showered, dressed, and ready to hit a five o'clock happy hour book signing across town. He is a free man for the night since Janice is staying over her mom's place.

The Christmas music on the other end of the line begins to agitate him.

He types the domain name of his bank into his computer in front of him.

Tuckford Bank and its logos pop up on the screen. A slideshow of pictures featuring customers along with quotes about their experiences with Tuckford Bank rotate on his screen.

"Tuckford Bank helped us buy our first home."
Sylvia Hall

Stay at home mom in Tuckford County

"Tuckford Bank helped my wife and me get ready for our first baby."

John Sanchez

Electrical engineer, father, husband in Tuckford County

"Tuckford Bank helped me recover from my college credit card debt."

Lori Ramsey

Graduate from Tuckford College

Lloyd rolls his eyes and enters his user identification and password into the prompts.

USER ID: LLOYDG
PASSWORD: 2654STANTONSTREET

His online banking account information pops up onto the screen. The music switches to the next Christmas song.

Lloyd clicks onto the "Make Payments" option and pays $99.22 to his overdue cable bill.

He scrolls to a medical insurance payee and clicks onto it. His last payment was two months ago.

Lloyd's heart rate starts to elevate.

He scrolls to his credit card payee. His paper credit card statement sits next to him.

Current account balance: $2,843.66

He clicks onto his online banking balance.

Current account balance: $1020.46

Lloyd's face starts to feel warm. He doesn't have enough money to pay his credit card bill.

A woman on the other end of the line starts speaking.

"Thank you for calling your reliable Tuckford Bank. My name is Loretta. How can I assist you with your banking needs today?"

"Hi, Loretta. Is that really your name? *Loretta?*"

Before she answers, Lloyd jumps in. "Never mind. I have several questions about my account and possibly taking out a line of credit."

"And what would this line of credit specifically be used towards?"

"To pay off a credit card debt and a cash advance."

"Well, I can certainly answer any questions. However, I must first warn you that currently due to difficult economic times, Tuckford Bank is not providing cash advance or credit card transfer-type loans."

"I have seen loans recently coming out of our bank; however, they are for things like home loans, education, or cars."

"Yeah, I saw those people on your website."

"Those stories are something new we added for our customers to see how Tuckford Bank can help them."

"There was one man talking about getting money to help get ready for his new baby," says Lloyd.

"Sure, sure. But that's a home improvement type loan. Are you in a similar situation?" she asks.

"Sort of, yeah! I'm not looking to improve my house. But things like medical care, hospitalization, that kind of stuff is what I need help with."

Lloyd stares at his overdue medical insurance bill sitting on his desk.

"What type of medical care is this for exactly?"

"Pregnancy. Childbirth."

"Well, I've seen loans available for catastrophic medical emergencies. But if you're just talking about prenatal care, childbirth, and hospital stays for routine pregnancies, we don't loan money for that. We have educational workshops encouraging our clients to become health insured so they are not shouldering the burden of these costs to their family, but other than...."

Lloyd cuts her off, enraged.

"What if you don't have insurance and you're expecting a baby?" he starts sarcastically. "Then what? WHAT. AM. I. SUPPOSED. TO. DO?" he continues hotly.

"Sir. Please calm down. I'm just letting you know what services our bank provides. You're welcome to check with other banks or lending services. I'm sorry to hear that you're in a bind and we understand here that sometimes unforeseen situations arise. But we don't have the lending power to loan money in that fashion. It's too high of a risk for us."

"You have the lending power. You just choose not to use it that way. Isn't that right?"

"Sir, I don't want to address the policies of our bank. I'm only a loan officer. I don't make the final decisions when it comes to loans. You can certainly fill out the appropriate paperwork and submit it. I'm just letting you know the likelihood of the outcome, so you're not wasting your time."

"You're right, *Loretta*, you *are* a waste of time," Lloyd snaps before slamming down the phone.

14

ENGAGEMENT

Lloyd sits in his car in the parking lot outside the Tuckford Botanical Garden, a large arboretum of plants and flowers. He's waiting for Brandy, a girl he met last night at the book reading in Salga, a town neighboring Canyon Base. They agreed to meet here and then walk through the Arboretum as soon as it opens.

The tall trees lining the parking lot boast an infinite density of nature, extending into a dark forest all the way up to the Arboretum, which is at the base of the mountains. Lloyd spent most of the morning researching the area.

There is a creek about five hundred yards up, which is a few feet deep in some areas and has a hiking trail around it, which is usually busy on weekends but very sparse during the week, especially in the mornings. The area is so isolated and untraveled by hikers that people have been known to get engaged here.

Brandy pulls her small Honda Civic around the parking lot in the direction of Lloyd's car, which is the only one on the lot.

Lloyd recaps everything he learned about Brady last night while mingling with her at the book reading. She's an aspiring screenwriter with an MFA in Creative Writing from Tuckford University. She is twenty-six years old and came to this area from across the country to pursue her career aspirations.

To Brandy, Lloyd is a film director who could put her in contact with the people she needs to meet to make her dreams come true. It's all his facade, at least for this week.

Brandy pulls her car into the space next to Lloyd's. He watches her carefully.

To Lloyd, Brandy fits his mold. She is educated, blonde, fighting her restlessness in a marriage that isn't working anymore, and she's four weeks pregnant. Lloyd visualizes what her building contractor husband might look like. Lloyd is sure of one thing – Brandy must be out of her husband's league. Afterall, it's quite common in Tuckford County that beautiful women like Brandy wind up with blue-collar men like contractors.

Lloyd steps out of his car in time to open up Brandy's car door and greet her with a big hug. A bit trepidatious, she smiles at him and obligingly returns the gesture by hugging him back. She seemed much more flirtatious last night, and Lloyd doesn't like her hesitancy right now.

"So, I just read on the entrance sign that the Arboretum doesn't open until noontime today. Should we do our hike first?" she asks.

"Yes, let's," says Lloyd fakely, trying to forget about her perceived slight and apprehension towards him.

Brandy pops the trunk of her car. She removes the furry tan boots from her feet and replaces them with her tennis shoes. She slips out of her cashmere sweater wrap and scarf, folding them neatly into a pile and places them on the baseboard of her trunk, before pulling out an athletic sweater she plunges her arms through.

Lloyd's eyes are glued to her.

Once her head makes it out through the neck hole, she slowly shakes her head back and forth, causing her long blonde curls to fall down her back.

She begins to pull up her hair into a high ponytail, combing all her loose strands up into the rubber band tie.

"Hey, hey. Leave it down," Lloyd insists, gently.

"Why? We're going for a hike," she replies, playfully.

"It's more like a brisk walk," he says.

"Fine," she relents, letting go of her hair, which cascades down her shoulders.

"Is that how you like it?" she says flirtingly, shaking her head side to side and deliberately posing her body towards Lloyd.

"Exactly," he says, feeling himself erotically turned on.

Lloyd goes back to his car, removes his sweater from his waist, and replaces it with a fanny pack. He reaches over his water bottle in the center console and into the glove compartment. He grasps for and tucks a small roll of plastic bags, big enough to fit a human body, into his hand and stuffs them into the zipped pocket area of the fanny pack. Next, he grabs the mini roll of duct tape and places it into the pack, before closing the glove compartment box and zipping up the fanny pack.

The two begin their walk, deep into the woods, with Lloyd leading the way he had mapped out, directly towards the creek in that isolated spot where couples often become engaged. But today, the only thing Brandy and her unborn child are going to become engaged to is the possibility of death.

15

FIRST SEARCH

Lloyd walks around Canyon Base Lake at sunset. The longer he can wait to return home, the longer he can avoid seeing Janice or having to explain to her the scratches on his hands. Brandy fought hard this morning trying to peel his fingers away from her throat as he attempted to compress her larynx.

The trees are bare of autumn leaves and most of the grassy areas around the lake have turned yellowish-brown. Search crews have been walking through the neighboring areas for the past day in small groups.

Lloyd uses his binoculars to get a closer view of the search crews, moving them up to his eyeglasses. Other local neighbors stand in the general area, discussing the terrain, the possibility of where clues could be hidden, and speculating why the police were making search efforts on the lake.

"Maybe they're looking for the old murder weapon," says Lloyd, not being able to help himself from joining in on the speculation and gossip.

"Possibly. I did see a dive crew gearing up near the lake house," says a male neighbor.

"I think they're looking for a body. I heard a fisherman reeled in some hair and called the police," says a female neighbor, sipping from her Coffee Grind cup.

"What color hair?" asks Lloyd, curiously.

The woman looks at him wondering if he really wants to know the color of hair.

"I don't know," she says, horrified. "But that woman was killed ten years ago. Maybe it's linked to that," she continues.

Lloyd returns back to his binoculars.

"Did you know her?" asks Lloyd, sounding concerned.

"No, but a lot of my neighbors did. Said she was a real nice lady. Some are saying she was murdered right in front of her daughter," she replies.

"Ten years ago you said?" confirms Lloyd.

"That's when it happened."

"He's long gone," says Lloyd.

"They'll catch him," she snaps back.

Lloyd chuckles at her and returns to his scene watching.

Voices on the opposite side of the lake echo back towards Lloyd and the onlookers.

"I bet that's the prosecutor," an onlooker says, pointing across the lake.

A man with light brown fatigues and a dark green reflector shell with "TCPO" slapped across it walks around, surveying the area. Tuckford County Prosecutor's Office.

"I know that guy. I was a juror once in a capital case he handled. Man, is he good," says a male neighbor.

Lloyd zooms the focus of his binoculars onto the prosecutor. He's a tall, good-looking, dark-haired man in his forties, with light skin.

Prosecutor Jack Moore is a top prosecutor in Tuckford County. He is only assigned to big cases, usually the ones that the elected prosecutor thinks will have a lot of media exposure.

"Interesting," says Lloyd, still fixing his binoculars on the prosecutor, feeling a bit nervous and a bit excited at the prospect of an important attorney being called to the scene to investigate.

Investigator Marty Kaplan begins gathering a group of men from the Canyon Base Police Department, the Special Homicide Team, and the Tuckford County Dive Team.

After ten minutes of huddling in a circle, pointing to maps, and drawing on clipboards, the investigation group begins to disperse.

The dive team takes their positions and begins to enter Canyon Base Lake.

An hour passes of search and rescue attempts. Finally, a rolled floor rug emerges from the water, with ropes wrapped around it. Gasps of air break the silence.

16

FIRST LOOK

A few hours after watching the body being lifted from Canyon Base Lake, Lloyd sits at Hal's Diner in the same booth where he first met Annabelle. He feels naked, not wearing his hairpiece or his glasses. A part of him is starting to get used to these things. But he can't run the risk of being identified at Hal's.

Men with cameras try to push their way past an otherwise busy entranceway of people waiting to be seated. Lloyd had a twenty-minute wait, but it was all worth it. To return to the initial scene of seduction was to relive the entire experience, from the first meet to the last breath of a victim.

The voluptuous hostess near the front door turns away the media after a few minutes of back and forth argument.

"Respect our space!" she yells at a videographer getting in her face.

Investigator Marty Kaplan and Prosecutor Jack Moore are greeted by the host, who motion over to the empty booth in front of Lloyd.

Neither one looks at Lloyd while they are seated.

Annabelle's husband Tim enters the dining room from a swinging door off the kitchen. He walks past Lloyd and up to the investigator's booth, wiping his hand on his white chef's apron.

Marty and Jack stand up and shake his hand.

"Hi, there. I'm sorry. I lost my cook. He quit on me unexpectedly this morning. I think it really got to him. So I had to get back in the kitchen and pick it up for a bit," Tim says. His chef's apron covers his belly, which once protruded the day Lloyd saw him at the diner with his daughter. And he looks as desperate as the day he fell to his knees in the middle of the street when police visited his house recently.

Lloyd strains to hear every part of the conversation.

"No worries. This is Prosecutor Jack Moore. He's on the case. Take a seat, we just have a few questions for you," says Marty.

"Thanks, man, for taking some time to talk to us," says Jack, shaking Tim's hand.

"Anytime, man. Anything I can do. I want her killer found. I've been waiting years for this," says Tim.

"Well. We can't make any promises about that," says Marty.

Tim studies Marty's face.

"Please don't say it. Don't tell me he killed that woman who was found in the lake. I can't stand thinking he's out there doing this to other women after all this time," Tim says.

"We're still investigating that. We're on our way to inform her husband after we leave here," says Marty.

"Man, that poor guy. I can't even imagine. Who's doing this shit? He should be beat, shot, whatever you can do when you get a hold of him. I'm going crazy. Today would have been our fifteen-year anniversary. I'm hearing rumors again she was seen with a man, here at this diner. I don't know why she would've gone with him, whoever he is," he carries on.

"Is there any chance... Well, is there any chance..." starts Marty.

"No way. No way. What are you saying? That she was having an affair, stepping out on me?" says the chef angrily.

"It's just something we have to ask. We were never able to pinpoint anyone that had it in for her. No enemies. No threats. It's just something we need to ask again. None of her friends knew her to be having an affair. We're just trying to rule out all possibilities again," says Marty.

"No. No. There's no way," he says indignantly.

"Fine, we just had to put that out there," says Marty.

"Is there something you know? Something suggesting that?" asks Tim.

"No, nothing we're aware of," says Jack.

"Look, we're doing everything we can to find out who did this. This case has always been in the back of my mind," Marty says reassuringly.

"What was her pattern when she left work?" asks Marty.

"Just always went home. Remember I was working in construction at the time she went missing. I was out of town at a job site. I first thought things were off when I was calling her and she wasn't responding. That was close to seven the same day she went missing. It wasn't like her," he says.

"That mother... shit, you don't know how bad I want to get my hands on his throat," he says, gripping his hands tightly together and shaking as though Annabelle was just killed yesterday.

Red scratches on Tim hands catch Marty's attention. "They're cuts from a new Japanese knife I've been using," Tim offers.

"Yeah, takes a while to break it in," says Jack.

"Did you ever look at that one lead I gave you? Years ago?" says Tim, changing the subject.

"We looked at everything at the time. We're combing through all of it again," assures Marty.

Tim's clenched jaw shifts into a grind.

"I know, I know. Let it out, man. It's okay," says Jack consolingly.

"How's your daughter man?"

"She's brave, she's always been strong. I have her in a writing club. It's been good therapy for her. She was doing fine this whole time, but lately she's been having these nightmares. Bad ones. I think with the case being reopened and all."

"Man, I'm sorry. When she's ready, we need to talk to her again. See if she remembers anything. I know it's hard, but I've always suspected she walked in on things," says Marty.

"I'll talk to her. Do you have anything else for me? I have to get back in there," Tim says.

"No, man. Get back in there," says Jack.

Tim looks directly at Jack Moore. "Find him. Or I will," he demands sternly.

Lloyd watches Tim make his way back towards the kitchen and glances back towards Jack and Marty.

Marty stares right at Lloyd.

"I don't think he's involved," says Jack.

"Definitely not. I've never suspected him," says Marty confidently.

The conversation between Marty and Jack becomes muted. Lloyd strains to hear what is being whispered below their breaths.

"May I take your order, sir?" asks a waitress.

Lloyd, startled, looks up at a young waitress.

Lloyd looks down at his menu.

"Excuse me ma'am, may we have a moment with this gentleman?" says Marty, now standing with Jack at Lloyd's table.

"Lloyd Gil?" asks Marty.

"Yes," Lloyd confirms.

"This is Jack Moore, the county prosecutor," says Marty, pointing at Jack.

"And I'm Marty Kaplan. Tuckford County Homicide Investigator," he continues, before pausing.

"Mr. Gil. We'd like a chance to speak with you about a possible homicide."

"Who was killed?" asks Lloyd.

Marty and Jack look at eachother before asking Lloyd to accompany them to the police station.

17

FIRST INTERVIEW

Lloyd sits alone in a small room at the police station, waiting to be interviewed. Since he was approached by Marty and Jack forty minutes ago, thoughts have been racing through his mind. Mostly he wonders why they are treating him like a suspect, putting him in a room for questioning. If they believed he was an innocent man, shouldn't they have him wait in the lobby or explain what's going on. That's what they did in the movies.

Whatever is about to happen, Lloyd is ready for this. He has spent time preparing himself. He knows what to say and not to say during an interview with police. He is being watched for verbal expressions, emotion, inflection, and deception.

Marty walks in and sets a small microcassette recorder on the table in front of him and hits the record button.

"Mr. Gil. As you know, I'm Marty Kaplan. I'm the lead investigator on a recent homicide," he says.

"I'd like to just ask you, is there anyone you know that would want to hurt your wife?"

"No one. Everyone loves her. What's this about?"

"Was she seeing anyone?" asks Marty, retuning back to Janice.

"No, no one I was aware of."

Marty focuses on Lloyd who looks confused. The two remain silent until Marty takes a deep breath and begins to reveal.

"Well, Lloyd, it appears Janice was killed this morning, shortly before we found her body. It was just by chance we located her. We were searching for evidence in another case," says Marty solemnly.

Lloyd processes this news for a moment, waiting for emotion to come over him. But he has none.

He forces himself to well up his eyes with tears. He tugs at his hair.

It's all part of the look of a distraught husband who just lost his wife. And Lloyd has to fake it. Because he feels nothing, even at the idea of having just lost his wife, whom he married seven years ago and who was pregnant with his unborn child.

"My condolences, sincerely. I know this is difficult," Marty says.

Lloyd plays the part. He covers his face with his hands, he rubs his eyes, he sniffles loudly. He takes a deep breath, as if to calm himself.

"I swear you look familiar to me. Have we met before?" asks Marty, changing the subject.

"I don't believe so," says Lloyd.

"Hmmm. I usually never forget a face," says Marty.

"Neither do I," retorts Lloyd.

Marty studies Lloyd's face carefully. Lloyd stares right back at him, unafraid.

"Hmmm," Marty says curiously. "So we've been out in your neighborhood looking at some new information we received in the murder of a pregnant housewife ten years ago. She worked in the same diner we were just in. Hal's in Killmore," says Marty, pausing to again study Lloyd's face.

Lloyd doesn't react.

"Does that have anything to do with Janice?" asks Lloyd.

"We don't know at this point. Do you have a reason to believe it does?" asks Marty curiously.

"Other than similar location, no. I mean, I don't know. This is what you guys are paid to figure out, right?" asks Lloyd sarcastically.

"Why would you believe they were close in location?" asks Marty. "Are you familiar with the murder of the waitress?" Marty questions suspiciously.

"No. I hadn't heard of it. But you just said she went missing ten years ago. You said you were investigating that again," asks Lloyd.

"I don't believe we gave you that information, that there was any connection between the two cases. I don't release that type of information on a pending investigation," says Marty firmly.

"Maybe I overheard you at the diner. Plus, that old murder has been all over the papers lately. Like you guys were opening back up the investigation," says Lloyd. "I don't know," he continues dismissively. "Do you have any other questions for me?" he asks impatiently.

"When was the last time you saw your wife?"

"Yesterday. But I talked to her on the phone earlier today. She was at home. She had spent the night at her mom's. She wanted to sign up for search crew efforts for..." says Lloyd before stopping himself.

"Search efforts for evidence in the waitress case?" asks Marty.

"We just assumed they were combing the area for clues in that case where the woman was killed up the block. The one in the papers. Janice wanted to get involved, to help out in some way. That was just the way she was," says Lloyd.

"Were you having problems in your marriage?" asks Marty.

"No. None at all," says Lloyd.

"Are you sure about that?" asks Marty.

Lloyd scans over Marty's expressions and eyes for any hint of him knowing any private details about him.

"What kind of problems are you talking about?" Lloyd asks.

"The typical kind. Extramarital affairs. Domestic violence. Financial. Anything really," says Marty nonchalantly. "I mean, we all have problems. You guys were married, what, for seven years?" he continues.

"Yep. Seven exactly. No, everything was great," says Lloyd.

"How are you feeling right now? About hearing all this? I haven't seen you express any emotions really," says Marty suspiciously.

Lloyd starts inhaling loud sniffles and wrinkling his eyes shut. It is all contrived.

"I gotta be honest with you, Mr. Gil. There is no perfect marriage. At least that I've seen. There is always something to complain about. And the fact that you're not complaining about anything and telling me that everything was perfect, is raising a flag in my mind," says Marty. "I'm not here to judge. We all make mistakes. Men step out on their wives, who they love, when nothing is going wrong, all the time. It doesn't make you a bad person. But we need you to be honest with us. Otherwise, it's looking like you're trying to hide something from us," says Marty accusingly.

"Nope. Nothing going on. No affairs, no mistresses. All was good, sir," says Lloyd. "On that note, you know what? I feel like I'm being treated like a suspect. I just lost my wife and I feel like you're giving me the fifth degree. And if that's the case, I'm entitled to a lawyer.

"I did not kill my wife. Do you hear me? I did not kill her. She was pregnant with my child. I would not do that to her. I don't know who the hell did this, but it wasn't me. I'm not going to speak with you or the prosecutor. I don't want you coming to my house. I don't want you asking me any more questions. Do you understand me?" Lloyd says, staring down Marty.

"How do you explain that the rug she was wrapped up in came from *your* dining room floor?" Marty asks.

"This interview is over. You're going to have to speak with my lawyer," says Lloyd, flicking a worn business card on the table.

Marty clicks off the tape recorder and reads the card:

Richard Hill
Hill & Associates

"Wow, you must think you did something really bad," says Marty sarcastically. "If you're hiring the Hill firm," he continues.

"He's my stepbrother," Lloyd snaps back.

"I don't know who the hell you are or what the hell you did to your wife, but you can be sure as shit that I'm going to find out. Figure out another place to stay for the night. You won't be allowed back into your home for twenty-four hours. We're writing paper on your house right now. We'll have a search warrant within an hour," says Marty, picking up his recorder and leaving the room, before slamming the door behind him.

18

FIRST MISTAKE

Lloyd rinses his face with cold water inside the bathroom at Eva's house. He looks at his watch. It's only been an hour since his interrogation.

"Sweetie, are you okay in there?" calls out Eva from her bedroom.

"I'm fine. I'll be right out," says Lloyd.

Lloyd pulls off his pajama bottoms and turns the sink on. The water gushing loudly masks the subtle sounds of groaning pleasure he releases while stroking his penis heartily. His pleasure from watching it grow elicits a large grin across his face reflecting in the mirror.

Within a minute, he ejaculates into a hand towel, trying to muffle his heavy breathing and grunting by shoving the back of his hand into his mouth.

He slips back into his pajama pants and returns to bed with Eva.

"Sweetie, how are you feeling?" she asks, combing his chest hair with her fingers.

"I'm okay. I think I'm still processing everything. It just happened so suddenly," he replies calmly.

"Are you sad?" she asks.

"Well, of course. I mean, we were together for a long time. She was a good woman," he says.

"But you were going to leave her," she says.

"Yes, I was," says Lloyd.

"Lloyd, did you still love her?" she asks.

"No. It wasn't like that," he says reassuringly.

"It's been a long time since I've had that feeling with her. I can't say I was in love with her. I loved Janice, but I wasn't in love with her," he replies shallowly.

"So then what did you feel for her?"

"It's hard to explain. I felt indebted to her. I signed up for that. I married her," he replies unemotionally.

"That's not how a marriage should be. Like a debt. That just sounds terrible. I'm sorry you were in that position," says Eva sorrowfully.

"Well, it's over. It's all over," says Lloyd thankfully.

"Have the police given you any information about who they suspect did it?" Eva asks.

"They haven't. They asked if she was having an affair or if I knew anyone that wanted to hurt her. But really, she had no enemies," Lloyd replies.

"Do they suspect you at all?" asks Eva curiously.

"Why would you ask that?" questions Lloyd, annoyed.

"Well, don't they always suspect the spouse?" replies Eva matter-of-factly.

Lloyd thinks back to the interview with Marty Kaplan and his last words to him about finding out what Lloyd did to his wife.

"Perhaps," Lloyd responds.

"Did they give you any details about what happened?" asks Eva. "And I'm sorry, sweetie, if you don't want to talk about this. I just think it might help," says Eva sympathetically.

"The only thing they said was she was wrapped up in a rug from my dining room. They were going to search my house tonight. I'm sure once I get back inside, the house will be a mess. I'm not looking forward to going back," he says.

"Do you want me to go back with you?" she asks helpfully.

"I'm not sure that's a good idea. I didn't tell police about us. In fact, I denied having any marital affairs," says Lloyd hesitantly.

"Why didn't you just tell them about us? It's not like you have anything to hide. Your marriage was on the rocks. You didn't kill her. Why lie at this point? You should tell the truth; if not, one small lie can look suspicious," she warns.

"Eva, I don't need the police in my affairs. It's none of their business. And you're right. I did not kill Janice. I'm not worried about being on the hook for that. But the moment you give them anything to question or to look into, it's over. They'll keep fishing for information, write more search warrants, and wreck your life. It's what they do.

"And this asshole who's in charge of the investigation, Marty Kaplan, has a hard-on for me. I can just tell. This is his specialty. I don't know what his problem is with me, but he was treating me like a suspect in my interview. He crossed the line," Lloyd says angrily.

"Well, don't take it out on me," says Eva defensively.

"You brought this up," he replies.

"What should I say if they question me?" Eva asks nervously.

"Why would they talk to you?" he questions suspiciously.

"They'll find out somehow, that we're connected. What if they look at phone bills or search your computer?" she says.

"Shit! My computer! I forgot about my computer," yells Lloyd.

"They might check our emails," says Eva.

Lloyd thinks about all the words he has written in search strings on his computer in the past week about smells of bodies and dumping in lakes.

"Dammit!" screams Lloyd.

"Calm down. Calm down," says Eva.

"Screw this. If someone pins this on me. This murder. I swear I'll lose it. I didn't kill my wife," says Lloyd adamantly.

"I know you didn't. And you didn't kill your child, either. You didn't," says Eva reassuringly, holding Lloyd's hand tightly.

Lloyd pauses, staring directly at Eva.

"How did you know about Janice being pregnant?" asks Lloyd suspiciously.

Eva pauses and searches the room with her eyes as though looking for answers.

"You told me when I visited that night, I thought," she finally says.

"I don't remember that, Eva," he says sternly. "How did you know?" he demands.

"Really, Lloyd.   You told me when I was there... I thought," she says nervously.

Lloyd searches his mind for any memory of their conversation at the door, not recalling any moment he told Eva about Janice's pregnancy.   He can't recall telling her afterwards at any point, either.

He sits upright on the bed and again demands knowing how Eva has this information. His face begins to turn red and he raises his hand to strike her.

"Okay... okay... I overheard.   I overheard, Lloyd," says Eva frightfully, noticing his impending rage.   "I was outside your home that night.   I heard everything.   I'm sorry.   I just needed to know the truth."

19

FIRST REVELATION

Lloyd stands in the bookstore browsing the aisles. A part of him wonders if he should be missing Janice. Another part of him doesn't care. It's only been a day since he learned of her death.

Lloyd scans the aisles, not worrying about how late it's getting. Earlier today, his boss gave him a week of bereavement time off.

Fiction.

Non-fiction.

Cooking.

Autobiography.

Travel.

Lloyd ponders the lifestyle of a man on the run, a fleeing felon, a wanted man. A cowboy.

Lloyd looks around the aisle he is standing in. He has thirty minutes before closing time.

He scans the books in the self-help aisle. He reads each title.

Look Me in the Eye.

I Hate You.

The OCD Workbook.

The Mindful Path to Self-Compassion.

The Manipulative Man.

Lost in the Mirror.

He stops at one that immediately rings familiar.

The Psychotic Break.

Lloyd picks up the book and reads the jacket.

Twenty-five percent of people are sociopaths, have no conscience, and can stab you in the back without ever feeling bad about it. Break the cycle.

Lloyd scans the book, pausing to read in detail about the close similarities between high-powered corporate executives and criminal sociopaths.

They show no remorse.

They cannot love.

They cannot see their own faults.

They can be your coworker.

They can be your parent.

They can be your friend.

Lloyd puts the book back onto the shelf, in no particular spot.

He continues scanning the shelf and reads more titles to himself.

5 Stages of Grief.

Pain & Loss.

What to Expect When Losing a Loved One.

He picks that one up.

He reads from the inside jacket of the book.

Notify people.

Accept help for funeral arrangements.

You may experience crying, difficulty sleeping, guilt, or anger.

Avoid places that remind you of the loss.

Take advantage of bereavement and support groups within your community.

Lloyd is interrupted by a store clerk.

"Sir, we'll be closing in fifteen minutes," she says.

Lloyd turns toward the young blonde, who is in her mid-twenties.

"I'm sorry, I didn't mean to disturb you," she says, embarrassed.

She looks at the title of the book Lloyd has just shut.

What to Expect When Losing a Loved One.

"No, don't worry. It wasn't your fault. You're just doing your job," says Lloyd sincerely.

"Well, I meant..." she says, pointing at the book.

"Oh this. It's nothing. I'm a grief counselor. I see this stuff all the time. It means nothing. I read this stuff to grasp what is going on in my profession," says Lloyd nonchalantly.

"Oh wow, that's great," she says, twirling her hair.

Her milky skin, her flawless complexion, her tight jeans and her firm stomach protruding ever so slightly from beneath her semi-cropped top harden Lloyd to erection.

"My dad is a therapist, so I find all that stuff really interesting," she says.

"Are you in school?" asks Lloyd.

"I'm trying. I'm applying to Tuckford Med School right now. What about you?" she asks.

"I graduated from Yale," says Lloyd deceptively.

"My dad is from Connecticut," she replies approvingly.

"Not many people know where Yale is. That's quite impressive, especially for a young, beautiful girl," replies Lloyd seductively.

She smiles flirtatiously.

"So you're applying to med school, huh? That's great. One of my closest friends is actually on the admissions board at Tuckford Med."

"Really?" she says eagerly. "Do you think you can talk to him for me?" she asks immaturely.

"I'm sure we could work that out."

Lloyd's deceit is intentional and manipulating.

"Hey, what time are you off? Maybe we can grab a drink," he says, focusing his gaze on her neck.

The chills trickling down from her shoulders cause the thin hair on her arms to stand as Lloyd's stare violates her.

Looking down at her watch, she blurts out, "My boyfriend is waiting for me in the parking lot. Maybe another time."

"I'd love to take you out. And, you know, talk about Med School," says Lloyd, watching the young clerk walk away.

A warm flash sweeps across his body as he rages inside from the rejection. Feeling like he is being submerged in water, he counts to ten.

"Let it go. Let it go," Lloyd whispers to himself. "Breathe," he says, trying to calm his anger, as he breathes in and out of his nose until it subsides.

20

FIRST READ

Three hours after leaving the bookstore, Lloyd reclines back into the bed pillows alone on Eva's bed. He has thirty minutes until she's expected home.

He cracks open his newly purchased book, *The Psychotic Break.*

He reads from it starting at the introduction.

Acknowledgments.

Thank you, Investigator Marty Kaplan and the Special Homicide Team of Tuckford County. Your wealth of knowledge was priceless.

He continues reading the book.

Sociopaths exhibit anti-social personality traits at a young age. They may begin truant behavior, cutting class, not caring about the rights of others, hurting animals, or lashing out at other students. They don't necessarily exhibit such characteristics; however, oftentimes they do.

He reads on.

Some sociopaths act out, when it could otherwise be controlled with therapy, due to parental neglect or dysfunction.

What does Marty Kaplan know about this? Lloyd wonders.

He flips though the book and stops at a chapter entitled *Marty Kaplan*.

He reads on.

One of the most notable homicide detectives in Tuckford County. He specializes in sex crimes and has investigated high profile serial killer cases. When asked what he thinks drives people to murder, he states, "It could be addiction, greed, rejection, pride, power, and control. There's many things. But what drives someone to become a serial killer is different. That's someone who cannot stop killing because they keep chasing the thrill and excitement of it."

Lloyd removes the duct tape and the tarp from the hardware bag he brought into Eva's home.

He glances at the alarm clock on the nightstand.

1:13 a.m.

Lloyd closes his eyes and starts unwinding the duct tape quickly. The ripping sound from the tape he is rolling around his hand begins to excite him as he fantasizes about taping up the bookstore clerk's body, binding it and rolling it up in a tarp. His fantasy then turns to Eva.

Lloyd's heart rate elevates, before he forces himself to calm down.

"Quiet, quiet down," he whispers to himself. "Calm down," he continues, throwing the wad of tape down onto the carpet.

"I can't do this. I can't keep doing this," he tells himself, rolling over into his pillow.

"Make it stop. Make it stop," he pleads softly to no one, desperately, hoping something or someone will make his evil thoughts stop.

21

STAINED

Lloyd unlocks the front door to his house and makes his way through the front tile area leading to the living room, in complete darkness. This is the first time he's returned to the crime scene—his home.

Lloyd feels the nearby wall for the light switch, but once he finds it and flips it on, he only hears a clicking sound without any light illuminating. He stops after switching it on and off ten times while still in darkness, before pounding on the wall angrily, wondering if police broke it during the search yesterday.

"SHIT!"

He walks straight in, slamming the door behind him, and throws his keys forcefully against the baseboards of his living room wall. His shoes click against the marble tile leading to his kitchen, where he flips the light on, illuminating his surroundings.

The fluorescent lighting takes a moment to reach its maximum potential and by that time, he's at his refrigerator.

Black fingerprint dust covers the refrigerator handles.

"SHIT!"

Lloyd stares at his neatly lined and stocked refrigerator.

Diet iced tea.

Flavored waters.

Flat waters.

Sparkling waters.

Bottled beers.

Wine bottles.

Milk. Almond. Soy. Vanilla soy. Lactose free.

It's all perfect, left in the exact way Janice typically lined the fridge with Lloyd's favorite things.

Lloyd despises it all.

He twists off the top of the raspberry flavored water and gulps it down like he hasn't drunk any liquid all day.

Lloyd leaves the kitchen and walks to his bedroom, not even observing the living room area.

He removes his overnight bag from below his queen size bed and begins packing it.

His socks line his dresser drawer perfectly. Black. Brown. White athletic.

The drawer below that boasts his underwear, cotton briefs. Black. White. Tan.

He packs one of everything, not sure how long he'll be away.

He moves to his closet, which is color-coded entirely. He focuses on the blue section of his dress shirts and picks two. Then he picks a white dress shirt, with a black silk tie from his tie rack, and a black, single-breasted Hugo Boss suit for tomorrow along with his black, leather shoes.

He pauses at his nightstand and looks at the wedding picture of him and Janice.

Her smile lights up the picture and Lloyd looks into his own eyes in the picture.

The uncertainty and unhappiness is apparent, even on their wedding day. He picks up the framed photo and studies it closer, wondering for the first time if his unborn child could have been enough to distract him and fix his life.

He throws the frame down aggressively at the oak nightstand.

"SHIT!"

After grabbing the silver, metal flashlight from his nightstand, he walks towards the living room, carrying his overnight bag.

He flicks on his flashlight, looking around the living room.

The dining room rug is missing. Chairs are knocked over and the table is sitting on its side.

The candles and coasters that once sat on the coffee table are strewn across the floor.

He follows the light from his flashlight towards the front door and tries to remember where he threw his keys, moving the light in every direction where the keys may be.

"SHIT!"

He focuses in on one area close to a baseboard near the front door. The shiny reflection from the keys catches his attention.

Blood stains the tile entry near the front door.

He reaches down for his keys and takes a close look where the tile meets the crown molding near the ground.

A handful of Janice's dark hair sits in a pile on top of Lloyd's keys, fixed to the wall by scalp membrane and a clot of blood.

Lloyd's stomach turns and acid regurgitation creeps its way up his throat, setting in a vomit taste in his mouth.

He flips off the flashlight and reaches through the chunk of hair to grab his keys.

He swallows hard.

"SHIT!"

22

FEIGNING GRIEF

Eva stands near Lloyd's fireplace mantel, looking at his family photos. Lloyd allowed her to come over and help him clean up the mess after seeing Janice's clot of hair against the baseboard last night.

She picks up a framed photo of Janice and Lloyd, asking if she could take it down.

"Eva, put that down. Please," says Lloyd, frustrated.

Eva looks at him with distrust.

"Eva, her murder is still being investigated. I don't want to look like I've already moved on. If it means anything to you, I'm not leaving them up because I want to. It's just the perception of it," Lloyd says with a slight detection of emotion.

Eva looks at Lloyd, puzzled.

"Do you have any photos of your family, without her, that you could put up instead? Like your mom or brother?" she asks, insistently.

"No. You know the story about them. Plus, I don't want any photos of them up," he says defiantly.

"But what if they can help you?" she pleads.

A knock at the door interrupts his concentration.

It is the young girl from Hal's Diner, dressed in her school uniform. Lloyd smiles at her, introduces her to Eva, and explains how they met.

"So, I'm selling these water bottles," the girl says, awkwardly removing one from her cloth shoulder bag.

As her long bangs fall in front of her face, she struggles to push them behind her ear, causing another bottle and a couple pens to fall from her sack.

The three stare down at the mess, but no one moves.

"I'm raising money for kids. Kids who have lost their parents and the ones who have been abandoned," she says with conviction.

Eva listens patiently, staying quiet.

Lloyd walks to his bedroom to retrieve his wallet and looks through it.

He overhears the young woman and Eva speaking to one another.

"What was your mom like?" asks the girl.

"Well. My mom. Let's see. She was not a nice person," replies Eva.

"I'm sorry. Was she mean to you?" the girl inquires curiously.

"She was more than mean to me. She abused me. She did things that no little girl should have to go through," Eva says sadly.

"I'm so happy you are a survivor," says the girl sympathetically.

"How do you deal with what happened to you?" asks the girl.

A long pause follows. Too long. Making the silence uncomfortable for Lloyd, still in the next room, away from the two women. It's so long that he walks back out to the living room area to interrupt the silence.

Tears have begun to stream down Eva's face. She is looking down, still facing the girl at the entranceway.

He walks up to the girl and hands her a five-dollar bill.

"I'll take one of the water bottles," says Lloyd obligingly.

Lloyd smiles at the young girl, noticing her dimples for the first time among her freckles.

The young woman reaches up and gives Lloyd a hug, elevating herself on her toes to reach his neck.

Lloyd pauses, wondering if anyone is watching him from the neighborhood. He wraps his arms around her. She holds onto him, nuzzling her nose into his neck reflexively.

She releases her heels down to the ground.

Lloyd doesn't want to let go. Her developing breasts pressed up against his chest excite him. The softness of her sweater and sweet smell of a hint of rose captivates him.

Eva watches the two embrace. Her tears stop and she smiles nervously at both of them, whose bodies are now disconnected except for their touching hands.

Eva studies the two, confused.

"Thank you so much," says the young woman graciously, before turning to leave.

Eva watches Lloyd, who is oddly grinning and focusing on the girl's backside and tiny waist as she walks away.

23

OPEN LETTER

Lloyd sits at Eva's dining room table watching her move from the kitchen to the table as she gets breakfast ready. The smell of bacon fills the room, reminding Lloyd of Janice, whose home-cooked meals filled his home each night with aromas he has already been missing. It's only been a couple days since her death.

Lloyd thinks for a moment what life would look like later down the road with Janice. She'd get further along in her pregnancy, probably start to have some morning sickness, and her body would begin to change. She'd have to shop for a new wardrobe, spending more money. She'd need to decorate a baby's room; more money wasted. She'd need the stroller, new car that would fit everything, and then the hospital bills would set in.

Lloyd hadn't been paying for medical insurance over the past several months leading up to her death, but Janice didn't know that. The expense was becoming too much and it was one of the things Lloyd decided to cut.

Eva moves delicately from room to room in her plaid apron with ruffled fringes, not saying anything to Lloyd as he opens up the Tuckford Press.

Lloyd reads the front page, which features a couple articles on plane mishaps. A man had fallen from the stowaway cargo area of a plane that was landing at the Tuckford International Airport. They yet had to identify the man, whose body was so deformed from the impact to the ground.

He was found in a neighborhood in Killmore and residents had to bring children inside, so they didn't see the carnage. The article mentioned how oxygen is limited at certain elevations and how weather conditions affect stowaway humans.

Eva glances at the headline, telling Lloyd how tragic that must be. She comments that is a terrible way to die, wondering how the man would have climbed into that area of the plane or why he would do that. She wonders if he was trying to run from something, was a convicted felon, or an undocumented person trying to get into the country.

Lloyd stays silent, not addressing any of Eva's concerns, entirely uncaring about the dead man. He thinks to himself that he'd do the same thing, running from police or trying to get to another country for a good enough reason.

The next article on the front page details an out-of-country plane crash where a female country singer had died. She was only forty years old and had just signed a deal to star in a movie.

Eva again comments on the tragedy for the singer's family, wondering about the details of the crash, and why her life would be taken at such a young age when she had so many things going for her. Eva rattles off all the number one hits the singer had, her route to stardom, her movie credits, and the fact she had three children.

Lloyd is listening to none of this. He has tuned Eva out. Eva sits down next to Lloyd and holds his hand, obviously upset at the singer's death and the fact Lloyd is not responding to her. Lloyd doesn't care about any of this. He stares at the paper, reading the details of the crash, and the statements from the friends and family of the country singer.

"Eva, can you bring me some coffee?" Lloyd asks calmly.

"Of course," she says, standing up and making her way to the kitchen.

Lloyd takes a closer look at the article on page three of the newspaper under the "local news" heading.

It's an article entitled "Open Letter," followed by "Letter to the White Picket Fence Killer."

Lloyd thinks back to Annabelle's house, which had a white picket fence.

He thinks about his own house, which has a white picket fence.

He reads on.

Like the rest of Tuckford County, I am deeply angered by the White Picket Fence Killer. He recently killed another innocent woman. He has left the entire community terrorized, wondering when he's going to strike next.

Serial killers like this are reminiscent of psychopaths and sociopaths like Ted Bundy. They will keep killing until they are caught. The police needs your help to stop his killing spree and seek justice.

The below letter is written as a fictional letter, so you know what we're dealing with. Spread the word and report anything suspicious.

If you have any information which may help police, please contact them at 343-2301.

Open Letter From The White Picket Fence Killer

Dear Victims, Friends, Family & World,

I'm an anti-social sociopath.

I've had a pattern since childhood of disregarding others, even though you didn't notice.

I could never keep a friendship going, because I didn't care about people's feelings.

All I care about is me, even though I hate myself.

I can't stand being frustrated when something doesn't go my way, so I deal with it using violence.

I unleash my rage and violence against women, especially the pregnant ones who are perfect and sit behind white picket fences, which is where I got my nickname, White Picket Fence Killer.

I choose my victims because I resent their lifestyles. It's a deep-seated hatred stemming from my own childhood.

And when I kill, I don't feel guilty. I don't even know what that feels like.

To rationalize my actions, I believe my problems are everyone else's fault, even when they're not.

There's nothing you could do to stop me, because I don't respond to punishment.

THE SUBURBAN SEDUCCIÓN

It will take me decades to come to terms with what I'm doing and understand what causes me to think this way. Don't waste your time trying to make sense of any of this, because I won't be.

I don't even know what remorse or empathy is. I may never understand how to put myself in someone else's shoes.

Don't blame my family. They raised me the best they could. And they'll carry the guilt from my actions for life.

Do pray for them along with my victims and their families, because I won't be. I'll be feeling sorry for myself and thinking how the world is still against me.

Do tell them to forgive me; not for me, but to free themselves from the prison I've sentenced them to.

Don't blame yourselves for leaving the victims alone or unarmed.

No matter what measures could have been taken, there will always be a place for me to carry out my anger against women and expectant mothers. Antique shops, art stores, bookstores, poetry readings, museums, wine galleries, restaurants—I would've found another victim.

Don't blame police for not finding me. I work carefully, leaving no traces behind.

Do take me serious, because I will strike again.

I'm like an aggressive cancer, viciously destroying your community.

Do report anything suspicious you see or hear, because I'm out looking for my next victim.

Do take seriously anyone who has a problem with anger or rage. Because killers like me have a problem dealing with loss, rejection, and failure.

Do carry out the maximum appropriate punishment against me under the law. It honors what our society stands for—life, liberty, and happiness—what I took away from my victims.

The best place for me is in prison. But even there, I'm capable of harming the people around me and the people in charge of taking care of me. Consider seriously the death penalty. After all, I'm a rabid dog that needs to be put down.

And to those who are hesitant about coming forward to police to report me, realize that you are contributing to the irreparable pain I'm causing. You're enabling me to carry out my serial murders. Even if you are my friend, family member, or representative, the blood is on your hands, too.

Do something to stop me—because you or your loved one will be my next victim.

From,

Your White Picket Fence Killer

Lloyd quickly closes the newspaper as Eva returns to the table with his coffee. He begins a discussion with her about the plane crash, while raging inside and feeling insulted from being called a "cancer" and "rabid dog."

24

ESCAPE

Eva stirs a pot of chicken noodle soup. The smell of the herbs, broth, and vegetables seep from the kitchen.

Lloyd rests his head back and counts in a slow fashion, trying to get his mind to stop racing about the Open Letter he read this morning.

Eva yells from the kitchen.

"How was your day?"

"Exhausting. I had to pick out a plot, a casket. I was trying to remember if Janice wanted to be cremated or buried," he says emotionless.

"When is the funeral?"

"I'm not sure yet. Her autopsy is delaying things."

Eva walks over to Lloyd, removing her old-fashioned, homemade apron with a fringe of cotton lace. She drapes it over a chair at the dining room table and sits on the armrest of the couch closest to Lloyd.

Eva's once strong arms are beginning to look thin. Her face looks more gaunt than it was just a week ago.

Lloyd doesn't move, but sits with his neck still held by the back of the couch and his eyes closed.

She begins to rub his forehead, touching her lips to his forehead and kissing him.

Her kisses are tender and loving.

"I know this is hard for you, Lloyd. You look really stressed out," she says. "Maybe we can plan a little getaway."

"If I leave town, it's going to be for good. It's going to be to get away to the furthest possible place," he says.

"What would happen to us? You would just leave and never come back?" asks Eva, sadly.

"Is this something you'd really do?"

Lloyd pauses.

"Sometimes, I wish I could get away from all of this."

"All of what? The investigation? Don't you want to find out who did this to her? Don't you care?"

"Eva..."

"Lloyd, I need to ask you something. I need to know. I need to know if you murdered Janice. It's eating me up inside. Look at me, Lloyd. I haven't eaten in days. I'm just having a really hard time with this," she says.

"I did not kill her. Why are you accusing me?"

"You can tell me, Lloyd. I'm not going to tell anyone. I promise, I promise," she says pleadingly.

"Eva, stop," he says.

"What about that other woman? What about her? The waitress, the lady down the street, the one we went to the scene," she says.

"No, I didn't kill either of them. Get that through your head. And don't ever accuse me again of this. What's gotten into you?" he says.

Eva begins crying softly.

"I can't do this anymore, Lloyd. I can't act like nothing is wrong. And I can deal with it, but I need to know the truth. Tell *us* the truth. I told you that first day you hurt me in the bedroom that I would never tell. I just asked you not to leave me. Don't leave me," she says desperately.

"Eva, you said something right now. You said to tell *us* the truth," says Lloyd. "Who is *'us'* Eva?" demands Lloyd suspiciously.

"I didn't say that. I said *I* need to know the truth," she replies defensively.

"Forget it. I need to get to the store. Can you watch the soup? It's on simmer," she continues quickly before removing her apron and grabbing her purse to leave in a hurry.

25

REPLY

Within minutes of Eva leaving to the grocery store, Lloyd opens the Tuckford Press again. He hadn't wanted her to get a glimpse of the letter he had been insulted by this morning.

He pulls his steno pad close to him and twirls his silver pen around his fingers, thinking how to start off his letter. Lloyd elevates his feet on Eva's couch and rests his back into a corduroy pillow, removing his glasses and massaging his temples. He replaces his glasses and begins to write.

To Whom it May Concern:

The following is to inform you that I am responsible for the missing body of Annabelle Phillips. For many years, I've thought of it as a work of art.

THE SUBURBAN SEDUCCIÓN

Tuckford law enforcement is very incompetent. I walk around town a free man while investigators search for clues.

I'm the "White Picket Fence Killer." I confess, I like my nickname because it suits my victims. I have indeed painted a white fence red with blood.

I am very upset with the people from Tuckford County. I demand an apology letter by the person who wrote the "Open Letter" and the press for printing it. I am neither a "rabid dog" nor a "cancer." I also demand the letter to be unpublished.

Additionally, I demand that the killer of Janice Gil be brought to justice. If the police did their job, they would uncover the real killer.

As I write this letter, I'm fighting an urge to kill I have that I can't understand. It's just there. It always has been.

Until next time,

White Picket Fence Killer

26

DEMONS

Lloyd sits with Eva on her couch listening to cassette tapes from her new therapy class. Lloyd strokes Eva's hair, as she is still catching her breath from their quick lovemaking session after she returned from the store. The reply letter Lloyd just wrote sits on the coffee table in front of them in an envelope.

Dr. Lehr speaks slowly with a thick accent from the recorder.

"Most men are born with demons or inherit them at a young age. Some are created from their upbringings, while others are from mental or physical illness. We should accept this as a society. But what we shouldn't accept is when that person has failed entirely to keep these demons properly managed," says the voice on tape.

Eva stops the old-fashioned, black, plastic cassette player.

"Lloyd, do you agree with that?" she questions in a professorial tone.

"What is this, a counseling session?" he retorts.

Eva reminds Lloyd of his agreement to have nightly talks with her.

She hits play on the cassette player.

"Women who allow these men to continue to repeat unhealthy patterns become enablers," the voice continues.

"So, Lloyd. What *is* going on with the investigation?" she asks curiously.

"I don't know. My guess is that Marty Kaplan, the investigator on it, is going to try to pin Janice's case on me. He's an asshole."

"Why would he do that, Lloyd? This is your life they're messing with."

"Cuz they have no other leads. They have to."

"Eva, can I ask you a question?" he asks, changing the subject.

Eva agrees to entertain it.

"Why are women attracted to me?" he questions.

"Well, I can tell you why I was attracted..." she begins.

Lloyd cuts her off from answering it that way, "No, not you in particular. Why are *other* women attracted to me?"

"Lloyd, you're very handsome... and intelligent. You listen to what we say, you pay attention to our needs. A lot of men aren't good at that. And you can be really thoughtful. You're genuine. Real,"

"Then why am I so indifferent about Janice's death?" he says brokenly.

"Because, like the tape, you're not properly managing what's going on inside of you. Maybe it stems from your childhood," she says.

"Why do you put up with me?" he asks.

"I don't know. Well, I mean, I do, but I don't. That's why I'm taking this class."

"Do you think I should run from you?" she asks kiddingly.

He pauses, unsure of the true answer to this question before answering.

"No. I told you I'm not a monster," he replies, grasping her hair between his fingers and smoothing it down to the roots, softly.

"Eva, I didn't kill Janice," Lloyd says convincingly.

"How did this happen to her?" she asks.

"Maybe she was just there and an intruder came in. Maybe the guy had no other choice. Maybe he just reacted," Lloyd says sadly.

"He didn't *have* to kill her," says Eva.

"Maybe she was just there. Maybe she just walked in. Maybe he had no idea she was home," Lloyd protests.

"How could he not know?" Eva presses on, challenging him.

"Eva. Who knows. I have no idea," he says angrily.

"Lloyd, do you ever think things happen for a reason?"

"What do you mean?" he questions.

"Well, you're saying maybe it was an accident. But maybe it happened for a reason."

"Reason for what?"

"To help you *feel*. You've talked about not being able to feel, or have emotions. Maybe it happened to help you experience. To empathize."

"Maybe," he responds, thinking deeply about what Eva just mentioned.

"Maybe like you, *he* didn't have that growing up. The ability to feel. To love. To experience loss," she says.

"But neither did you. You grew up being abused, not loved," he says.

"We're not talking about me, Lloyd. We're talking about you," she replies.

"Why do you think whoever it was went to your house?" Eva asks, changing the subject.

"I don't know. Maybe he knew her. Maybe he was looking for me," says Lloyd, shifting his gaze away from Eva towards the fireplace mantel of photos.

"Look at me," she says aggressively.

"I am," he says, returning back to face her.

"Why did Janice die?" she demands.

"I told you, Eva. I don't know. I didn't kill her," he says sternly, slightly raising his voice.

"You said you would answer my questions honestly," says Eva, matching his tone.

"I *am*. What do you want to know?"

"Who would kill her? You have to think hard," she demands.

Lloyd stares away from Eva, clenching his teeth together, tightening his jaw, causing his face to flush from the blood rushing in and his ears to ring loudly.

"Don't challenge me, Eva," he says, aggressively, releasing all the tension.

"What? You can't answer me, Lloyd?" she asks sarcastically.

"You want me to believe you're not a monster. How is that possible when you can't even answer me? You have demons, really deep ones," she screams meanly.

"Don't belittle me," he yells back, standing up.

"I can't do this anymore, Lloyd. I can't."

"Eva. Stop. Stop," says Lloyd, returning back to the couch and cradling her head into his chest.

"I don't want to believe you're capable of this. But everything says you are. It feels like a dream, like it's not real.

"Investigator Kaplan called me yesterday asking about us. I don't know what to say anymore," she finally pours out, before losing herself in a crying spell.

Lloyd sits and feels nothing but anger about hearing Marty's name, wrapping his arms around her until she stops.

He starts kissing her softly, starting with her forehead, then moving to her lips, and each cheek.

"Eva, look at me," Lloyd says, gripping her chin and pushing it up so her eyes meet his.

"I love you," he says, waiting for a reaction.

"I love you, too," Eva finally says, obligingly.

"I need you to help me, Eva. I need you to NOT talk to anyone about my case, especially police," he says sternly and steadily.

"About what?" she asks, surprised.

"About everything, what I did to you, how we met."

"But..." she starts, before being silenced by Lloyd's finger up against her lips, motioning for her to stay quiet.

"Eva, it's just a matter of time before they're arresting me. What happened with us is no one's business. Promise me you won't tell anyone," he says, waiting for a response from her.

Eva looks around her living room searching for words. She glances toward her coffee table, the living room furniture, her bookshelf, then the photos and Christmas lights lining her fireplace mantel.

Her eyes stay glued to the family photo with her sister.

"I won't. I told you from the start I'd never tell. You don't need to worry about me," she says, still staring at the photo.

27

JAIL

Lloyd walks into the general population jail cell of the Canyon Base Police Department. Even though he tried to get mentally prepared after his conversation with Eva last night, there's something about the reality of an arrest that he couldn't prepare for, like the coldness of the handcuffs when they are initially slapped on his wrists.

He wipes the black powder still fresh on his fingers onto his orange jumpsuit. This jail sits on the border of two cities and typically houses the rougher criminals.

Over the next thirty minutes, two more men are added to the cell tank, making it five. It is never a good idea for the numbers to be uneven. Immediately, when someone is added to the tank, the others size him up, decide whether they could out-strengthen him or team up together to outnumber the rest. The blacks go with the blacks, the Hispanics band together, and the whites could band together or join with either side. There are no Asians in Tuckford County, or at least it is rare.

At least three men in the tank are Hispanic, tattooed, and have shaved heads. Two of the other men are white and older. After Lloyd makes small talk with one of the white guys, he learns he was booked for a DUI earlier in the day.

Lloyd picks an empty corner to stand in and within a minute, stares down the Hispanics before dropping to the ground and doing pushups against the concrete. He moves to sit-ups, making sure he is facing the Hispanics, who are in the opposite corner. He doesn't for one moment take his eyes off the Hispanics. He needs to know where they are at any given moment.

One of the white guys looks like he is about seventy years old. Lloyd doesn't even bother speaking to him, feeling he is useless to team up with or befriend. Even though Lloyd is half Hispanic, he knows he fits in with the whites more based on looks. The seventy-year-old slowly makes his way to Lloyd, seemingly to befriend him after the Hispanics begin hopping around pretending to air-box with one another.

"They think they're Oscar de la Hoya," the old man says to Lloyd.

"I'm not sure who they think they are, but they aren't coming over here," replies Lloyd.

"Exactly, boy, now you're talking," says the old man.

"What are you in here for?" Lloyd asks.

"My son stabbed my wife. Bitch didn't die. I shoulda pulled the knife out. Maybe she woulda bled to death. Cops think I'm involved. But I'm not. I didn't even see what happened. They were always fighting," the old man says, emotionless.

Lloyd doesn't react.

The Hispanic men stop play boxing with one another and begin whispering to each other. Lloyd's stomach tenses up, more than just from the sit-ups he's been doing. The old man looks toward the Hispanics.

"I've seen this look before," says the man to Lloyd, worriedly.

"What's up?" says one of the Hispanics to the old man.

"Hey man, chill out," the old man says, trying to calm the atmosphere.

Suddenly, one of the Hispanic men removes his knee high sock and drops something inside. He slowly walks towards Lloyd and the old man, with the other Hispanic closely behind him.

"Hey man, what you in here for?" the Hispanic asks, focusing on Lloyd.

"Murder," says Lloyd fiercely.

"Wow, murder, huh?" the Hispanic says mockingly, looking at his partner.

"You look familiar," the first Hispanic says.

"We're in here for murder, too," says the second Hispanic.

"I've seen you before," insists the first Hispanic.

"Who'd you murder?" the second Hispanic asks.

The first Hispanic motions for him to back down and stop talking.

Lloyd doesn't move his stare off them. The old man retreats to the iron bars.

The first Hispanic man starts twirling the sock-filled weapon.

"We murder people, but not the kind you do. That's where I saw you, in the paper. You been killing women," says the Hispanic, beginning to pummel Lloyd with his weighted sock.

He swings his sock and beats Lloyd mercilessly, mostly focusing on his face, over and over again. The old man looks away as Lloyd yells for help and the second Hispanic yells encouraging words, as though he's watching a boxing tournament.

28

CHANGE

Lloyd sits across from Eva at the visiting booth of the South Tuckford County Jail. Other inmates sit in orange jumpsuits two feet away on both sides of Lloyd. Friends and relatives of the inmates talk into phones on the civilian side of the booth, separated by glass, speaking to the inmates on the other side.

Lloyd's face is black and blue from the Hispanic men beating him relentlessly yesterday. His eyes look like swollen balls, and he has bandages on some of the more blackened areas of his face. The codeine the jail nurse gave him seems to be working enough to dull the pain from yesterday's beating.

Lloyd holds the receiver to his ear.

"Lloyd, how did this happen? Where were the jail deputies?" Eva asks.

"I don't know. They were there, but by the time they got the asshole off of me, he had taken at least ten swings.

They don't care. There's a whole investigation going on," says Lloyd, in frustration.

"I can't believe they got that thing into the cell," says Eva. "Lloyd, you still haven't told me why they arrested you."

"They're trying to pin Janice's murder on me. We shouldn't be talking about this. They could be recording our conversation right now," he says angrily.

"I'm sorry. We don't have to talk about it then," she says hopelessly.

"Look, Eva, I need your help. Look at me," he says desperately, fixing his eyes on her, looking for any sign of sincere sympathy.

Eva takes a deep breath and examines the markings on his face.

"What do you want me to do?" she asks.

"Believe in me, Eva. I need you to not lose faith in me. I didn't do this," he says.

"But you had that tape and..." she starts.

"Eva..." he says firmly.

"I know. I'm sorry. It's just that..." she says.

"Eva, I've changed. I wasn't honest before with you. I'm not going to make it out of here alive. Look at what this place is doing to me," he pleads.

"I need your support. I need you to get me out of here. I need you to post my bail. My arraignment is set for tomorrow afternoon. I need you to contact my stepbrother, Richard Hill. I need him to represent me," says Lloyd desperately.

Eva looks up to the ceiling, her eyes starting to water.

"Eva," starts Lloyd, demanding her attention. "Look at me. Do you want me to stay in this cage. This place is like a zoo. It's for animals. I don't belong here. They're trying to get me killed, putting me next to these people," he says desperately, motioning with his eyes to the inmates around him.

Eva looks at the family members and spouses next to her that are communicating with the other inmates. A Hispanic woman in her twenties with three young sons each under five years old sits beside her blowing kisses into the phone to an inmate on the other side of the call booth, who has tattoos all over his face.

Eva looks to the other side of the booth. There is a Hispanic mom in her seventies, praying with her head bowed down into the phone receiver she is holding. The inmate on the other side of the booth is mirroring her position, bowing his head into the phone. He has a shaved head with a big "L" tattooed on the side of his head.

"Do you see what I mean, Eva?" Lloyd whispers into the phone, convincingly.

"Tell me how to contact him," Eva says compliantly.

29

FIRST APPEARANCE

A criminal courthouse is a place you never want to visit, unless you have to, for a loved one, for your own case, or to work. Department Three is busy with its usual afternoon business, while waiting for Judge Cohen to make his post-lunch appearance.

Lloyd sits in an orange jumpsuit alone in the jury box, with two deputies closely watching him.

The South Tuckford County Courthouse is one of the nicer ones in the state. Its historical embellishments and refurbishing it underwent recently gives it more of a French palace feel than a stomping ground for criminals.

Aside from the scenery, the government does nothing to make the courthouse comfortable for the public to loiter around. The hallways have very limited seating, so people have to stand. Even inside the courtrooms, there are long, hard, wooden benches to seat the audience, rather than cushioned seats. It's like a church with hard wooden pews for Catholics being forced to kneel and repent for their sins.

The coolness from the winter afternoon air seeps through the doors every time they are opened to allow criminals to enter the building. There are no heaters warming the halls or the courtrooms. All of it is intentional. It's supposed to be a place that you don't want to come to unless you're ordered to. Everyone who works in the courthouse has grown so accustomed to the lack of hospitality; the attorneys wear gloves, scarves, and wool coats, and courtroom staff curl their feet up to small space heaters below their desks.

"Remain seated, come to order, court is now in session," the deputy yells.

In the audience section, a couple of local news reporters sit, along with Eva, who sits in the last row, and a couple of attorneys in suits sit in the middle area, observing the proceedings. Janice's mother sits in the front row behind Richard.

In the front row of the audience section behind prosecutor Jack Moore sits Investigator Marty Kaplan in a dark suit.

"We are on the record in People versus Lloyd Gil, Case Number TUCK1933. All parties are present, including Mr. Gil, who is seated in the jury box in custody," says Judge Cohen.

"I have a Complaint in front of me, charging one count of first degree murder upon Janice G. Have you received a copy of this?" Judge Cohen asks, directing his attention towards the public defender.

"I have, Your Honor. I have advised my client of his rights and we are ready to proceed with arraignment. On his behalf, I'd like to enter a not guilty plea and set an immediate date for preliminary hearing on this case," says the public defender, who is clueless about the circumstances of the case, yet sounds confident.

Just as Judge Cohen is about to speak, the courtroom doors open and a man in a neatly tailored, dark grey designer suit with black, leather shoes and a white, pressed shirt and skinny, black tie enters.

The courtroom grows quiet.

"I apologize, Your Honor, for my tardiness. Consider this the first and last time something like this will happen. Richard Hill on behalf of Lloyd Gil. I'm requesting your permission to substitute in as his counsel," this man blurts out, focusing his attention only on Judge Cohen, despite the crowded nature of the courtroom.

"Hand your card to my clerk," says Judge Cohen. "She'll need it for the file."

The embroidery spelling out "HILL" onto his white shirt cuff peeks out at Lloyd briefly from beneath his jacket sleeve as he hands her his business card.

Judge Cohen's eyes remain fixed on Richard as he moves around the courtroom confidently and in control of every movement.

"Mr. Hill. I'm well familiar with you. And know from personal experience when I worked with you in Loft City, that tardiness is not a habit for you. So I'll accept your apology this one time."

"Thank you your honor," says Richard, making a movement holding his chest as though he is slightly bowing at the judge."

"How do you wish to proceed?"

"I'd respectfully request to have my client arraigned on the charges. And set dates forthwith."

"I don't see any reason why we can't proceed in that manner," says Judge Cohen. "Mr. Gil, do you have any objection? I expect you were prepared for this. The substitution on your behalf?" the judge says, directing his attention towards Lloyd.

Lloyd studies Richard, his stepbrother he hasn't seen in years.

"No," he replies.

"Mr. Moore. Any comment?" asks Judge Cohen, looking at Jack.

After asking for a brief moment, Jack turns back to speak with Marty.

Lloyd looks around the courtroom and sets his eyes on Eva, who looks nervous. She is wearing a wool pencil skirt, something that is not her usual style, which looks like she either borrowed it or bought it after realizing she needed to come to court. Her cream silk blouse and black cashmere sweater are also not her type. It looks fashionable and Lloyd likes the look. She has on high-heeled, suede, black pumps and dark grey stockings. Seductive and again, not her usual look.

Jack pulls away from Marty and returns back to his side of the counsel table. Marty squints his eyes at Lloyd and while no one is watching, mouths the words, "Fuck you."

"I'm ready," says Jack to Judge Cohen, who is still sitting in his black robe up on his bench.

"Your Honor. We are asking for you to set no bail," says Jack calmly.

After a long pause, Judge Cohen muffles the words, "Not today, counsel; file your bail motion."

"Mr. Gil's bail will remain as fixed at one million dollars, in accordance with the bail schedule."

"Your Honor. My firm is prepared to post bail immediately," says Richard.

"May I be heard?" yells Jack, who then continues without permission.

"My office is currently considering filing special circumstances against Mr. Gil. That alone makes him an extreme flight risk, considering the possible penalties," pleads Jack.

"Then file them and we'll take up the bail issue at that point. Until then, bail remains as set. Mr. Gil, as part of your bail, I'm setting a few conditions. One, you are not to leave the jurisdiction of this county, except to reasonably prepare for your defense and for work-related reasons. Second, relinquish your passport to my courtroom clerk no later than tomorrow morning," says Judge Cohen.

"I don't have a passport," says Lloyd.

"Fine, then you've complied with that condition. Third, you will be receiving a phone call by the end of each day by my courtroom clerk. She will verify your whereabouts, so be sure to answer calls coming from our area code. Do you understand?" says Judge Cohen.

"Yes, we understand and agree to all that," replies Richard quickly.

"Very well. You'll be released later today. We're done here," says Judge Cohen, slamming his gavel down loudly before leaving the bench.

30

FIRST REUNION

Lloyd drives through the busy streets of downtown Loft City, which sits an hour from Tuckford County and is the metropolis of the state. The finest financial institutions, restaurants, and corporate businesses are housed here.

Lloyd drives slowly, looking for street addresses of each of the sky-rise buildings. He is still groggy from not being able to sleep much last night after being released from jail. Homeless people push carts through the streets, while well-dressed, thirty-something-year-old executives walk briskly down the sidewalks, holding electronic tablets and talking on cell phones.

Lloyd looks up through his front windshield and reads the signage on the top of a building. One word says it all:

HILL

Lloyd pulls into a metered spot, fills it with change, and dashes up to the fifty-second floor to Hill & Associates. Within minutes, he is being offered any beverage of his choice, including alcohol, and an array of cheeses, crackers, and mixed nuts.

Lloyd sips from his dirty martini before following a blonde in her mid-twenties, who is guiding him to Richard's office. He spills some vodka on his hand as he moves his focus from his drink to the woman's tight leggings and high red and black heels.

They turn the corner into Richard's office. Richard rises from his leather desk chair to greet him.

"Lloyd. It's been years. Have a seat. Thank you, Darlene," says Richard, motioning for her to close the door on her way out.

"I see you took advantage of our beverage selection," says Richard.

"She insisted and said there was a firm happy hour going on," says Lloyd.

"Yes, Darlene is hard to say no to," laughs Richard suggestively.

"Wow, you haven't changed much," says Lloyd.

"And you haven't, either," says Richard playfully.

Richard sits down, motioning for Lloyd to do the same on the guest chair.

Richard's office view boasts the tallest high-rises in Loft City along with Loft Stadium, practically allowing a full viewing of a professional football game.

Framed photos of Richard's wife sit on a credenza behind his desk.

Prestigious awards and framed newspaper headlines of high-profile cases fill one wall. Diplomas fill another wall.

Stanford University – Political Science Bachelor's of Art

Yale Law School – Juris Doctor

He had accomplished everything Lloyd had not. Richard's photographs adorn magazine covers, which are framed and set on another wall.

Top 40 under 40
Loft City Lawyer
Trial Lawyers of the Country
Litigator of the State
The Board of Trial Advocates

Lloyd stops reading, noticing the obvious silence as Richard sips on his bourbon, watching Lloyd. Richard breaks the silence.

"Lloyd, I just want to throw this out there. We've had our differences. And Mom sends her best. She's had much regret about the distance between us over the years.

"None of us have any ill feelings toward you. You're family. You're part of *our* family. And I've always believed that families should stick together, especially in times like this. We are all deeply sorry about Janice. She seems like she was an amazing woman from what I've read about in the papers. I'd be honored to help you in any way possible. You're my brother," says Richard sincerely.

Lloyd hangs on to every word, listening for any sound of insincerity in Richard's voice.

"I'm assuming when you came yesterday you realized the extent of the case," says Lloyd with trepidation.

"I figured. I've already spoken with Investigator Kaplan. He told me you gave him my card.

"I'm honored, Lloyd, that you would ask and trust me with your defense... your life," says Richard honestly.

"Of course I will. I've discussed this possibility with Mom and we both agree, it's the right thing to do," continues Richard.

"I don't want you to represent me because it's the right thing to do...." starts Lloyd, in a distrusting tone of voice.

"That's not what I meant, Lloyd. I *want* to represent you. I feel I could help you. And I think you need me. Otherwise you wouldn't be here right now," says Richard paternalistically.

Lloyd glares at Richard, not disagreeing.

"But I have one caveat, Lloyd," continues Richard. "I'm not accepting any money for your case. I'd expect this to go to trial. I'd assume you're not looking for any plea deal. And I expect us to push this forward, aggressively. My time is valuable," says Richard sternly.

"Why'd you post my bail?" asks Lloyd.

"Don't worry about that. Mom committed to putting that up. I'm telling you, she feels a lot of guilt and regret for the loss of your relationship and your loss of Janice. I haven't seen her this distraught in a while," says Richard.

"Well, that's awfully kind of her," Lloyd says.

"There's a couple more things," says Richard. "I tell this to all of my clients, so don't take it personally.

"My job is to defend you. Zealously. This means that I become your biggest advocate. I'm not one of those attorneys who simply wants to provide you with an adequate defense. I represent you to win. And winning means something different in each case. What it means in your case, Lloyd, is to save you from the death penalty."

"Death penalty? What are you talking about?" says Lloyd, surprised.

"That was what the prosecutor was mentioning yesterday. The special circumstances. Janice was killed at home. This is either a first degree burglary or someone lying in wait. Either scenario qualifies you for the death penalty.

"I have no doubt, Lloyd, they're going to seek death in your case. They'll find a way. A pregnant housewife killed in her home is every community's worst nightmare. And the cops may try to feed the idea that you're responsible for another murder they've reopened the investigation on in the same area. I've been following the case closely. The police are starting to feel pressure because they don't have any leads on the other one. The police chief opponent vowed to solve that case once and for all," says Richard.

"But I didn't kill Janice," Lloyd yells.

"Let's get one thing straight, Lloyd," says Richard firmly, while standing up and moving closer to Lloyd, pointing his finger in the air towards him.

"I don't ever want to know whether you committed this murder or not. Or any murder for that matter. I don't want to hear you did or did not do it.

"I will ask the questions that I need answers to. I can't do my job if I begin to think that you're responsible. So never, ever talk about it again. Not to me. Not to anyone. It hurts us both. Am I making myself clear?" Richard demands.

"I understand," Lloyd says, defeated.

"When you leave here, you will need to go immediately to Dorner & Sons. It's at the corner of Fifth and Park. Ask for a guy by the name of Sam Hunt. He's a professional lie detection expert. He'll be expecting you.

"Other than Sam or my investigator, don't talk to anyone about anything pertaining to your case. Even at the funeral. Or on the phone. Especially if you get arrested again. Calls from jail are recorded. And the police could be behind anyone calling or visiting you at *any* point, in or out of custody. They like to do pretext calls. Behave the entire time. This is a marathon, Lloyd, not a sprint. Do you understand me?" asks Richard sternly.

Lloyd shakes his head in agreement.

"If you need a break. Or need to get out of town, feel free to use the firm's condo in Springset Falls. It's only an hour and a half away, but feels like you're in a different world."

"Thanks."

"I've also spoken with your boss at Software Solutions. You've officially been placed on administrative leave. I negotiated that instead of a firing; but if I were you, I'd be prepared for the worst."

Lloyd looks at Richard, shocked.

"When's Janice's funeral?" asks Richard.

"Day after tomorrow."

"Okay. I'll be there."

"Is mom coming?" asks Lloyd.

"She can't make it. But Olivia and I will be there."

Lloyd stares at the framed newspaper headline on Richard's wall:

Richard Hill
"The Undefeated"

"Tell mom I said thank you," says Lloyd.

31

FEAR

Lloyd drives to The Joint, a hamburger diner Eva requested they meet in front of to discuss "things." He's been avoiding her since he met with Richard yesterday. She didn't say what in particular she wanted to talk about; but her tone was rather short and Lloyd didn't like the feeling that gave him.

Lloyd pulls his car into a spot in a parking lot near the restaurant, turns his ignition off, and waits. There are no other cars in the lot.

Eva pulls her car into the parking stall next to Lloyd, quickly exits her car, and knocks on his window. Within minutes, the two are walking around downtown Canyon Base. The smell of burning wood from the homes in the vicinity competes with the waffle cone ice cream store on the corner they pass by. If it hadn't been for the obvious tension between Eva and Lloyd, the smells would have returned them both to a rare, fond childhood memory from the small pleasures of things like waffle cones and ice cream. Neither grew up with money or parents doting on them.

Although Eva's mother had the means to spoil her, the only love she gave her involved excessive whippings. And Lloyd's mother, although she never laid a hand on him, seemed to spend most of her time trying to fix a past that Lloyd never fully understood. She remained single during most of Lloyd's childhood, which worked perfectly fine for him. But when she met Michael Hill, everything changed; for Lloyd at least.

The two walk past the ice cream store and think about stopping in, almost pausing, but neither does. Eva breaks the silence.

"Lloyd, I've been thinking a lot," she starts. "You've suddenly gotten distant. Are you seeing someone else?" she asks.

"No, Eva, I'm not. I just have a lot on my plate with the case now. I care about you, but I think it's best we go our separate ways," he says softly.

Eva takes a deep sigh.

"You promised you'd never leave me," she retorts hopelessly.

"We can't be together. I feel like police are watching my every step. The media's been swarming," he continues.

"So because of that, you're going to end it?" she asks sadly.

"Look, this is hard on me and it's making matters worse when we're spending time together. It's not good for my case," says Lloyd.

"You can communicate with me," insists Eva.

"No, I can't Eva. I'm not supposed to be discussing my case with anyone," he responds.

"Lloyd, what is this really about?" asks Eva disbelievingly.

She removes a Kleenex from the pocket of her black, hooded, wool coat and begins dabbing her eyes with it.

"Are you seeing someone? Do you want to leave me so you can spend the night with someone else? Because if that's what it is, go ahead, Lloyd. I can accept it if we're done," she says.

"Could you really accept it... if I *was* seeing someone else?" he asks disbelievingly.

"I could. If that's what it is, I would want to know," she says. "Because I haven't been with anyone else," Eva insists.

"It's not that. I'm not seeing anyone else. But I would like the space to deal with my case," he says.

"You lied to me," she says. "You said you'd never leave me," she says uncontrollably.

"Eva, you're scaring me. Calm down. This is bordering on stalker-like behavior," he says.

"You've changed, Lloyd. It's like you don't even care about me anymore.

"What is it? What have I done?" she says in an insistent tone of voice.

Lloyd looks at his reflection in a store window as they pass by. He looks down at the ground, avoiding puddles remaining from the early afternoon rainfall.

"It's just that I need my space. I think it's best we never speak again," he continues.

"Lloyd, don't do this. You're all I have," she pleads.

Lloyd stops at the corner of a lighted intersection where no one is around and Eva faces him. She grabs for his hands desperately, but he refuses.

She whispers sternly, "Lloyd, I know you've killed them.

"And dumped their bodies. I saw the duct tape... the pink duct tape. You said it was to fix your window. There never was a broken window. I never saw it when I was there, even before Janice died..." she says suspiciously.

"Eva, were you trespassing around my house? Were *you* the one that killed Janice?" he asks threateningly.

"Lloyd... You know that's not true. You killed her. And I'm worried you won't stop. Let me help you."

32

GRIEVING

Lloyd stands in the cold morning stillness at Canyon Base Cemetery and watches Janice's casket sway back and forth as it is lowered by cemetery staff. The sturdy ropes seem unbreakable and the procedure seems as routine to the two male workers as deck hands docking a boat.

Lloyd feels nothing.

He clenches his fist tight inside his pants pocket and has a quick flashback of Eva's accusations yesterday.

His mother-in-law stands next to him, sobbing into her white, embroidered handkerchief. He forces himself to put his arm around her to console her, and she quickly uses his support to brace all of her weight against him.

Marty stands on the opposite side of the grave watching Lloyd's every move.

Janice's cousins and in-laws all stand dressed in black around the gravesite, each holding a red rose.

A priest dressed in a white robe shakes his silver aspergillum filled with holy water towards Janice's casket as it is lowered into the depths of the open plot.

The priest recites a prayer:

Lord, ever caring and gentle,

As we mourn the sudden death of our sister Janice, show us the immense power of your goodness and strengthen our belief that Janice has entered into your presence.

May we also commit to your love Janice's little one, Baby Gil. Enfold him in eternal life.

We pray for our surviving father and husband, Lloyd Gil, who is saddened by the loss of his unborn child and wife.

Give him courage and help him in his pain and grief. May they meet one day in the joy and peace of your kingdom.

We ask this through Christ our Lord.

Everyone, except Lloyd, says "Amen" in unison at the end of the prayer.

Lloyd looks down, squinting his eyes, pretending to care.

Everyone is so serious and Lloyd can't see the point in any of this. He thinks back to an article he read.

Everyone grieves in their own way. Some people are immediately affected by loss. Others remain in denial, unaffected, and grieve privately on their own.

Does this make him a bad person, Lloyd wonders. *Why can't he care? Why does he feel, nothing.* A flashback to water filling his ears, warmth, and a heartbeat fill him with comfort. Then a sudden jolt startles Lloyd, as his eyes reset from the blurry cemetery grass to the sharp view of Janice's casket, which continues downward into the earth as her mother's cries become louder. The pain of a parent having lost their child too soon, without notice, and by murder unleashes perhaps one of the most untamable breeds of grief. The sorrowful moans from Janice's mother cannot be calmed no matter how tightly her family holds her.

Marty, seemingly tuning her out, watches Lloyd's every move.

Feeling Marty's attention on him, Lloyd removes his handkerchief from his blazer jacket and begins to pat his dry eyes. But there are no tears to wipe.

Richard walks up to Lloyd and puts his hand on his shoulder and squeezes it.

Lloyd appreciates his brother's gesture for no other reason than to look like a grieving spouse in front of Marty.

Janice's casket makes it to the bottom of the grave and her family tosses their red roses downwards at it.

When Lloyd hears the sound of the last rose plopping against the casket, he throws in his white rose. Janice's mother throws hers last and she begins to compose herself.

The cemetery staff hurls shovels of dirt on top of Janice's casket and the roses in a slow and methodical way.

The guests begin to walk away quietly, heading to their cars parked on a nearby road leading through the cemetery.

Janice's mother turns to Lloyd and grabs both of his hands, facing him.

"Lloyd, I know you didn't kill Janice. I know it in my heart you didn't. Why are they charging you with this? Why are they doing this to you? I don't understand," she whispers.

"I can't talk about this right now," says Lloyd, frustrated.

Richard steps in and speaks for Lloyd.

"We really appreciate your support. We need it. And if you can come to the hearings and support Lloyd, that will really help him. It's important for his defense," Richard says.

"But why, Richard? Why can't you tell them he's not responsible?" she asks.

"This is common. Spouses are always the first to be looked at in homicides. We'll get his name cleared," says Richard confidently.

She looks back at Lloyd.

"I know you loved Janice and you'd never hurt her," she says.

"I'll be there to support you," she continues, looking straight at Lloyd with her glassy eyes.

He shifts his look away from her, hoping she's not detecting his lack of emotion. It doesn't seem to phase her and she releases his hands, turning to walk to her car.

Marty doesn't take his eyes off Lloyd until Lloyd looks over at him.

Marty mouths, "Guilty."

"Fuck you," Lloyd mouths back, turning around to walk away.

33

SEDUCTION

Lloyd looks around the wine bar from his stool. The women in Springset Falls were much more sophisticated than the Canyon Base kind. They were also much happier with life. They appreciate good wine and good conversation.

Richard agreed yesterday after Janice's funeral to allow Lloyd to use the firm's Springset Falls condo to get some rest, but Lloyd has a different plan.

He removes a book from his satchel hanging below a sprawling, dark wood bar facing a selection of wines, each sitting on a stainless steel perfectly pressurized bar that is modern and classy.

The blonde woman next to him removes her electronic tablet and begins scrolling through her screen applications until she arrives at a large, pink Venus sign, which she clicks on.

A large calendar pops onto her tablet along with a keyboard, and she starts typing a note into the calendar.

The only word Lloyd catches is "sex."

She closes the cover of her tablet and takes a sip of her red wine with her fake, bulging lips.

The canvas cover of her tablet boasts a large red stamp of wax with the letter "T" in the middle of it.

Old world personalization, thinks Lloyd, before "T" starts the conversation.

"The Book of Sand and Shakespeare's Memory," she says, reading Lloyd's book. "I don't think I know that one," she continues.

Lloyd carefully puts down his wine glass on the soft paper coaster in front of him.

"Borges definitely does it right in this one."

"Who is Borges? I've heard the name, I'm just not that familiar."

Lloyd jogs his memory for his prepared explication.

"He was from Argentina; a writer, poet. This one is a collection of his short stories. He's big on having the reader figure out the mystery in his story. He likes telling readers to look beyond restrictions we place on our lives and see the world for what it really is," he says confidently, before taking another sip from his wine glass.

"Fascinating. By the way, I'm Tiara. It's a pleasure to meet you."

"Jack," he says convincingly, extending his hand across his body towards her. "The pleasure's all mine."

"That must be what the 'T' stands for," he says, directing her attention to her tablet cover as she smiles, holding in the last sip of wine she is swirling around in her mouth.

"I must confess. I was peeking at your screen. What's with the Venus sign?"

She begins chuckling.

"It's a fertility thing. It helps track ovulation; when you can get pregnant," she says.

"Wow, they have those things now?"

"Yeah, it's great. When you hit my age, you need to pay attention to these things. I'll be forty in a month and I'm not getting any younger."

"Who's the lucky man?" Lloyd asks, noticing her left hand ringless.

"Oh, there isn't one. *Yet.*"

"I find that hard to believe."

"Me, too," she says, taking a deep sigh. "I moved here to find one, but the pickings are slim," she says, directing his attention around the bar, which is empty aside from an older couple in the corner and a woman at the end of the bar.

"Interesting. So why have a child?" he asks.

"It's kind of a natural instinct, especially at my age. My clock's slowing down."

"Why would you want to bring a kid into this world anyway?"

"I keep asking myself the same question. But at the end of the day, I don't want to be childless. What if I got sick? Who would take care of me?"

"What if it wasn't meant to be?"

"True. But I'd rather freeze my eggs now just so it's an option."

"Why not just find a donor? Or get pregnant now?"

"Are you offering?" she says flirtatiously.

"Well, maybe. Would that count as an act of love to this insane world?"

"It depends. Bringing a kid into this world could be a good thing or a very bad thing. It depends on the parents who raise it."

"What kind of parent would you be?" he asks.

"I think a good one. Plus, it would help slow me down. I'm getting too old for all this. Work, travel, sitting in bars like this."

"What do you do?"

"Medical sales. I sell supplies to plastic surgeons," she says as Lloyd begins to focus on the plumpness of her lips and the expression missing from her face while she speaks.

"And you? What kind of parent would you be?"

"I've never thought of that."

"Never? You've never fathered a child?"

"Nope," he says deceitfully.

"Have you ever tried to?"

"I can't say I have. But there's a first for everything," Lloyd says, holding Tiara's sexual gaze while they sip from their glasses.

She raises her eyebrows at him above the opening of her glass, still held up to her mouth.

"Well?" she says seductively, causing Lloyd's heart rate to elevate and his groin to pulsate.

"Bartender! Can we get another round!"

34

FIRST CALL

Lloyd reclines back in his bed at the Hill firm's condo and puts down his magazine to study his ringing cell phone and the unfamiliar number. It's a Tuckford County number. It's not the court clerk checking up on Lloyd's whereabouts; that call already happened when he was leaving the wine bar an hour ago.

He lets it ring and allows his voicemail to pick up.

He returns back to the article he was reading on *A Man's Guide to a Fuller, Richer, Informed and More Rewarding Life* before picking up the phone to check his voicemail.

It's Marty Kaplan.

He hits the play button on his phone.

"Lloyd Gil. It's Investigator Kaplan here. When you get this message, I'd appreciate it if you would return the call. I just have a few questions for you. It's about seven-thirty in the evening. My call back number is 909-2483. Feel free to call anytime. We both know I'll be working around the clock."

Lloyd's phone buzzes again. It's Tiara.

He reads the text:

Your condo in 30 minutes?

Women around here know what they want, that's for sure.

Lloyd replies:

That sounds wonderful. See you soon, beautiful.

P.S. Have you been craving our intoxicating chemistry as much as I have over the last hour?

His phone buzzes with a reply almost immediately. He reads it:

Yes, I've been craving it almost as much as what's about to come. FYI, I like to "come" at the same time, together, loudly. ;-)

Lloyd's groin moves involuntarily as his lips settle into a smile.

He scrolls to the last missed call on his phone and sets his phone screen to send a message to Marty Kaplan. He writes a text:

I got your message, Marty. I'm going to be occupied with personal matters for the rest of the evening. I'm sure you can find your answers.   You're a smart guy.   You're one of the most notable homicide detectives in Tuckford County.

Lloyd hits the "send" button.

A reply message returns within seconds.   It's from Marty.

That's what I've been called.

Lloyd replies:

So then start solving my wife's case. I didn't kill her.

Marty replies:

I will once I stop you.

Lloyd turns off his phone, infuriated. He closes his eyes and rages in his mind about everything and nothing for twenty minutes until a knock at the door interrupts him.

Within fifteen minutes, Lloyd is penetrating Tiara. Unprotected sex was always such a joy for Lloyd. The feeling of being deep inside a woman without any barriers was something he enjoyed.

He watches her as he pounds roughly into her.   She seems to enjoy it, moaning at every entry, over and over again.

Her taut breasts, filled with silicon, jerk back and forth with each jolt.   He takes pride in watching her quick breathing and listening to her erotic noises.

He moves his hands up towards her neck and brushes her collarbone softly with his fingers. He repeats this after each time he thrusts into her.

He jabs into her with his hard penis at a quicker pace, increasing the speed.

He stops and looks around the room for something to wrap her in, staring down at the bed sheet, with homicidal thoughts.

"Why are you stopping?" she asks, frustrated.

The condo phone rings. Lloyd answers it. It's Marty Kaplan.

"Lloyd, you're screwing with the wrong person. Let's get that straight. You and I both know what you're capable of. Think twice before your next move," says Marty threateningly.

"Make an arrest then. Be the heroic cop. You piece of shit. You have nothing on me. You wanna play games? Maybe you don't realize who *you're* screwing with," says Lloyd, slamming the phone down.

He turns his anger towards Tiara, who is already partially dressed, looking fearfully at Lloyd.

"Get out of here. Get out now, you whore!" yells Lloyd, before the gushing sound of water fills his ears.

35

FIRST RISK

Lloyd waits for the sun to set from his car. And he watches her. His rage hasn't subsided after receiving the call from Marty while in Springset Falls three days ago. Instead, it has festered.

Marty Kaplan's wife moves from the living room to her dining room, removing silverware from a china hutch and placing it neatly on a table. She's home alone.

The white, wooden fence that surrounds the perimeter of the house appears unsecured. It's a one-story house with an abundant flower garden butting up against the fence. A security sign sits at the front of the house near the entrance door.

Southland Security.

Lloyd reads the sign out loud and laughs.

A small, black security camera hangs from the tip of the roof protruding out over the front porch.

Lloyd takes out his binoculars and focuses them towards the side of the house.

Two German shepherds prance back and forth towards, then away from the side gate.

Marty's wife moves to the kitchen.

She has long flowing hair, just the kind that Lloyd can't resist. Her flowing top drapes lightly over her pregnant stomach. She is Marty's second wife and much younger than his first.

A car pulls up to the driveway of their home.

It's Marty Kaplan.

"FUCK!" says Lloyd.

Marty gets out of the car, grabs his briefcase from his trunk, and walks inside. The porch light illuminates. Greeted with an affectionate kiss from his wife, it all appears perfect.

Marty releases his gun from his waist holster, places it into a small closet near his front door, and walks down a long hallway.

Lloyd loses sight of him through the binoculars.

Marty's wife continues setting the table and brings a large casserole dish to the table. She pours two glasses of sparkling water.

He watches Marty and his wife sip their water. Marty reaches over and kisses her behind her ear.

Lloyd places his binoculars down and studies his clenched fists.

His bitterness sets in. His mom used to make a tuna casserole he loved, at least before his stepdad took her life over. She wasn't allowed to make that type of family style food, which his stepdad called "poor man's food."

He looks around the neighborhood. All the houses look the same. White picket fences. Families eating at their dinner tables. Cars in the driveways. People spending time together.

Lloyd resents the perfection of it all. It represented the fake life his mom had chosen over him.

Lloyd picks up his binoculars and focuses them back at Marty's home. The couple is no longer at the table. The dining room and kitchen are empty. The front porch light is off.

Lloyd hears the sound of a text message coming in on his phone. He reads it. It is an unknown number. He opens it and reads it:

Stay the hell away from my house and my wife, you sick shit. Or else...

36

FIRST SITE

Lloyd sits at Janice's gravesite at Tuckford Cemetery. He goes through his mental list on everything he was supposed to do.

Visit the gravesite. Accept help from friends.

It's only been a week since her funeral, but he's trying to play the part of a grieving husband. So he vowed to make daily visits to her gravesite. The perception of all this was important.

He kneels down at her gravestone.

RIP
BEAUTIFUL DAUGHTER & WIFE
JANICE GIL
&
BABY GIL
KEEP SMILING DOWN AT US

Janice's smile *was* infectious. She lit up any room she walked into. When Lloyd first met Janice, he actually felt something for the first time in a long while. She made him laugh, smile, and open up about things he had never shared before, especially about not knowing his father.

Janice had always been able to make Lloyd feel protected and safe. But over the years, this began waning. Lloyd studies the words "Baby Gil," before getting interrupted.

"Hi, Mr. Gil," a young woman's voice says.

It's the young woman who recognized Lloyd at Hal's Diner and showed up at his house. She walks over and kneels at the gravestone alongside him, bowing her head and closing her eyes, holding her hands in a praying position close to her heart.

"What are you doing here?" he asks.

"Visiting my mom," she says.

"She's here, too?" he asks, confused.

"Yeah, she was buried here a long time ago. Since I was little," she says sadly.

Her soft long curls are neatly smoothed down the front of her shirt.

"How often do you come to see her?" asks Lloyd.

"Every day on the way home from school," she replies proudly.

"Why that often?" he asks.

"Because I miss her. It makes me feel close to her. Plus, it makes my dad happy. He can't come cuz he works. So when I get home, he'll ask me. He'll say, 'How's Mom doing?' So I don't wanna let him down. It's a regular thing I do," she says.

"Well, that's a real nice thing to do for your dad. I wasn't that mature at your age," he says, laughing.

The last time Lloyd naturally did things for other people because it made them feel good was too far in the past for him to remember.

"I'm really, really sorry for what happened. My dad told me. They said my mom was killed the same way. But they never caught him," she says. "It's been ten years," she continues with a hopeless sigh.

The young girl fades into a white fog as a dull ringing sound pulsates Lloyd's eardrums and a flash of Lloyd dumping Annabelle Phillips' body in the Orange Groves startles Lloyd.

"How was she killed?" he asks, trying to snap himself out of the fog.

"I don't really remember. I don't want to know," she replies sadly. "It really messed my dad up. They say he's not the same. And it's been really hard on me, not having my mom and all. People say I look a lot like her," she says, tugging at her long, blonde hair and dusting off her school uniform skirt.

Lloyd studies her face.

What was the kid's name... Sadie? Stella? Sarah? Lloyd thinks to himself.

"I just wanna know why. Why he did that to her. Why did he take her away," she struggles asking.

Lloyd looks at her. A tear welling up in her eye finally breaks free. It falls down her milky skin and over her freckles. Lloyd's eyes travel downwards, past the tear stream. Her uniform skirt rests against her legs, which are exposed and bare.

She struggles to study Lloyd's eyes.

"You still look really familiar to me. I know you live near us, but I feel like I've seen you somewhere else," she says.

"So you miss your mom a lot, huh?" he asks awkwardly, changing the subject.

"Yeah, especially her hugs. It's really all I can remember about her," she says.

"The best ones were when she got home from work. Cuz she worked a lot. She had just started waitressing at Hal's," she says fondly.

Lloyd swallows hard.

"What's your last memory of her?" he asks.

"When she put me down for a nap. That was right before she was killed," she says. "They say I heard the whole thing and saw the guy. But I've blocked the whole thing out. I was only four. I don't want to remember any of it," she says sadly.

"By the way, I'm Selena," she says, extending her hand.

Lloyd cracks a smile.

"I'm Lloyd, nice to meet you."

37

SUSPICION

Lloyd sits alone in his boss' office on the tenth floor of Software Solutions, Inc. He is waiting for his boss to get into the office for a meeting he was called to after leaving Janice's gravesite.

The office wall is covered with articles on Software Solutions, Inc. being one of the top companies in the state. Lloyd has been a big part of the company's success.

For ten consistent years, Lloyd had won top salesman of the year, winning a cruise of his choice for Janice and himself each year. One year it was Alaska, another year it was the Caribbean.

Lloyd managed a team of salesmen and his region consistently achieved top sales numbers in the country. His commissions helped him buy his home in Canyon Base. His bonus provided the down payment on Janice's Range Rover and afforded him a modest monthly payment.

Lloyd was proud of his status at the company. But he never was quite able to use his status and money the way he wanted to. Now, with Janice gone, he would have the opportunity to finally do what he wanted to do. And it didn't involve a fancy house, car, or vacations the way she preferred or the kind expected in suburbia.

For the first time in ten years, he skipped the company holiday party. He had been on administrative leave.

Lloyd stands up as his boss walks into the room.

"Lloyd, how are you man?" his boss Chuck says.

"Good, good man," replies Lloyd.

"You hanging in there?" Chuck asks.

"As best I can," Lloyd says.

Lloyd returns back to recline into his seat as Chuck makes his way to his.

"Look, you've been an asset to this company. You know how much you've done for us. We couldn't have grown the way we did and expand into the regions we did without your service to this company," Chuck says formally.

"Thank you," says Lloyd.

Chuck pauses before continuing on.

"Look, I know what you're thinking. You've heard this over and over in the last decade. But this isn't one of those conversations. This isn't about the bonus or the end-of-the-year award. This isn't about any of that," Chuck says, starting to comb his hair back with his fingers, nervously.

Silence fills the room.

"I gotta let you go, Lloyd," he says finally.

"What do you mean?"

"Just that. You can't work here anymore," says Chuck.

"What is it? Were numbers down?" Lloyd asks.

"No, no, nothing like that."

"Then what? I've worked my ass off for this company, Chuck. The least you can do is let me in on what's going on."

Chuck pauses and looks around the room, patting his hair.

"They said I can't talk about this," he says, not looking at Lloyd.

"It will interfere with their investigation," continues Chuck.

"What investigation? I'm already facing charges. You know this. We discussed this. You said you were with me until something happened at trial. And that's a long time from now, Chuck. What's this really about?" asks Lloyd desperately.

"The case looks bad, Lloyd. They shared some of the details with me," he says.

"They're trying to turn you against me. They're trying to make my life a living hell. They're doing this to break me down, because they have no friggen case, Chuck. You're a smart man, you should be able to see through their bullshit," says Lloyd dramatically.

"You know I'm the last person to side with law enforcement. I know there's dirty cops out there. We discussed this. Them trying to pin the case on you," he says.

"Then what is it? They can't force you to fire me. They can't do that. Richard said they can't. It's my livelihood. I need a means of living. Surviving. The community needs to see that I'm going about my life. I can't do that without you. I need my job back, Chuck," he says, trying to lay a guilt trip on him.

"They won't get out of my hair, Lloyd," he says.

"Why fire me?"

"They're starting to subpoena all our business records, even from years ago. Ten, twelve years ago. They want to know your whereabouts way back then. What accounts you were working on. I can't afford to have our company involved in this stuff. They've even been asking for business records from a woman who's computer system you installed and turned up dead years ago. And I can't afford to be involved in any kind of lawsuit. My attorney and insurance company made this call, Lloyd. I didn't. You know how I feel about you. I think you're a stand-up guy. I know you didn't kill Janice. This is purely a liability thing," he says, exasperated.

"I can't change your mind?"

"No, Lloyd. I'm sorry, man. Consider it a lay-off. Collect unemployment or whatever you need to do. You'll be escorted out right now," says Chuck, looking up as two security guards walk into his office asking Lloyd to accompany them.

38

DOMINATE

Lloyd stands in line at the unemployment office. He didn't waste any time deciding to put in an application after he was laid off an hour ago. The buzz of people waiting in line irritates Lloyd along with the small children running in circles around the roped poles restricting the line of people. But the purpose of being there is worth the hassle.

A blonde woman with long, curled hair smoothed over her chest walks up and stands behind Lloyd. The alluring smell of her perfume steals Lloyd away from his irritation. Her scent reminds Lloyd about Eva in a mysterious way.

Her matte, ruby red lips match the red and black pattern of her bustier top holding up her perky breasts, which sits under her dark brown leather jacket. A brown, leather belt cinching her tiny waist gives her an hourglass shape. Black, leather boots ride high up her long legs above her knees.

She smiles at Lloyd, who can't take his eyes off her. This stunning woman, who looks to be in her late thirties, begins talking to an older man who walks up to stand in line behind her.

The idea of attracting this woman and having sex with her distracts Lloyd from the crying baby near him. Her smell overpowers the scent of the unbathed man in line in front of him.

She smiles again at Lloyd.

"Is it always this busy here?" she asks to no one in particular, her focus obstructed by her oversized, dark sunglasses.

The hint of her Spanish accent seduces Lloyd and he jumps on the opportunity to answer her.

"This is my first time here," he says with a big smile. "Are you from around here?" he asks.

"I'm just visiting. But I'm picking up some paperwork for a friend. She lost her job," she replies in a friendly tone.

"What are you reading?" Lloyd questions curiously.

"It's a collection of love sonnets," she replies.

"Do you speak Spanish?" Lloyd asks, speaking Spanish.

"I do," she replies back seductively in Spanish. "And what brings such a sexy man in here?" she continues in Spanish.

"I didn't understand what you said," says Lloyd in English, laughing and recognizing he was caught.

She laughs back with him. "Well, you could have fooled me. I said a couple things. That you were sexy, being one of them," she says.

"I'm Diego and part Mexican," says Lloyd, extending his hand to her, who touches it softly with her perfectly manicured hand. She begins to shake it, before Lloyd grabs it and kisses it.

"I love it. So sensual and forward," she says in English with a sexy Spanish accent. "I'm Demitra. And from South America," she says seductively.

A woman with a baby in front of Lloyd glares at Demitra before being called by the government clerk to the next open station.

"Are all the women as beautiful as you in South America?" asks Lloyd flirtingly.

"South American women *are* beautiful," she replies confidently. "And we love men," she continues.

"I'd love to share a drink with you," says Lloyd, insistently.

"Only if it's back at my hotel," she says confidently.

Lloyd smiles. "Well, if you're pulling my arm," he says jokingly.

"I'm at the Gable House on Main Street. I'm here for a week," she says, winking and slipping him her card. "There's a bar inside. The Tavern," she recalls proudly.

"NEXT IN LINE!" yells the clerk, motioning for Lloyd to come to her counter.

Lloyd walks to the open station and studies her business card while waiting for the clerk to process his application. One side is in Spanish and the other, in English.

Demitra

House of Pain

South America's Fearless Dominatrixes

Demitra@HouseofPain.com

Demitra, standing at the counter station next to Lloyd, flirts with the clerk deliberately and provocatively. While turning to leave, she winks at Lloyd, who smiles back and says, "See you in thirty."

39

HOUSE OF PAIN

Lloyd became curious about BDSM shortly before Janice was killed. Mostly, he was curious about domination, submission, bondage, and discipline.

He had watched BDSM pornography, but never had sought out the services of a professional dominatrix.

Demitra walks up to the wooden bar at The Tavern. When Lloyd goes in to kiss her on the cheek, she stops him. Her control, confidence, and composure is intriguing yet puzzling.

Demitra reminds him that he is late for their agreed meeting time and quickly informs him that she will dictate any touching between the two.

"BDSM is about control, Lloyd. And in this relationship, if there is going to be one, the power lies with me. I'm a dominatrix. And I'm assuming you have already gathered that by my card," she says sternly.

"I have," says Lloyd, smiling at her.

The two sit at the bar, learning about each other. Lloyd drinks his Argentine Malbec and Demitra sips her espresso. He pushes his wine to the side after a couple sips and noticing Demitra's annoyance over his drinking. It's hard for her to assess his submissiveness if he introduces alcohol into the date.

"You will learn the rules," she assures him. "I'm giving you some leeway this session. Because we just met. Plus, you seem like a good candidate. I'd hate for you to become discouraged. But I can tell this goes against your grain. You're used to being in control. You must let go. And don't forget, always respect a domme's time and role. Figure it out before you meet with one again, including me," she says aloofly.

Lloyd remains intrigued and Demitra begins to share her story.

She was born in South America and lost her parents at a young age. They died in a plane crash, and it left her an orphan. She was raised by her aunt, who groomed her into a dominatrix. Her aunt owns House of Pain, where she's been working since she was nineteen years old. She's thirty-two now.

Lloyd shares a revised version of his own life. He had lost his wife in a car accident five years ago. Ever since then, he has tried to pick up the pieces of his life. In the last year, he's been able to move on.

Demitra questions Lloyd about Janice's murder and the cold case, having just read about them in this morning's paper. Without disclosing his relationship to Janice, they chat briefly on the profile of the White Picket Fence Killer. Before casually changing the subject, he told her it must be someone who needs to get caught.

Demitra's clients were mostly powerful and successful men who wanted to be submissive during their free time. They didn't want to be in charge in the bedroom. They wanted someone else to dominate them.

Demitra's clients had all kinds of strange fetishes. One man had paid her two thousand dollars an hour to come to his hotel room and blow smoke from her cigarette in his face.

A different man paid her to dunk his head repeatedly in the hotel bathtub.

Some wanted her to urinate on them.

Another man would call her and ask her to verbally insult him. She would put him down over the phone, telling him what a piece of shit he was and how he would never amount to anything. She received one thousand dollars an hour for that.

Other men just wanted to lay over her lap and be paddled in between their daytime corporate business meetings.

Demitra had worked hard to become one of the top dominatrixes in South America. Men traveled from around the world to be dominated by her. And many of these men were like Lloyd, from America. She had serviced politicians, lawyers, doctors, pilots, vice presidents, and CEOs.

Demitra stops talking about her experiences and entertains Lloyd's attempt to negotiate.

"How about I pay you five hundred dollars for a session?" he offers.

"What kind of session?"

"Domme. Sub. Then switch," says Lloyd, using his newly discovered vocabulary.

"I don't switch."

"Never?"

"Never."

Lloyd stays quiet for a few moments before looking directly at her.

"Do you have a maternity top or one of those baby doll dresses?" he asks.

Demitra pauses as if to think for a second and replies.

"I do. Is that what you want me to wear?"

He studies her and replies back.

"Yes."

She says nothing.

"*Please*," begs Lloyd desperately.

"No!" she says firmly.

"I need you to. It's the only way I'll get aroused."

She pauses for a moment.

"That's going to be extra. Five *hundred* extra."

Without hesitating, Lloyd agrees.

Within five minutes of Lloyd paying the bar tab, Demitra lights several candles, removes a large suitcase from under the hotel bed, and takes out a neck restraint, handcuffs, a blindfold, and a paddle.

As she is closing the suitcase, Lloyd asks, "Where's the dress?"

She removes a baby doll shirt from the suitcase and puts it on. It's a spaghetti strapped top, see-through kind with small polka dots and the extra material allows it to flow down past her belly button, as if to replicate something a pregnant woman would wear. Lloyd grins excitedly.

Demitra explains the rules to Lloyd. They agree that the safe word when he wants her to stop would be "red." Emotions or memories can be triggered by some of a dominatrix's actions and words, so the safe word can be used anytime. The point of BDSM was to be pleasurable, not tortuous.

Within minutes, Lloyd is naked on the floor on his knees with a dog collar around his neck, which has a leash attached to it that Demitra is holding as he is blindfolded. He's eager to remove the blindfold to get a glimpse of her maternity top in the mirror.

But Demitra forbids him from removing the blindfold and instead, proceeds to spank him. The spankings escalate in force and pain, until the point he yells, "RED!"

Demitra turns the lights on and faces Lloyd, who is still on the floor.

"Can I remove my blindfold?" he asks timidly.

She unties her silk blindfold wrapped around Lloyd's eyes.

He eagerly faces towards her, but she yells at him, "I didn't tell you it was time to look at me."

"I'm sorry," he says and quickly faces back towards a wall-to-ceiling mirror resting on the floor.

Demitra's baby doll top rests below her breasts, fully exposing her hard milk chocolate colored nipples. Her black, thigh-high stockings held up by her garter belts and red heels overwhelm Lloyd.

"I said it was not time to look at me," she yells after noticing Lloyd watching her in the mirror.

"I just..." he starts trying to explain.

"I don't want your excuses, you piece of shit," she yells at him.

"Get out of here," she continues.

Demitra walks over to a chair next to the mirror and sits down. She lights her cigarette and opens a nearby window and begins puffing smoke out the window.

Lloyd begins dressing himself and removes the dog collar from around his neck while Demitra keeps her back towards him. She sits stiffly upright with her breasts still exposed. Silence fills the room, until Lloyd's belt buckle clinks.

"Demitra, can I talk to you?" he asks.

There is only silence, except for her deep exhales of smoke into the cold December air.

"I really enjoyed this," says Lloyd sincerely.

She says nothing.

"Can I see you again?" he asks desperately.

"Get out," she says sternly.

"Can I..."

"LEAVE NOW!"

Lloyd clenches his fists tightly and focuses his stare at her neck, fantasizing about strangling it. The sound of water fills his ears.

Demitra turns around and looks at him directly.

"Did you not hear me, you worthless piece of shit. GET OUT NOW!" she demands fiercely.

Lloyd grabs his sweater and leaves the room.

40

FIRST CALL

Lloyd comes to a stop in his Toyota Camry at an intersection in Springset Falls, where he is back in town avoiding the press and police who have been swarming his house. He feels at ease, except for the stinging sensations still lingering from yesterday's paddling.

Lloyd fantasizes about driving and driving and never returning to Canyon Base. But Richard had warned him against this, telling him that no one can disappear or erase themselves from society. It is unusual and takes a great deal of sophistication or police help to change an identity completely. He had only seen it done through a witness protection plan.

But Lloyd still thought about it regularly, imagining going into a bustling city and blending in large crowds, changing his look, and never being caught.

Lloyd looks at his ringing phone and sees a number. He notices it is a Canyon Base phone number, recognizing the area code, but nothing else.

He picks up, remembering the judge's order to answer all calls from this area code.

"Lloyd Gil here."

"Hi Lloyd, it's Selena. Remember me? I'm the girl from the cemetery. I sold you the water bottle," she says timidly.

"Of course, sweetie, I remember you," he says, looking over at the water bottle set in a cup holder attached to his dashboard.

"How did you get my number? And where are you calling me from?" he asks, suspiciously.

"Oh, this is my aunt's home phone. She lives down the street from me," she replies.

"How did you get my number?" he repeats.

"Eva, your friend, gave it to me," she says.

"When did you see her?" asks Lloyd, fishing for more information.

A long pause follows and Selena finally breaks the silence, answering, "I can't remember."

"So what's up?" asks Lloyd, changing the subject.

"Well, I was wondering. Now that you mentioned Eva, I wanted to ask you how you met her?"

"Why do you want to know that?" Lloyd asks back.

"I don't know, I'm just curious. I was thinking maybe I could get to know her better or help her," says Selena.

"I think you're going to have to talk to Eva about that. That's between you guys," replies Lloyd.

"Okay. I was also wondering... Do you remember how I told you about my mom and how she died? How I supposedly saw the whole thing?" she asks nervously.

"Yeah, I remember you saying something like that," he replies.

"Well, remember I told you that you looked familiar?" she says quietly.

Lloyd vocalizes in agreement.

"Well, I wanted to tell you that I think you're the guy—*that* guy," she starts.

"Selena!" says Lloyd exasperatedly, cutting her off.

"Hear me out. I think you're the guy that did that to her. I'm almost positive. And I'm worried that the police will find out it's you. So I wanted to know, what should I tell them when they ask me?" she questions.

Lloyd listens, shocked by what Selena is telling him.

"I mean... I *know* it was you. You're the guy who killed my mom," she says decisively.

"Selena, why would you want to get me in trouble?" he asks, disappointed.

"I don't want you to. I like you. That's why I'm calling you. To see what you think I should say if they come and talk to me and ask me questions," she continues concerningly.

"Tell them you don't know anything," he says desperately.

"But that's not true," she says pleadingly.

Lloyd stays silent.

Richard's words revisit his thoughts.

Don't talk to anyone. Do you hear me, Lloyd? No one. Don't answer calls from numbers you don't recognize. And don't speak to anyone, when you're in or out of custody.

"Lloyd, are you there?" she questions, breaking the silence.

"Selena, I don't know what you're talking about. Why are you calling me?"

Silence fills the line.
Selena's breathing interrupts the quiet.
"Should I hang up?" she whispers.
Lloyd ends the phone call and screams.
"Dammit! Pretext call!"

41

REJECTION

Lloyd walks away from the local grocery store in downtown Canyon Base. It has been a media frenzy recently inside and around the bead store. Policemen in uniform walk around the media vans. Lloyd pretends to be just another curious onlooker. Bystanders hold their Coffee Grind cups and chat among themselves, speculating and trying to figure out what's going on.

A homeless man, carrying a sign asking for spare change, pleads with a police officer, telling him he needs to speak with the lead detective. The homeless man is slurring his words, holding a paper-bagged bottle, and appears intoxicated. The police ignore him.

Selena and her father briskly walk across the street to the same side as the bead store. Selena has her backpack on. They stand about ten feet from Lloyd, and Selena elevates herself up on her tiptoes, trying to get a view inside the news van.

Selena's dad sets his eyes on Lloyd. What starts as a stare, turns into a harsh glare. It is a look that can cut. His eyes stay glued to Lloyd as Lloyd looks everywhere else but at them.

Selena taps on the shoulders of a couple people in front of her as though she's asking them what all the commotion is about.

No one answers her.

Her father's eyes continue the intentional stare-down at Lloyd.

Selena turns to look in Lloyd's direction. Selena's dad grabs her shoulder and whispers something to her, causing Selena to wave at Lloyd, who looks away. Selena's stare remains fixed on Lloyd. Lloyd turns pale, as though he has just seen a ghost.

Selena's father looks at his watch and whispers something to her, before turning to walk away. He gives one last look in Lloyd's direction, but Lloyd is already starting to move among the crowd. He wants to avoid them.

A police officer summons for the homeless man to step aside to give a statement. But Lloyd is not worried about that. The man is an obvious drunk.

Selena is just tall enough to stand out in the crowd and look over the tops of the heads in the crowd to see Lloyd, who is making a dash through the crowd away from her. She searches for him desperately, spotting his movement amongst the crowd and follows in his direction along the sidewalk where she can avoid obstructions.

When they both get to the end of the crowd, Lloyd makes a move into the street and Selena catches up to him as he is about to get into his car parked against the sidewalk.

"Lloyd," she starts, placing her hand on his shoulder from behind. "I just noticed you were here," says Selena.

"Don't touch me," he snaps back.

"But, I... I just wanted to talk to you," she says.

"There's nothing to talk about," he snaps back.

A car door slams and Selena's father storms toward Lloyd, sweeps around the backside of his car and places both of his hands on Lloyd's shoulders from behind.

"Don't ever touch me again!" Lloyd yells and continues on. "Stay away from me!"

"Why don't you just get out of here. Leave! Get out of Canyon Base. Get out of Tuckford County! YOU'RE NOT WELCOME HERE!" Selena's father screams at Lloyd, calling the attention of everyone in the nearby street.

Selena pushes her father away from Lloyd, telling him to stop.

"Don't waste your time, Dad," she begins. "He's not worth it," she says, looking back in complete disgust and glaring at Lloyd, like he wasn't even worth her breath.

42

UNCHANGED

Lloyd opens the New York Times at The Coffee Grind. He skims through the articles, feeling frustrated that the news never seems to change. The Republicans and Democrats can't agree on anything, the unemployment rate keeps rising, and holiday shopping projections are not being met.

Lloyd's nerves are not seeming to calm as he was hoping with the chamomile tea sitting in front of him, which he has been sipping on over the last hour, trying to forget about the confrontation he had with Selena and her dad yesterday. He removes his new book from his brown leather briefcase and places it on top of the newspaper.

The House of the Spirits by Isabel Allende.

Within moments of removing the Chilean novel, a beautiful, blonde woman rests herself into the wooden coffee bar stool next to Lloyd and reaches for a hook under the wooden table to secure her Louis Vuitton purse.

"The House of the Spirits. That looks interesting," she says, reading the cover and Spanish translation on the front of the book.

"It most certainly is. I'm sure you'd enjoy it," he says flirtingly.

She bounces her bottom searching for a more comfortable position on the stool and once she finds one, removes her cream-colored pea coat and her tan, leather gloves. This fashionably dressed woman wearing tan riding boots and expensive camel–colored, wool leggings, sips from her latte, gazing at Lloyd through her dark-rimmed glasses into his.

Lloyd sizes her up within moments, concluding she is the materialistic kind.

"Hi, I'm Veronica," she says, extending her hand out towards Lloyd.

"I'm Marty," says Lloyd deceptively.

"So what is that book about?" she asks curiously.

"Well, I don't want to ruin it if you plan on reading it. But I'm sure I can give you a sneak preview of it," Lloyd starts, looking around the coffee shop.

The woman repeats Lloyd's head movement and also looks around the coffee shop.

"Are you meeting someone here?" she asks.

"Yes, I am. My mother actually," he replies.

"That's so sweet," she responds endearingly.

"What do you do for a living?" she asks.

"I'm a real estate investor."

"Oh wow. Do you work on your own or with a company?"

"On my own. I manage a lot of my mother's finances and travel around the world taking care of her properties."

"That's really nice."

"If I take care of them, they become mine."

The woman's eyes almost sparkle at Lloyd. She's obviously unaware this is all an effort to seduce her.

"In fact, my mother should be here any moment," he says curtly, enticed by her obvious interest in him.

"Oh," she says.

Noticing her slight disappointment, Lloyd makes an offer.

"Why don't we do this? If you're interested, and only if you're comfortable with it, I'd love to take you to lunch once I'm done here," says Lloyd smoothly.

"I'd love that. I'm off today, so I'm just going to be shopping around here," she says.

"Great, let's meet back here in an hour, we'll go to lunch and go from there. What do you say?" says Lloyd confidently.

"Perfect," she says, standing up like Lloyd is doing and taking her cue to vacate the barstool.

Lloyd's eyes are glued on his mother, who has just walked into the coffee shop and is heading to the order line. She doesn't notice him and Lloyd is not entirely sure if she would even recognize him.

"And why don't you take this book with you? You can read a bit and return it to me when we see each other again in a little while," he says, handing her the book and smiling at her after she shrugs her shoulders and laughs giddily.

Lloyd sits and watches his mother from across the coffee shop for the next hour. First, she cracks open a book.

Gabriel Garcia Marquez' *One Hundred Years of Solitude*, a Colombian novel that tells the story of seven generations of a family.

Mrs. Hill, Lloyd's mother, is much more frail than Lloyd expected her to be. Her wrinkled skin sags from her bony hand, which shakes as she turns each page. Her black, long-sleeved flannel shirt has caught her short-haired animals' light-colored fur.

Her black pants are lifted six inches above the ground as she sits back in the brown, quilted leather armchair in the corner of the coffee shop. The shortness of her pants reveals white socks and light brown nursing shoes.

She is not the sight Lloyd expected to see. The last time he saw her was by chance in town five years ago when he was shopping for a Christmas gift for Janice. She was in a boutique gift shop in Canyon Base, with shopping bags fastened around her arms. She was wearing a fancy Christmas sweater, gold earrings, and pants that were hemmed to fit over her black, high- heeled leather boots. Her blonde hair was short and appropriately coiffed. But today, it is shoulder-length, partially greyed, and stringy. She pushes her gold-framed reading glasses, which hang from a neck chain wrapped around her ears and the back of her neck, up to her nose.

She flips through her pages briskly. She was always a speed reader, a voracious one, having the capability to take to her Hispanic novels with lighting speed. She prided herself on this.

As Lloyd watches her, every five to ten minutes she writes something into the pages of the novel, perhaps a note, a reminder to look up a particular word, a memory, or emotion. She had always been determined to understand novels completely, something Lloyd never cared to do.

He only focused on pronouncing the author and characters' names correctly, and memorizing a couple talking points about the books he carried around to seduce his victims. That was all that seemed to be needed with the women he met, to build a rapport, appear educated and trustworthy. The whole facade worked on average one out of every ten times he would try it.

Lloyd removes the letter he received from his mother, unfolds it, and reads it again, for the tenth time this morning.

Dear Lloyd,

I hope this letter finds you warm and safe. I wouldn't want it any other way. Richard has kept me updated about your case, including the recent developments. Day by day, I've watched your case unfold. I've been reading most of the articles. We feel this will be a positive thing for the firm. Richard has done well with the firm and it remains as esteemed as when Michael, my late husband, ran it.

I am very sorry about Janice and your child. After losing Michael, I can partly understand the pain of your loss. But I am not sure you are capable of experiencing such pain. I always remember what Dr. Blanchart used to tell us—I would always have to feel the emotions for you, because you have none.

If you recall, he assessed you when you were 17 years old, after you hurt that woman and her child on your paper route. This is something I've never shared with anyone, but I feel much regret for not getting you the proper help it appears you may have needed back then.

I am conflicted as to whether I have done the right thing by you and our community by posting your bail. When I began learning about some of the evidence in that old murder of Annabelle Phillips, I began wondering if you were involved in that. She was last seen with a man, who fits your description. When I read that and after hearing you were arrested for Janice's murder, my heart began to sink. I am not the same woman I was since Michael's passing. All I have is Richard and I made one promise to Michael before he passed—that I would do anything to help Richard and the firm. This is why I posted your bail. And it's the only reason why I've agreed to have the firm take your case. It will be our first capital case, and I'm confident Richard will be successful at winning it.

I feel responsible for how you turned out. I endured a lot when I was pregnant with you. I feel terrible.

I feel that I know better than anyone else what you're capable of, Lloyd. Your brother Richard does not. If you continue on the wrong path, I may have no other choice but to inform Richard, revoke the bail money, and tell police about your past. You need to control any urges you have. You must get help. Otherwise you will turn into a cancer. You will become a rabid dog if you allow your anger to get the best of you. Unchecked anger breeds hate. Please, prove my worst fears wrong. Don't become like your father. Please consider getting help. You are a bright man.

Signed,

Loretta

Lloyd stares at the words "cancer" and "rabid dog" and reads them to himself over and over and over again, infuriating himself until he becomes so enraged he clenches his fingers together simulating a strangling motion. The sound of water floods his ears.

Once the building pressure falls, he folds the letter back up and places it in his pocket. Veronica walks towards him, holding the book he lent her an hour ago. She has several bags looped around her arms.

He looks towards the corner Loretta was sitting in. She's gone. He searches the entire shop for her; but finds her nowhere.

He clears his throat, smiles insincerely at Veronica, who is eager to discuss the excerpts she has read from *The House of the Spirits*, and escorts her out of the coffee shop.

43

INTERRUPTION

If Mrs. Hill had spent any time thinking about the ramifications her letter would have on Lloyd, perhaps she would have chosen her words more carefully. The letter almost served as a new fuel to unleash the mysterious rage he harbors.

While Veronica lays her shopping bags out on the bed of her upstairs guest bedroom, Lloyd sits in her downstairs bathroom and takes the letter out, reading it twice more. He tears down the middle of the letter, making sure to rip through the words, "rabid dog."

Lloyd studies his face in the mirror. Dark circles under his eyes are beginning to set in. He shakes as he holds his mother's letter. He takes several deep breaths, releasing each one in a controlled fashion. None of the inhales or exhales brings down his heart rate or calms him. His adrenaline is rushing wickedly through his body, reddening his face. He understands none of this, other than he has become accustomed to it every time he thinks of his mother or biological father. A water swishing sound as though he is being drowned fills his ears. He doesn't stop and try to comprehend any of these physiological signs. He can't. A sense of fear follows his anger.

He tries several deep breaths again, finding some relief in the last one. He cools his face with sink water and sets his face close to a small open window and lets the air sweep over it. All of this calms him down enough to rejoin Veronica on her couch.

The two sip chardonnay from their wine glasses after toasting to "new friends."

Veronica has one brother and she has continued living in Tuckford County while pursuing interior design. She is waiting to meet the right man to sweep her off her feet, so she could settle into one of the craftsman houses with a white picket fence nearby. What Veronica hasn't planned for is the only thing Lloyd is fantasizing she will be settling into—her coffin.

It takes no more than a glass of wine for Veronica's eyes to begin fluttering and her face to become quite flush. She jokes for a brief moment, asking Lloyd if he slipped something in her drink, to which he reminds her that she poured their glasses; but he uses her flirting comment to aggressively move his body towards hers. Grabbing her neck, he French kisses her deeply and his erection grows as she pleasingly responds.

Within a minute of kissing her, his hands are under her blouse, unfastening her bra, and pinching her erect nipples. Lloyd wraps one hand around her throat, pacing his squeezing fingers with her labored breathing, allowing her air every few seconds. Veronica attributes Lloyd's sexual aggression towards her as his response to her complaints all afternoon about her ex-boyfriend's lackluster and vanilla lovemaking skills.

Lloyd begins to squeeze her neck tighter, not letting go, and slowly starts to restrict her breathing.

She begins to struggle, trying to figure out whether the pressure is for pleasure or pain.

Within a second of Veronica beginning to struggle, the front door begins to open. Lloyd is caught off guard, not having heard the keys fiddling in the door lock right before.

Lloyd straightens his hair and watches a young woman in her teens with short, blonde hair cut into a bob walk into Veronica's condo. The young woman releases a leash attached to a small beagle dog. The white, black, and brown fur ball on paws begins scampering around the condo.

"Yes, you're home, you're home, Buckley," says the young girl in a high-pitched, immature voice ringing loudly in Lloyd's ears.

The young woman looks up. "I'm sorry...," she begins to say, looking startled and recognizing Lloyd.

It's Selena.

"No, no sweetie, it's okay," answers Veronica as calm as she can, still out of breath and fumbling for her clothes.

Selena stares at them both. "You're...you're..." she begins fearfully, before Lloyd interrupts.

"I have to go," he says, getting up and leaving the condo quickly.

44

QUESTIONING

Within seven hours of leaving Veronica's, Lloyd sits in the passenger seat of Richard's car in the parking lot of the Canyon Base Police Department.

Richard is dressed impeccably, the way Lloyd used to when he had a job and travel benefits. Richard has on a dark grey suit by Hugo Boss, tailored precisely to flatter his fit physique. His red tie with a small pattern sits nicely against his striped blue and white shirt. His gold cufflinks and tan shoes are from Marc Jacobs.

Richard looks towards the Police Department entrance, trying to gauge where Marty Kaplan and the prosecutor are.

"Look, Lloyd, I want this to be brief. I've already told you I do NOT want you answering any questions about these new allegations. There's just no way it could help you. They'll twist your words and it will wind up hurting you. Trust me on this. I've seen it happen before.

"They're going to want to know if you know the victim. I guess it was a woman you were seen with. They're gonna want to know your whereabouts. They'll probably ask you to take a lie detector test, which you're NOT doing. I don't care whether you want to or not," Richard explains.

"Why wouldn't I just take one for Janice's murder? That will clear me," Lloyd asks.

"Because they're never a good idea. Plus your overall impressions with Sam, the lie detection expert, weren't that favorable to us," responds Richard.

"But I'd pass," Lloyd retorts defensively.

"They can ask you about *anything* once you agree to take it. It's just never a good idea," insists Richard.

"I thought they weren't admissible in court anyway," says Lloyd.

"The results aren't, but some of your answers may be. We have to be careful. Look, Lloyd. Let me be the attorney. You be the client. Okay?" says Richard.

"Okay," Lloyd says sarcastically. "I thought I was doing that pretty well," he continues.

"Well, do it better!" Richard snaps back.

"How?"

"Stay out of goddamn trouble. Stop getting hauled in for interviews like this. And follow my damn advice. Stay away from women for Christ's sake," continues Richard angrily, watching and waiting for Lloyd to react. But he doesn't.

"Here. I need you to sign this admonishment form that says you've decided to go against my advice and it's your sole decision to speak to the police," says Richard, handing Lloyd a pre-prepared form.

Lloyd stares at it for a minute, then signs it decisively before the two sit in silence until Marty Kaplan waves at them from the entrance door to come inside the Police Department.

Marty escorts them back into an interview room, where the three sit close together at a round table.

Before Marty has a chance to say anything, Richard takes control of the interview.

"Look, I am only here at my client's insistence.   He wanted to come down and speak with you, but I've advised him repeatedly against giving a statement.   It's simply standard procedure.   I tell all of my clients the same exact thing, so it's nothing specific to Lloyd or any disrespect to you," Richard says, extending his open palm towards Marty.

Marty cringes, then sits back and studies Lloyd while Richard rants on about shoddy police investigations in his past homicide cases, which wound up being the demise of the cases he defended.

Having a defense attorney in an interview prevents Marty from asking the tough questions, using an interrogation style that he is famed for, which has awarded him the best confessions from the toughest defendants over his career. He's never once gotten a defendant to confess when a defense attorney is in the room.

Marty doesn't look at Richard at all during his rant, until Richard blurts out, "Why do you have a hard-on for my client, Marty? I'm watching you stare him down and that's enough. I have a dinner meeting back in Loft, and I have no interest sitting here watch you eye-jack my client."

"Are you done?" asks Marty sarcastically.

"Look, the reason I asked you two to come in was to get some help in solving an old homicide we've reopened. It had a couple similarities to Janice's case. Of course, it could just be a coincidence, but we're covering all bases.   And we wanted to rule you out, Lloyd.   That's all you're here for," says Marty calmly, shifting his eyes between Richard and Lloyd.

"How do you plan on ruling me out?" asks Lloyd.

"Well, first off, let me ask you—did you know Annabelle Phillips?" questions Marty.

"It was a woman who lived in your neighborhood ten years ago with her husband and young daughter at the time," says Marty.   "Here, I got some photos," Marty continues, removing two from his manila file sitting on the table and slapping them down in front of Lloyd.

The outside of the large Craftsman house with a porch and white picket fence brings Lloyd back to that day.

Annabelle's vintage portrait photo with her long soft blonde hair excites Lloyd.

Lloyd stares at the photos.   A minute passes and the silence in the room becomes uncomfortable.

"No," says Lloyd.

"You don't recognize her, Lloyd?" asks Marty suspiciously.

"What about her," says Marty, slapping down a photo of Selena.

"Her daughter," Marty continues.

"You don't know this girl, *do* you?" suggests Richard in a leading tone, causing Lloyd to reply, "no."

"I mean...yes," Lloyd corrects himself.   "She's a neighbor. Yes, I know her quite well. And I've even met her dad," he continues on.

"That's right, Lloyd! You killed his wife Annabelle ten years ago, remember?" asks Marty sarcastically.   "And now you have killed your wife. And I bet you would have killed Veronica, had Selena not interrupted you. What did she do, walk in on you when you were starting to strangle Veronica? Just like she walked in when you were murdering her mom? Is that what happened, Lloyd?" yells Marty in Lloyd's face while repeatedly pointing his finger in the air towards him.

"This interview is over. Back away from my client, Marty. This interview is over. He's not answering any more questions," says Richard, standing up to leave. "Let's go, Lloyd. This is exactly why I told you not to talk to him," Richard continues, walking himself out of the room.

"Prove it! You're one of the most notable homicide detectives in Tuckford County. Prove it!" yells Lloyd mockingly.

"Walk out, Lloyd," screams Richard, already in the next room. "WALK OUT!"

45

LEGAL DEFENSE

Lloyd follows the blonde woman with big breasts dressed in a cream bodysuit who escorts him down the hallway of Hill & Associates to Richard's office. She holds his coffee, which he requested be infused with a shot of Baileys Irish Cream. He needs something to take the edge off this morning, especially after last night's showdown at the Police Department with Marty.

Lloyd is offered a seat in Richard's office, where he sips his coffee over the next ten minutes, while Richard yells into the phone at a client who obviously had not paid his bill or has any intention to. He slams the phone down, apologizing to Lloyd for the waiting and the aggressive tone he was using on his former client.

"There is one thing that bugs me more than anything. It's something I usually tell my clients from the start. I didn't tell you because you are not a paying client. But I tell everyone else, when I send you a bill, there's two rules. The first is to pay it! I don't care where you get the money, just friggen pay it. The next rule is to not tell me where you got the money from. Two simple rules, but these bastards just don't seem to get it," Richard rants unbelievably.

Lloyd sits in amusement of his brother before chuckling.

"Lloyd, I don't like to meet with my clients too many times before we get close to trial. The reason I asked you to come in this morning is to talk to you about new potential charges the police are looking at. Marty alluded to this yesterday during the interview. At the same time Marty was harassing us, my investigator was sitting down with your boss Chuck and got some more information on that old murder," says Richard.

"You're being investigated for the murder of a waitress at Hal's who was a former client you had about ten years ago. The same lady Marty mentioned, Annabelle Phillips. She was strangled and dumped over in the Orange Groves," he says.

Lloyd looks down, trying to mask any possible reaction. He hadn't practiced this one and didn't want Richard picking up on any clues of his guilty conscience.

Richard studies Lloyd's reaction, waiting for him to lift his eyes from the ground. Lloyd doesn't ask or say anything.

"Good job, Lloyd. I know at least you were paying attention to the rules I initially gave you. Don't discuss any murders. I ask the questions," says Richard.

"It takes most of my clients a while to grasp that rule," he continues. "But it seems you have been practicing it," finishes Richard.

Richard explains to Lloyd what to expect over the next few days, including a possible second arrest and more attempts to question him by police. Richard repeats the rules back to Lloyd, highlighting the one to not speak to anyone, especially the police.

The game plan is to sit and wait. Lloyd is directed to go about living a normal life, running errands, visiting Janice's grave, and staying out of trouble.

"Lloyd, I also want to start talking about the evidence in your case. Let's just assume you are charged with this new murder—and of course Janice's. You had no motive to murder them, correct?"

"No."

"I've been thinking. Maybe there was someone close to you that wanted to hurt Janice."

Lloyd stares at his brother confused before processing that this is a game he needs to go along with.

Lloyd thinks for a minute before finally blurting out, "Eva may have."

Richard reclines back into a resting position in his chair and studies Lloyd.

"Did Eva seem like a woman scorned?"

"Yeah, she did."

"She was the jealous type, wasn't she?"

"Even jealous of Selena when she came over to my house."

"She could have killed Janice out of jealousy and rage. Isn't that possible?"

"For sure."

"That's exactly what happened in that case up there," says Richard, proudly pointing to a framed article with a headline saying, "Defendant Blames Mistress for Wife's Murder."

"Did Eva ever do things that suggested she was obsessed with you?" asks Richard.

"I found her snooping around my house the night before Janice was murdered. That really happened. She was desperate, wanting to know if I was married. She even knew Janice was pregnant. She had been eavesdropping outside during our entire conversation that night. The lady is obsessed with me.

"Selena came over once and Eva got jealous over her, too. She's unstoppable," says Lloyd, trying to sound as if Eva's crazy.

"All this is good, really good," says Richard.

"But the only way this is going to come in during a trial is one of two ways. First, if you testify. And I want to keep you off the stand at any cost. The other way it comes in is if Eva testifies. But I don't want her anywhere near the courthouse," says Richard. "You're not still speaking to her, are you?" asks Richard.

"No," says Lloyd hesitantly.

"I don't want you anywhere near her. No speaking, calling, meeting, nothing, Lloyd. Your life depends on it."

"How are we gonna explain this new case, Selena's mom?" asks Lloyd.

The two look at each other, waiting for the other one to answer.

"Is it possible *her* husband did it?" asks Lloyd finally.

Richard smiles and says, "Now you're thinking like a lawyer."

"You were the one that said the husband *always* is the first suspect."

46

THE PRACTICE

Lloyd reclines back in a sitting chair at Richard's home during a holiday party. Lloyd thinks of all the years he hasn't been a part of his family gatherings, the holidays, and the reunions. Cousins, nephews, in-laws, and everyone at Richard's house seems to be doing exactly what families do—catch up, talk about sports, business, family affairs and reconnect with each other.

Richard thought it was best for the public perception and the trial if Lloyd started reconnecting with his family, especially since their discussion yesterday at the law firm about him being investigated for Annabelle's homicide. The media had started swarming again at Lloyd's home, so Richard agreed he could stay with them until it calmed down.

But Lloyd is out of place, off watching basketball on Richard's family room TV, with his feet up on an ottoman. A small boy, about four years old, walks over to him, confused as to who he is.

"What's your name?" the small boy asks Lloyd.

"Uncle Lloyd," he replies, first thing off the top of his head.

The young boy turns around, walking away hurriedly, and begins to cry, searching for this mom.

Lloyd hasn't been at a family event in over twenty years. He was used to Janice inviting her family over for the holidays, where he wouldn't have to socialize, but would rather stay in his bedroom or his office and pretend like he had to work.

Janice never seemed to mind, or at least she never complained. Lloyd missed the way of life he had, but he knew for his trial, he had to play this part of the "family man," "the grieving widow," and the "innocent brother, husband, and son." It was all part of the game, which was mostly Richard's idea of creating a winning defense, as he called it.

Everyone that mattered understands why Lloyd is at the party, including Richard's wife and the firm, Hill & Associates; some of the partners and associates are there.

As the party starts to wind down everyone thanks Richard and Olivia for getting everyone together and hosting the night. They congratulate Olivia and Richard again for the news that she is pregnant.

Lloyd hears it all but sees no reason for the niceties, grace, and thankfulness. He has really never seen the point in all of it. He watches disgustedly as Richard and Olivia, both visibly exhausted, extend their good-byes to each guest. He stares with disgust at her belly.

Richard and his firm partner approach Lloyd. The partner, a tall, slender white man in a cashmere sweater, glares at Lloyd before Richard asks Lloyd to join them in

Richard's study. Lloyd proceeds with them reluctantly while Olivia retires to the kitchen.

Richard's study has books lining each wall. Penal Codes, Traffic Codes, and Homicide Symposium binders fill the shelves. Films depicting the legal system are represented by framed movie posters throughout his office. Among these, he has vintage posters of old-time films, depicting the gravity of injustices.

A movie poster of "To Kill a Mockingbird" sits next to "It's a Wonderful Life."

"Have a seat, Lloyd," says Richard.

"I'm fine standing. I've been sitting all day," replies Lloyd defensively.

"Let's all have a seat. No need to get impatient," says Richard.

"Look, I don't want to. I've had a great time. You and Olivia did great. I miss Janice and the opportunity to host these types of things. My life is upside down right now. So I appreciate the invite," says Lloyd insincerely.

"Lloyd, what *are* you doing with all your spare time right now, or your 'life' as you say, that is causing it to feel upside down?" asks Richard suspiciously.

"That's none of your business," snaps back Lloyd.

"No, Lloyd, you're wrong. It *is* my business, don't you understand?" says Richard.

Lloyd glares at Richard.

"Now that we're having this discussion, let me ask you a couple things. I'd like us to think about what is going on in someone, mentally, that might lead them to kill innocent women; good-looking, pregnant, suburban housewives?" asks Richard.

Richard's partner stays quiet as Lloyd studies his face, noticing his high cheek bones glistening in the light.

Lloyd doesn't respond.

"Never mind. Don't answer that, especially if it's gonna take you this long. We'll let the psychiatrist answer that during trial," says Richard.

"That's one thing we're gonna need to work on—the way you answer questions. You look like a deer in headlights. You need to articulate responses for any question that's going to be thrown at you, Lloyd. Do you understand?" asks Richard, frustrated.

Lloyd stays quiet.

"Answer this, Lloyd," says Richard. "Why were you searching the depth of Canyon Base Lake from your computer? Why is Marty Kaplan saying that's the smoking gun?" questions Richard, with concern.

"Why, Lloyd? *Why*? *That's* the trick question. And what you need to know is that Richard is just doing this to prepare you for the obvious questions that are going to be brought up at trial. The jury will need explanations to things like this. Richard's right. So, listen to him," says the partner.

"Come up with something, anything, to every question you can think of. I don't have all the answers. That's the whole point of this exercise. And when you're answering me, make it seem like it's coming from the heart. Fake it if you have to. I don't want you to have any surprises. It's a long way from here—trial—but this is the start. Every time we meet, I wanna see that you've made further progress in coming to terms with it all. There's no reason you can't," says Richard.

"There has to be an explanation for all of this. It's a big misunderstanding. I'll figure it out, someday, I will," says Lloyd desperately.

"We don't want your explanation, Lloyd. We want you to get better and to just stay out of trouble, especially until your trial. We want police to stop calling with new accusations against you. Our firm cannot handle this level of attention," the partner says reluctantly.

"But you're the *Hill* firm," scoffs Lloyd.

"Exactly. And we don't want this level attention; not *this* kind. Defending the single murder of your wife is one thing, but a double homicide is quite another," the partner says sternly.

47

ANOTHER POSSIBILITY

Lloyd sits outside his brother Richard's house, waiting and watching for Richard to come home. Richard told Lloyd to meet him at his home to discuss something important. Since he's not allowed to be in the house when Richard is not there, he left early this morning.

Olivia, his sister-in-law, walks the grocery bags from the back of her station wagon to the inside of her house. She looks tired from yesterday's party. The coolness of the air floats across the top of Lloyd's forehead from his car window, cracked a couple inches open as he sits in the darkness of his car, completely invisible to anyone looking in.

He breathes methodically, nervous about the possibilities of why Richard asked to meet.

Lloyd watches Olivia return to her trunk and bend over to grab some flowers that had shifted further into the depth of the trunk. Lloyd grins at the sight of her round backside covered by her fitted red jeans.

An alarm system sign planted in the dirt next to a short staircase to the front door is illuminated from the halogen light in front of it. It's so obviously intentional. The white, wooden fence constructed in crisscross shapes with wood studs is illuminated by a second halogen light.

Before Janice's death, the last time he had seen Olivia was at his wedding. She looks the same and that was years ago. Her long, blonde flowing hair falls below her shoulders and whisks back and forth as she struggles with the last heavy grocery bag up to her front door.

It's six-fifty-five in the evening. The street is pitch black with very little light offered from neighboring porches. It's perfect, at least for what Lloyd imagines for a moment—an intrusion into the home, forcing Olivia straight down her hallway to the back bedroom, strangulation followed by an assault.

Snapping out of his fantasy, Lloyd clutches onto his silver flashlight.

The only problem is that Richard is expected home at any moment. At least that's what he said during his short conversation on the way over. Lloyd wonders for a moment whether he could pull off an assault of his brother's pregnant housewife.

Richard pulls his car into the driveway and he goes inside, not even looking towards Lloyd.

The moment he gets inside, Olivia and Richard start arguing with each other. Finally, Olivia rests one palm on her stomach, before throwing up the other in the air and moving to the back area of the home. The back half of the house goes dark while the front half stays illuminated.

Lloyd's phone rings. It's Richard. He answers.

"Lloyd, we need to meet another time. I'm sorry, but you can't come to my home. It's a long story," says Richard.

"I'm out in front already," says Lloyd.

"How long have you been here?" asks Richard.

"Not long," replies Lloyd.

There's a long pause.

"Meet me tomorrow at noon at my office. I'll explain then."

"What about a place to stay, Richard? I have nowhere to go. The media will be up my ass if I go home."

"I'm sorry, you can't stay here anymore. Olivia isn't comfortable with it; not anymore at least. I'm sorry," says Richard hurriedly before hanging up.

The rest of the lights go dark inside the house.

48

CONFRONTATION

Lloyd stands in Richard's office looking out the window extending from the floor to the ceiling. A light rain, looking like fast moving white balls of dew bouncing around each other, falls downwards.

A tall Christmas tree stands erect in the middle of the plaza stories below with a bright star beaming lights around the buildings surrounding it, including the Hill tower.

Richard sits at his desk taking bites from his specially prepared protein plate while thumbing through photos of Janice, murdered. Her face is so distorted from the elements she was exposed to in the Orange Groves. She is almost unrecognizable to Richard, who last saw her in person at Lloyd's wedding.

His only other contact with her was through her annual Christmas cards she would mail, usually adorned with photos of her and Lloyd on the annual work cruise or sitting on a bundle of hay at the local farm in Tuckford County.

But for those annual holiday cards, Richard would otherwise not have cared to remember he had a stepbrother.

Richard studies the close-up photos of the gash to Janice's head. He carefully watches Lloyd's back, making sure to only view the photos when Lloyd is not looking. Out of respect, he has not shown Lloyd any of the crime scene photos of Janice.

Lloyd remains still at the window, with his face an inch away from the glass and his hands in his pockets. The condensation from his breath fogs the window pane in front of him.

"How did you make it, Richard? How did you get this far?" asks Lloyd enviously.

Richard pauses before answering.

"A lot of hard work, Lloyd. A lot of hours. A lot of sacrifice," replies Richard proudly.

"A lot of men put in hard work, hours, away from their family. And they don't have a fraction of what you do. It's gotta be something more," replies Lloyd, complimenting him.

"You're right about that," starts Richard. "You're right about that," he again repeats, before clasping up the envelope of photos and reclining back into his leather desk chair, taking a sip of his coffee.

"I had my dad's footsteps to follow in. It takes money to make money. It's rare to do it alone," responds Richard.

"How do you think your dad made it?" Lloyd asks curiously.

"Well, he... *he* did it alone. He was driven, ambitious, he had your mom to support him. She's a great woman," says Richard endearingly.

"Just like Olivia supports me. I don't know how she puts up with me, with all the long hours. But she does. She always has. It's allowed me to accomplish all this," says Richard thankfully, directing Lloyd's eyes around his office with his hand.

"Why are you starting a family?" Lloyd asks curiously.

"It's what you do, Lloyd. It's what *we* do," says Richard patronizingly.

"Enough about me. Lloyd, let's discuss your case. We need the jury to know Eva was stalking you and Janice the night before her murder," says Richard optimistically.

"You haven't been in contact with her, have you?"

"Not at all," Lloyd replies. "She was trying for a while, but I've been avoiding her like you said."

"That's where I'm leaning with this case. Cast blame on her. The jury can sit and wonder if she did it.

"That's the one good thing you have going for you in this case," continues Richard condescendingly.

Lloyd freezes for a moment before reacting.

"Is that what you think of my case? That's the *one* good thing I have going in *my* case? This is *your* case, too! I thought you were defending me! You think I killed her, don't you?" Lloyd screams in frustration.

"It doesn't matter! I told you that I don't want to know if you committed these crimes," says Richard.

"I didn't kill Janice!" blurts Lloyd defiantly.

"You may have not killed Janice, but your name keeps coming up in the other case.

"I've seen a lot of spousal murders, Lloyd. But never with similarities linking to another case."

"That's what's most concerning to me as your lawyer. That's not to mention the woman you were with when the girl walked in; that woman believed you were capable of killing her too. I don't like that Marty Kaplan is calling me and telling me you struck again. He sure as shit has my number on automatic redial on his phone. That's what I have been dealing with since I agreed to represent you," screams Richard, exerting every last breath to get out his frustration without a pause.

"I didn't sign up for this. I didn't sign up to represent a serial killer. *My* brother, a *serial killer*," says Richard.

"I signed up to save you from death row. That's about all your piece of shit self is worth anyway," says Richard disgustedly.

Lloyd picks up the glass of water, slamming it against the window pane. It shatters into tiny shards of expensive glass, all which fall to the ground around a puddle of water that Richard quickly steps away from.

"Oh, did I stain your Gucci, leather shoes, Richard? Is that all you care about? Your reputation? Your next trial? Your firm?" says Lloyd, pointing at all the accolades around his office.

"Keep going, Lloyd. You *need* me. You need me to save your life. My dad warned me this would happen some day. 'One day, Richard,' he used to say. 'That long lost stepbrother of yours will come knocking on your door.' He warned me, 'It wouldn't be to apologize. It wouldn't be to join us for the holidays. Or be part of our family. It would be because he needs something.' And he would tell me, 'You're going to be in a position to help him. The question will be,' he would warn me, 'Can you afford to?' Not financially. Not professionally. But, emotionally, personally. 'Can your sanity afford to help him...?' he used to say," Richard says.

"I never knew what he meant, but he used to tell your mom the same thing," he continues, now up in Lloyd's face.

"None of us understood why you weren't part of the family. Why you decided to go your own way," blames Richard.

"I want you to think long and hard, Lloyd. Because I've been doing a lot of thinking for you. What kind of man are you trying to be? What are you trying to prove?" questions Richard rhetorically.

Lloyd backs away, infuriated.

"Don't try your cross-examination mind games on me. I'm your client; not the state's witness," says Lloyd righteously.

"I know you're good for some of this. Maybe not Janice's murder, but the other lady. Mom saw you at The Coffee Grind with that girl Veronica. She knew her, you idiot. You don't think I know you're watching Mom? You don't think she'd recognize you in your stupid hairpiece and glasses? Why? Because it's been how many years since she's seen you? She's your friggen mom and a mom doesn't forget the face of her son," protests Richard aggressively.

"I don't know what you're talking about," says Lloyd dismissively.

"Lloyd, when I hear these things, not only does it interfere with me legally representing you, it interferes with my motivations to defend you. I don't want to fight for you—and save you from death row—if I know you deserve it.

"I still have integrity. I have a wife I go home to every night. I still need her respect. We're bringing a baby into this world. And I want to earn his respect too. Because that's what I wake up every morning for and look forward to seeing in the mirror. A man with integrity, respect, and honor," says Richard condescendingly, standing a foot away from Lloyd, facing him.

Lloyd stands in silence, infuriated, with his body starting to warm up.

"Does any of this make sense to you?" asks Richard hopelessly.

Richard can't tolerate the silence, so he answers his own question.

"Maybe it doesn't, Lloyd. Maybe you lost your integrity, self-worth, and your wife's respect a long time ago, and that's why you can't relate to anything I'm saying. Is that what it is?" asks Richard sarcastically.

A ring interrupts them both.

"Richard, Marty Kaplan is on the line," says Richard's secretary.

"FUCK! Lloyd!" Richard says before responding to his secretary, "transfer him over."

"What can I do for you, Investigator Kaplan?" asks Richard, who is tapping the pads of his fingers on his desk.

"We need to speak to your client about some evidence turned over to us in connection with a theft and possible assault of a woman who worked in Downtown Canyon Base. A bead clerk," says Marty seriously.

"What evidence?" asks Richard, staring at Lloyd.

"An earring. An earring anonymously turned over to the police department. It's got Eva's DNA on it and the bead lady identified it as hers," says Marty.

"He's not talking to you fools anymore," Richard says before slamming the phone down.

"I...." starts Lloyd.

"Stop!" yells Richard. "I don't want you to address this. You see, Lloyd, these are the types of calls I'm getting on a daily basis from Marty Kaplan, as I sit here in the dark preparing for your defense. Why the hell would they want to talk to my client about an earring that was turned over to them? What connection does Lloyd have to the earring?"

"That...." starts Lloyd.

"Stop! I'm thinking out loud. I don't want to hear anything from you. I'm getting the investigator over here to speak with you."

"They're getting really close to charging you with Annabelle's murder, which makes perfect sense why they're suspecting you of other crimes, like this chick from the bead store now. I mean, do I really need to go on and on? They're tying them all together, Lloyd. It's just a matter of time. I know the feeling of an impending arrest. Marty's getting close; you can hear it in his tone. I need to..." says Richard hopelessly before Lloyd interrupts.

"What the hell, Richard? Are you saying you think I'm good for killing Janice?"

"I'm not talking about this. Opinions don't matter, Lloyd," says Richard dismissively.

Lloyd clenches his hands turning them into fists, causing his face to turn red.

"How can they do this? How can they charge me with these murders? I didn't kill Janice and I didn't kill the other one."

Lloyd starts pacing back and forth, talking to himself and completely out of control.

"Earring... earring," Lloyd repeats to himself, pulling at his hair as Richard heads for the door.

"Screw her. Screw her. That bitch. I just wanna take her by the..." Lloyd blurts out.

"Who are you talking about, Lloyd?" starts Richard, stopping in his tracks.

"Never mind. Don't answer that," Richard continues. "I don't want you around her, whoever you're talking about. Forget it! I don't want you talking to her. I don't want you talking to anyone, Lloyd. This is what the police do. They get people to start working for them. Don't fall into their trap. They'll have you fall into something you have no idea they're behind. Trust me," says Richard assertively.

Richard's phone rings into his office and within seconds, Marty is on speaker phone.

"Don't hang up on me, Richard. You'll want to hear this one. Your baby brother is going down. He tried the same thing on that bead clerk. He attempted to strangle her and threatened her. She could have been another one of his murder victims," says Marty, adding a laugh to the conversation.

"File the charges, Marty. Your threats mean nothing to me. Send over the reports," Richard says before hanging up.

Richard turns to Lloyd and stares directly at him to warn him.

"Stay away from this, man. And if you get arrested, remember our rules."

49

LAST CALL

Lloyd wastes no time to confirm his suspicions about Eva talking to police. Within two hours of leaving Richard's office, he sits on top of her on her bed, crushing her with the weight of his body as she begs for forgiveness for anything he suspects she's responsible for.

Lloyd can't hear any of it. Her screams are muffled.

There's nothing worse than a killer who knows that the police are onto him and his witnesses have turned against him.

"Lloyd, I swear on your life, I did not tell police about us. They're just saying that. Trust me. I'd never!" she pleads.

"You betrayed me, Eva," he blurts out.

He moves his hands to her neck and squeezes it until she screams for him to release the pressure.

Lloyd takes a couple deep breaths and sits on top of Eva, watching her struggle for her life.

He's cool, calm, and collected. A swishing sound of water fills his ears.

She protests about all the reasons he should spare her life, how they had a relationship, how they were friends, how they loved each other, how he promised her that he had changed.

"You promised when we first met that you would never leave me. You said you wouldn't treat me like my mother did," she pleads to no avail.

Her own struggling slowly wears her out.

"Do what you need to do. I'll forgive you, whatever you decide," says Eva guiltily, closing her eyes and submitting fully to him.

He stops.

"Eva, I'm not your mom," he says defensively.

"It feels that way. You're trying to kill me. You're turning against me like she did. You're turning into what she was. She destroyed me. She destroyed our family. You're no different. You're going to destroy me," she protests, with tears streaming down her face.

"I'm not your mom, Eva. I'm not your mom," says Lloyd, releasing the tension from his fingers around her neck.

"And I'm not yours, Lloyd. Neither are any of your victims," she says back defensively.

"You see your mom in all of your victims. You're like your dad who abused her. That's why you kill them. It's all because of your built-up hatred, your un-dealt-with issues.

"You don't want to kill me, Lloyd. You've told me that before. But now look at you. You have no conscience. No empathy. Don't you care about me? How good I've been to you. That's what kills me the most to see, how you'd just snap and kill me, just like that... after all I've done for you.

"To kill me because you think I betrayed you and I talked to police. What do you think, I'm some animal you can just kill?

"I didn't speak to the police. I didn't. I promise. I'm not that girl. I'm not that person to go and turn you in," she says desperately.

Lloyd studies her face and the displeasing red birthmark across her face that looks like a gaping wound has spilled out blood over her skin.

"Eva. I didn't kill Janice. You came to my house the night before Janice was murdered. You were the one that couldn't let go of the fact that I had a wife."

"How dare you," she says threateningly.

"Janice and that other woman were killed the same way. Wrapped in a rug and dumped. I know, Lloyd. I know it was you," she screams fearfully.

"I didn't kill Janice. I didn't. Why don't you believe me?"

Eva considers this possibility.

"I didn't kill her either," she says in a controlled tone.

The two look at eachother while several seconds pass.

"Then who did? Who killed her? Who killed my wife?" yells Lloyd, beginning to cry for the first time over Janice's death.

He finally stops asking after Eva embraces him tightly and rocks him back and forth.

50

STEER CLOSE

Lloyd drifts to sleep in his car two blocks away after leaving Eva's house, still sweaty from his struggle before he spared her life.

He pulls down the visor inside his car and stares at himself in the reflection of the mirror, asking himself repeatedly what the hell is wrong with him.

Was he trying to make every woman pay for his past? What was his past?

Feeling as though he is submerged in water, he gasps for air.

He questions whether he is some kind of avenging angel.

He sits in silence waiting for answers or emotion to come over him.

Nothing but silence fills the darkness of his car.

His appearance is pathetic. His clothes reek of body odor. He doesn't care anymore.

He hasn't had a haircut in months and his hair is overgrown, intruding into his ears, which is unsettling even to him.

He drifts off to sleep for a moment, before hearing a loud knock at his driver side window.

It's Marty. He rolls down the window.

"Wake up, you asshole," says Marty, demanding Lloyd step out of his car.

"You're under arrest for the murder of Annabelle Phillips. We've been looking 10 years for the White Picket Fence Killer. And all along, it was you."

51

FAME

Lloyd looks around the dayroom at the County Jail lying on his bunk bed, still upset over his repeated and ignored requests to be placed in protective custody since Marty booked him in last night. The last classification deputy told him it was because of jail overcrowding.

Another inmate lies down in his bunk directly above him. They watch a television broadcasting the local news and commercials.

"Man, you gonna be on the news?" asks Lloyd's bunkmate.

"I don't know. I don't watch this stuff," replies Lloyd, afraid his high publicity case may make him the target of a shanking.

The blonde news anchorwoman catches Lloyd's attention. Her long, blonde hair curled neatly down her chest and royal blue sweater turns Lloyd on.

"She pretty, ain't she?" yells his bunkmate.

"Mmmm hmmm," says Lloyd.

"What you think. She's about twenty-five?"

"At least, maybe thirty," answers Lloyd.

"Would you?"

"Huh?" asks Lloyd.

"Would you? Would you do her?"

"Hell, yeah!" Lloyd replies excitedly.

"Not so sure I would. I like the Latinas."

"Me too, the blonde ones."

"No fake blondes for me. That commercialized, Botox shit just doesn't do it for me. I'm into the natural ones, mostly brunette," says Lloyd's bunkmate.

"To each his own," says Lloyd.

"I think you gonna be on the news. Your case is big."

"Don't remind me."

The television projects a voluptuous, blonde woman headlining the stories for the evening news.

"Stay tuned with us for the seven o'clock news on Channel eighty-three. The White Picket Fence Killer has been captured. We'll have all the details right here, including a statement made by his attorney and the prosecuting attorney," says the blonde anchorwoman.

"At least *she's* giving the story," says Lloyd sarcastically.

"Seriously."

The news story returns within a minute to project Richard standing in his office lobby in front of bold letters spelling out HILL & ASSOCIATES.

A news interviewer stands with Richard, who looks impeccably dressed. The interviewer talks into a microphone.

"I'm here with Mr. Richard Hill, the brother and lawyer of The White Picket Fence Killer, Lloyd Gil. Sir, are you prepared to defend Tuckford County's most prolific killer to date?" questions the newsman.

"I am prepared to defend my brother, a man, a humble man, who lost *his* wife to a killer who is still on the loose. I am confident that Mr. Gil will be acquitted of the charges he is faced with," says Richard, smiling confidently into the camera.

"At Hill & Associates, we only take on selective cases where we feel that we can serve justice and help defend some of the most vulnerable people, whether they are large corporations or indigent defendants, who simply need adequate representation to ensure the criminal justice system treats them fairly and the interests of justice are served," continues Richard.

"Thank you, Mr. Hill. There has been a wave of fear in Tuckford County, and time will tell whether Lloyd Gil is the White Picket Fence Killer. Broadcasting live from Loft City, back to you Sandra," says the newsman as the camera focuses back on the voluptuous blonde.

Lloyd's bunkmate taps loudly on the bunk bed metal bars.

"Yep. You made it big. You're in the big league, man. When your case is on TV like that, you're in the big league," he says.

Lloyd steps down from his bunk and moves aggressively towards his bunkmate, who's still lying down.

"Don't fucken say, 'I'm in the big league.' I didn't kill my wife, man, you hear me? I'M NOT THE WHITE PICKET FENCE KILLER," screams Lloyd pulling on his bunkmate's county-issued orange jumpsuit.

"Chill out, man," says his bunkmate, starting to stand up, looking like he's ready to fight Lloyd.

"Don't EVER fucken say that again," yells Lloyd.

"Deputies, deputies!" yells his bunkmate.

Within seconds, the entire dayroom of inmates are in an uproar and a blast dispersion round is unleashed.

Smoke begins to fill the air.

52

ANOTHER

Lloyd sits handcuffed alongside two deputies waiting for the nurse to come in and examine the wheezing sounds coming from his lungs. Since Lloyd engaged his entire dayroom in a fight last week over his bunkmate's comments, he's complained of a shortness of breath. Normally, the blast dispersion rounds cause the inmates to close their eyes so they're not able to continue fighting. Tearing and burning sensations to their eyes usually result, but they typically dissipate.

Lloyd likes his visits to the jail infirmary, where he is treated for his chest congestion. Here, he could have human contact with Marie, the beautiful, blonde nurse.

The nice thing about her for Lloyd is that she treats him like a human being. Lloyd quickly learned she has a philosophy to not treat the inmates any differently. Her job is to heal them, not judge them. She treats them with sensitivity from the start of their visits.

And Marie believes that even killers, robbers, or spousal abusers are all humans, entitled to healthcare. So she has no problem administering aid to the inmates. In fact, she enjoys her job and working with the people that everyone wants to distance themselves from. It makes her feel useful and unique.

The nurse walks into her small patient room in the infirmary. Lloyd has been coming to her for the past week to receive breathing treatments. She administers a sophisticated nebulizer on him, filling his lungs with a liquid formula. Lloyd blames his condition on the blast, but the infirmary doctor refused to diagnose that as the cause.

"How are things, Marie?" asks Lloyd.

"Good, thank you," she says curtly.

When Marie's eyes meet Lloyd's, he smiles but she looks away quickly without smiling back. Something is off.

She's avoiding her usual small talk and directs him to sit on her patient table.

"How was your week?" he asks.

"Busy."

"Are you taking any vacations anytime soon?"

"No."

She hands the mouthpiece to Lloyd, expecting him to put it between his teeth, but when he sits and glares at her, a nearby deputy has to order him to put it in his mouth.

He clenches his teeth down hard, crushing the mouthpiece, which is connected by a large tube to the electronic breathing machine. Without noticing his firm grip, she reminds him to take a breath, holding it for a few seconds.

Marie's perceived rejection is entirely unacceptable to Lloyd.

While he follows her instructions, she takes out her stethoscope from the side pocket of her scrubs, puts the earpieces in, and places the pad against Lloyd's chest, listening for the level of clarity in his air tracks.

This starts to calm him.

Lloyd enjoys her physical touching and searches her face for any indication of what she is thinking. He studies her forehead as she focuses on the areas of his chest she is moving the surface pad around.

Her long, blonde, flowing hair, which drapes down over her shoulders and breasts.

Her white with baby blue polka dots scrubs fits her body perfectly, even over her slightly pregnant stomach. Lloyd rehashes her story in his mind.

Marie is about thirty-five years old and has been married for five years. She and her husband had been trying to get her pregnant for the past several years, and finally had luck three months ago after a couple miscarriages. She is determined to keep herself healthy.

Her husband is an aerospace engineer who travels to different rocket launch sites around the country to oversee test launches. He is busy and on the go, so Marie is used to being independent. She looks forward to him coming home each time because it makes the relationship feel new again.

There were a lot of other details Marie shared with Lloyd, but these were the things he chose to remember. He studies her face.

Marie's beauty is natural. Her full, shapely lips along with her flawless complexion and healthy hair are among his favorite things about her. All that looks the same as before, but something is different about her mannerisms and dealing with him today. He just can't figure out what it is.

He continues taking deep breaths as she directs him to. The sputtering sound of the nebulizer begins agitating Lloyd, instead of calming him. The ten minutes he breathes in and out help to open his lungs.

He feels more and more powerful with each breath. Her treatment is helping him, but none of this matters. He only focuses on her rejection.

Lloyd envisions a fantasy where without warning, he grabs the hair on the back of her head and wrestles her to the ground of her own patient room.

He imagines her squirming and trying and get away while he kicks her in the stomach, hoping she'll miscarry her fetus. Or perhaps he would try jabbing her head into the base of the patient table over and over again, until she is fully incapacitated. He imagines himself squeezing her throat asphyxiating her, cutting off all oxygen to her unborn baby. In his sick fantasy, correction deputies run into the room and wrestle him off of her, but it's too late. Marie takes her last breath in one of the deputy's arms.

"Mr. Gil... Mr. Gil," says a correction deputy.

Lloyd snaps out of his dream, noticing Marie move about the room and turn off the nebulizer machine. The visit is about to end.

She turns to him and gives him a fake smile.

The sound of water swirls in Lloyd's head. And a beating heart follows.

He makes his way off the patient table and heads toward the exit door.

"I'll have you next," he says, glaring at the nurse, then looking down at her stomach, says, "and him too."

Lloyd is shoved out of the room by a deputy who is tightly holding his hands cuffed behind his back.

53

SECURITY THREAT

Lloyd sits in the packed courtroom next to Richard, being carefully watched by the courtroom deputies as everyone waits for Judge Cohen to take the bench. Two correction deputies, including the sergeant in charge of the housing unit of the jail, sit in the front row on the prosecution side. A tall, lean, attractive man in his forties sits in the front row of the prosecution side, glaring at Lloyd.

Two days have passed since Lloyd threatened Nurse Marie.

"Remain seated, come to order, court is now in session," yells the correction deputy.

Judge Cohen begins the discussion.

"Before we address the security concern, I'd like to take care of another matter. It has been brought to my attention that an additional murder charge will be filed against Mr. Gil, is that correct, counselor? For Annabelle Phillips."

"Yes, Your Honor. I already informed counsel I will be filing that by the arraignment. I would have had the amended complaint ready today, but we are adding the threat to the nurse, so I'd rather have all the charges in one document," says Jack Moore.

"Very well. Let's get to the issue before us today. It is my understanding there is a rather serious security concern over the defendant's housing at the jail. Present with us is Sergeant Griff Andrews, is that correct, sir?" asks Judge Cohen.

The tall, lean, attractive man who has been sitting in the front row of the prosecution side glaring at Lloyd all morning stands up quickly, answering affirmatively.

"What is the concern of your facility?" asks Judge Cohen.

"Sir, we have received multiple security breach concerns stemming around Mr. Gil. The most serious ones being the threat to our nursing staff and his assault on another inmate. Both are currently under investigation," says the sergeant aggressively.

"Have there been any incidents since then?" asks Judge Cohen.

"Not that have been brought to my attention," the sergeant replies.

"What is his current housing situation?" asks Judge Cohen.

"He is being housed in a solitary unit and being fed the brick diet," replies the sergeant obligingly.

"How are medical needs being addressed?" Judge Cohen asks with concern.

"At the moment, they currently are not," he replies hesitantly.

Media representatives start scribbling down notes.

"That is completely unacceptable. Look, I don't want to minimize what's going on. And I'm sure there are people in this courtroom who think hurling a brick of food into a man's cell is a slap on the wrist. After all, they have all the daily nutrients. And I'm sure some think we should lock this man's cell and throw away the key, like prisoners were treated in the eighteen hundreds in this country. But we've come far from treating people this way, especially with depriving them of their medical needs.

"That's why there are lawsuits and judges like me who set the standards for their living arrangements. His medical treatments are a necessity. I understand the security concerns over the threat. However, I am going to order that Mr. Gil be provided with his necessary breathing treatments, and this will remain a standing order so long as he is under my jurisdiction. This is a direct order of the court. Do you understand me?" says Judge Cohen.

"Sir, we will do our best to accommodate all the necessary rights Mr. Gil has under the law," replies the sergeant defensively.

"I've seen your agency sued over and over again in class action suits where inmates' rights are deprived. If these medical needs are deprived to this man, I can guarantee a lawsuit will result," snaps back Judge Cohen.

"Sir, we don't believe he needs the breathing treatments anymore. And it's questionable whether he needed them the day he threatened our nurse. It may have been a ploy. That's how the investigation is unfolding. I can't give any additional information without compromising the pending investigation. But like I said, I will ensure that all his basic needs are met," says the sergeant matter-of-factly.

"I think the better way to handle Mr. Gil would be to keep him away from your female staff, especially the pregnant ones. Frankly, I'm not sure why he seems to target those that are pregnant and it's a great concern, no doubt, but I'm not entirely sure he's a risk to anyone else," says Judge Cohen sarcastically.

"You may have made your own risk assessments. Actually, I take that back; maybe you haven't," the sergeant snaps back, shifting his focus to the pregnant court reporter.

"I'm not privy to the same information you have. I only assess the threats to our facility and this is the conclusion I've arrived at. You run your courtroom the way you want to and let me run my jail the way *I* see fit. The risk Mr. Gil currently presents outweighs his need for treatment," continues the sergeant decisively.

"Very well, this hearing is adjourned. I'll see you next week for arraignment on all charges. Bail will remain revoked," says Judge Cohen, defeatedly.

54

UNRELIEVED

Lloyd sits in the courtroom close to two deputies, hoping for one private moment with his brother. But instead, Richard moves around, first talking to the clerical staff, then deputies and last, Prosecutor Jack Moore.

A happy staff, prosecutor, and judge mostly favor one person—the defendant. But Lloyd doesn't appreciate any of this. Instead, he believes that Richard's focus should be on him.

Richard lets out a loud laugh when speaking to Jack, which even catches the attention of the audience. Annabelle's husband, Tim, looks up from speaking with his mother-in-law Cybil and stares at Richard. Tim begins to stand, but Cybil grabs his arm, pulling him back down.

Richard notices none of this.

Lloyd begins to feel like an outcast and a black sheep. It's been a long time since he's felt this way and he can't even remember the last time he cared about how others perceive him.   But sitting alone, feeling like his only friend in the courtroom is Richard, begins to remind him that he actually cares.

Jack walks around the courtroom, talking to the court reporter and media representative. He is a well-dressed, dark-haired prosecutor. He has almost a perfect conviction record and is next in line to taking over the appointed prosecutor's position.

"Remain seated, come to order, court is now in session," the deputy barks.

"We're here in the matter of the People versus Lloyd Gil. This time, it's for a separate murder charge for Annabelle Phillips, and one criminal threat on a jail staff, in addition to the murder charge for Mr. Gil's wife," says Judge Cohen.

"That's correct," starts Prosecutor Jack Moore, jumping in to take control of the courtroom.

"We will be seeking death in this case. I'm asking for no bail to remain in effect. We have our notice of intent on seeking death, which has been filed with the clerk," says Jack Moore.

"Are you ready to proceed on the arraignment for these charges, counsel?" asks Judge Cohen, looking at Richard.

"Before we proceed, I'd like to have an ex parte closed hearing regarding representing Mr. Gil," says Richard hesitantly.

"Well, the only way I'm going to have an ex parte hearing is if your client is asking for it. Are you asking to represent yourself or be appointed with new counsel?" asks Judge Cohen inquisitively, looking directly at Lloyd.

"No, I'm not. But maybe my counsel is?" replies Lloyd sarcastically, looking at Richard.

"Very well. I'll consider your request, counsel, if you'd like to lodge your paperwork with my clerk," says Judge Cohen sternly.

"May we have a sidebar?" says Richard, frustrated.

"No. Anything we discuss should be on the record. What is your pleasure, Mr. Hill?" asks Judge Cohen.

"I'm asking to be relieved, Your Honor," says Richard awkwardly.

"Can you please elaborate?" asks Judge Cohen.

"I can't, without divulging certain confidences protected," says Richard reluctantly.

"Are you adequately prepared to represent your client? I mean, are there any concerns with resources or your ability to advocate for him as the law requires?" asks Judge Cohen.

"I can't fault this on resources or being unable to offer him an adequate defense," says Richard defensively.

"Well. Even though I'm a bit disappointed, sir, we *are* at an early stage of the proceedings. I'm inclined to grant your request if that's really what you want to do," says Judge Cohen.

"May I speak with my attorney for a moment, Your Honor?" interrupts Lloyd, politely.

Richard leans over to Lloyd and starts speaking with him.

"This will just take a moment," says Richard, motioning up with his finger towards the judge.

"Lloyd," starts Richard quietly. "We've had a breakdown in confidences. I'm not in the right ethical mindset to represent you."

"What breakdown in confidences have we had, Richard? What ethical mindset do you have? Fuck you, Richard," whispers Lloyd fiercely.

"Let's get one thing straight. I'm not risking my firm's integrity for you. Don't think for a second I haven't talked to Mom about this, you asshole. My wife can't even look at me anymore, knowing I am representing you. You're threatening jail staff! You're unstoppable. What's next, Lloyd? Me? Olivia?" whispers Richard threateningly.

Two deputies move closer to Richard and Lloyd as their voices get louder. Camera clicking sounds from the different media photographers distract Richard until he refocuses.

"I'm trying to get myself under control Richard. I knew you'd abandon this case. You're not strong enough, Richard. You never were. You can't hold the weight of a case of this magnitude. Fuck that, top lawyer, ha! Maybe in Loft. But you'll never make it in this county. I don't even know why I thought for a minute you'd be able to represent me til the end," says Lloyd sarcastically.

Richard stares down Lloyd.

"Go ahead, Richard. Abandon me. I'm used to it. I've been the black sheep of the family my entire life. Walk away from this case and never look back. They'll be a time you'll feel bad about it. You and Mom. It will probably be when I'm being strapped in the electric chair for something I didn't do. Is that when it will hit you?"

Lloyd's eyes begin to well up with tears and Richard studies his face. It seems genuine, but Richard is unsure whether it's   nothing more than pure manipulation.

"If you hurt anyone else in custody or pick up anything, even so much as an infraction, and I mean this seriously, I will get off this case," Richard warns Lloyd sternly. They glare at each other before directing their attention back to Judge Cohen.

"He doesn't want to waive time for trial, Your Honor. I'm ready to continue representing him," explains Richard, composing himself. "I'll withdraw my request," he continues defeatedly.

"Very well, are you ready to proceed?" asks Judge Cohen, relieved.

"I am.   I've had a chance to review the amended complaint and advise my client. Mr. Gil will be entering pleas of not guilty to all the charges. Waive formal reading of the complaint.   And we ask that dates be set forthwith.   No further time waivers," says Richard, still flustered.

"Very well, all statutory dates will be set, bail remains revoked, Mr. Gil is remanded back to the custody of the Sheriff's Department, and I'll see you back here in a couple weeks to certify the minutes," says Judge Cohen decisively, before leaving the bench.

Richard turns to Lloyd.

"We've got sixty days til trial.   I'll visit you in the next couple weeks to talk about the case.   Stay out of trouble."

55

STRATEGY

Lloyd sits at the County Jail attorney-inmate meeting table across from Richard, who is sorting through police reports organized in file folders in front of him.

Lloyd studies the criminal complaint Richard handed him to review, which was amended just a week ago adding the additional murder.

"Well, Lloyd, let's get this meeting started. We've got a lot of ground to cover today," Richard starts wearily.

"Can I get copies of that stuff?" asks Lloyd curiously.

"Not yet. I need to go through this stuff and redact it before I hand it over to you. We're going to push forward and demand the trial get started. I just got preliminary DNA results back. Your DNA has been positively matched in both Annabelle's and Janice's case. In Janice's, we can explain it away. You guys lived together. Plus there is another unidentified DNA profile present. But Annabelle's is a whole other story."

"My initial impression was they didn't have a whole lot on you, but that has changed. The question is no longer were you there. The question now is *what happened* when you were there," says Richard, matter-of-factly.

"You never had any motive to intentionally hurt these women, did you?"

"No."

"Okay. Did you meet Annabelle and befriend her as a client, and have a consensual relationship with her?"

Lloyd pauses and looks at Richard, who is shaking his head reassuringly and affirmatively.

"Pretty much."

"Okay. I'd like to shift gears and talk about what happened in *both* of these murders. Because there are findings on the causes of death documented in the coroner's report," says Richard before pausing and reading the autopsy summary.

"Lloyd, have you ever heard of the dominant's defense?"

"No."

"When a person in the BDSM culture engages in activities of domination and submission, sometimes things get out of hand. Is that possibly what happened with Annabelle and even the others, the bead clerk and Veronica."

Lloyd studies Richard, who is still looking down at the autopsy summary.

"I guess?" answers Lloyd, inquisitively.

"You *guess?* When I look at the injuries of Annabelle and the manner of death, it appears she was strangled and that is the first thing that comes to my mind, Lloyd. After authorities found her dumped in the Orange Groves, they did an autopsy. It appears, things just went too far. I mean, because, you didn't intend for her to die, did you?"

"No. No. Of course not."

"*Okay.* Then let me ask you again in another way. You met this beautiful woman."

"Yes."

"You enjoyed each other's company, spent time together, talked about life. She was curious about you, Lloyd. You're a handsome man. Her husband was away. We're not trying to say this lady was a bad woman. But she had sexual urges. You and this woman were consenting adults."

"Right."

"One thing led to another. You were about to engage in consensual sex."

"She wanted to," Lloyd plays along.

"Right. And she wanted to explore new sexual games with you, like role playing, submission, asphyxiation."

"I get it," blurts Lloyd.

"Lloyd, there's nothing to get. This is what happened, isn't it? Sex play that got out of hand. You may have just squeezed too hard. It all got out of hand," says Richard confidently, before looking up at Lloyd, awaiting his response.

"Absolutely."

Lloyd starts to play it out in his mind.

Richard pulls out the police reports and flips through them.

"You would use your bare hands, correct? No weapons. No ligatures, correct?" asks Richard.

"Correct."

"No necktie, stocking, rope, cord, or belt..." replies Richard matter-of-factly.

"Right."

"Very well," says Richard, looking up at Lloyd.

"We will present this in the guilt phase, hire a BDSM expert, go the nine yards and ask for lesser verdicts, such as manslaughter. Or at least second degree. That will give us a chance to beat the death penalty," says Richard.

"If it doesn't work and we proceed to the sentencing phase, we'll bring in a mitigation expert and psychologist to talk about your childhood and whatever else they find that may have caused you to commit these crimes."

"Okay."

"Aside from these woman, you've engaged in BDSM before, haven't you?" asks Richard, optimistically.

"Of course," says Lloyd, righteously. "I met a dominatrix when I was out of custody. A professional one. She was from South America," says Lloyd.

"Where was this at?" asks Richard, interestedly.

"She came onto me in line at the Unemployment Office. She was in line. One thing led to the other. Next thing I knew, she was handing me her card," says Lloyd proudly.

"And you had a session with her," says Richard.

"Sure did," says Lloyd.

"Something sounds familiar about this story," says Richard, concerned.

"I'm going to press Marty and Jack on this. They mentioned having some new discovery for me. Maybe it involves this," says Richard puzzled, searching his mind for a memory.

"Did you ever talk to her about the case?"

"No, not that I remember."

"Let me think about this. I want to make sure it doesn't hurt our defense. Give her information to our investigator. In the meantime, I'm sending a psychologist in to speak with you tomorrow. Please cooperate with him and answer everything truthfully.   I want to see if there's any mental health issues we can raise, which will work in your mitigation phase," says Richard, before ending the meeting.

"Mental health?"

"Yes, Lloyd.   You may have some mental health issues that are causing you to commit these crimes.   It's something that will mitigate the penalty," says Richard as he gathers up his paperwork.

Lloyd watches Richard, who doesn't look up at him before turning to walk away.

"I'M CRAZY NOW?" yells Lloyd, loud enough for Richard to hear as he moves closer to the exit door.

Lloyd repeats those three words over and over again until Richard is completely out of sight.

56

RISK ASSESSMENT

The jail inmate visiting lounge is sterile, undecorated, and provides the minimal basic needs for two people to meet. The closest thing to hospitality is the soda vending machine in the waiting room leading to the visiting area.

Lloyd stands and greets Dr. Matthew McDonald, a state-renowned, pro-defense expert. Prosecution-oriented people call him a "defense whore." Defense-oriented people call him "Dr. McDominator."

"Hi, Mr. Gil, please take a seat. How are you doing?"

"Better than last time."

"I was able to take the opportunity to listen to the entirety of our interview last week all over again. I generated a fifteen page report, which contains all the results of your psychopathy examination, your Static-99, which tests your likelihood of committing a sexual offense in the future, and the HCR-20, which examines all of the risk factors in your social history leading up to your crimes."

Dr. McDonald takes out the computer-generated report from his briefcase along with his reading glasses case and sets them on the table in front of him.

"You know, my eyesight has really declined in the last year. It's incredible. I mean, I've been seeing an eye doctor for twenty years, since I was thirty, and have always had the same prescription, but in the last year..." says the doctor, before being cut off by Lloyd.

"Doctor. Can you get to the point? I don't have much time for my visits, so I would appreciate you using our time wisely," says Lloyd meanly.

Dr. McDonald opens his eyeglass case slowly, wipes his glasses with the thin cloth inside, and pushes them up the bridge of his nose.

"Mr. Gil. I've been doing this a long time and my guess is that you have not. I've been working in the criminal justice system for twenty years. You have been engaged with it for months. You may have committed some of the most heinous crimes, but I have evaluated the perpetrators of those crimes for some time.

"I must warn you that your demeanor and attitude towards me will be reflected in this report. Your brother, Mr. Hill, has asked me to prepare an accurate report as to my assessment of your medical and mental conditions, if any, how they contributed to your committing the crimes you are charged with, and the likelihood of you committing them again in the future."

"So let's cut to the chase. What were the results?" asks Lloyd.

"Not favorable to you at all, sir. With all due respect, utterly unfavorable in all aspects of every test.

"You scored higher on the psychopathy checklist than seventy-nine percent of inmates similarly incarcerated."

"What does that mean? A checklist? Check the boxes?" says Lloyd, sarcastically.

"No, sir. It's not a 'check-the-box' list. It is a widely accepted test to see if you exhibit traits of a psychopath. And your result was on the higher spectrum of inmates."

"That's assuming I was truthful in my answers."

"Exactly. This examination is based on your answers to the questions. But I don't have any reason to believe you are not an accurate historian of your childhood, your crimes, and your responses. There's no reason for you to be untruthful. I'm here to help you."

"What else do you have, doctor?"

"Well, there's the HCR-20."

"Same result?"

"This test, I don't particularly care for."

"Why is that?"

"Because it only measures static factors, meaning those factors that will never change. This test takes into account your childhood issues, any abuse, any previous criminal activity, any drug use, et cetera. I mean, those things will remain for perpetuity, but they do indicate to us whether you are at higher risk to be a danger."

"I can guess those results, doctor. You don't need to tell me those. It's not very difficult to figure out."

"Well, those results were rather interesting. It's my belief your abusive father has more to do with your rage than your mother and based..." says the doctor, before Lloyd cuts him off.

"How can you say that? I didn't even know my father. My mom abandoned me. Why do you think I did this shit?"

"Lloyd!   By your own admission, you had a loving mother, you had, albeit a difficult childhood, with your mother struggling, but otherwise, she did the best she could. She provided for you. You were close.

"Your father was the perpetrator. After we met, I had the opportunity to interview your mother. She was his victim and a very submissive one. Your crimes reflect your rage and hatred over your father's abuse."

"I DIDN'T EVEN KNOW HIM!"

"I understand this, but what I've discovered from speaking with your mother is that she endured a lot when she was pregnant with you. Your father punched and kicked her in the stomach many times while you were in utero. I believe there's a connection between your rage toward pregnant women and your father's abuse."

"That makes no sense. I wasn't even born," says Lloyd.

"The early development of your brain such as your frontal lobe are at a critical stage while you're in the womb. You internalized all of your mom's fears, vulnerability and stress. After you were born, you were abandoned by both your parents–your dad physically and your mom emotionally. She was just trying to survive and save not only herself, but you. I believe your rage stems in part from these things.

"It is very possible that the injuries and the trauma you and your mother experienced, Lloyd, could be one of the causes of your anger."

Lloyd takes a moment to process this.

"Do you ever feel like you're in a womb or like you're underwater when you experience fits of rage?"

Lloyd starts hearing a water sound fill his ears and swirl around his head.

"I do. I'm feeling it right now."

"Take a deep breath. Breathe for a moment and tell me what you're experiencing."

"Numbness. Blackness. Suffocation. A smothering feeling. A sudden jolt," says Lloyd, closing his eyes, frightened.

"Is this why I am so fucked up?" says Lloyd, opening his eyes suddenly.

"Only you can answer that, Lloyd. You are the one that needs to look deep inside of yourself and answer that. I'd like to continue working with you, studying your progression. I'd like to refer you to a neurology specialist who can help you, scan your brain and see if my conclusions are correct.

"I'd like to help you rebuild your brain and address any degeneration that has happened as a result of this trauma. I believe I can help you. This is not who you are. But until you fix yourself, the only conclusion I can offer to a jury at this point is that you remain a serious danger to society."

57

DEFENSE

Judge Cohen's courtroom is filled with attorneys, media, and victims' family members. Although it was only five months ago that he was arrested on Annabelle's murder, it feels like it was five years ago for Lloyd.

People are trickling in from the afternoon break after listening to Lloyd testify in his trial all day. Lloyd stirs nervously at the defense table, for the first time wondering if it was a mistake to testify. Two deputies sit directly behind him for safety precaution. Annabelle's husband glares at Lloyd.

Lloyd turns to Richard.

"Why isn't Mom here?"

"We discussed this, Lloyd. We decided it's not a good idea."

"*You* decided that," Lloyd retorts.

"It's better she's not here. The news has been blowing us up, saying things like our defense is a family affair and how

Mom and I are enablers. It's best she's not here. Trust me, Lloyd."

"Remain seated, come to order, we are now in session," yells the deputy.

"We're on the record in People versus Lloyd Gil, resuming from this morning. All respective parties are present and in their seats. We're ready for the jury. Please bring them in," says Judge Cohen.

One by one, the twelve jurors and three alternates file into the courtroom and take their seats.

Tuckford County takes capital punishment extremely seriously. It is a conservative county made up of predominately Republicans, who are willing to openly voice their desire to enforce capital punishment.

Slowly over time, the county is becoming more liberal like the rest of the state. And perhaps one day, it will move in the direction of adjacent counties to a less serious approach to the law. But right now, the attitude is an aggressive one targeting gangs, domestic violence, drugs, sex crimes, and human trafficking. All elected politicians have consistently won on a platform of ridding the violence in this county.

Jurors in Tuckford County are predominately made up of retired schoolteachers and business owners, blue-collar workers, and the elderly, all of which have no tolerance for any violence-related crimes and even less for innocent women murdered in their own homes behind their white picket fences.

If you walk into the local courthouse, the most common type of juror would be dressed in an embroidered sweater handed down from generation to generation. These are the type of people who zealously protect gun rights even amidst the country's rising school and gun violence. They do anything to protect children against molesters and abusers, and fight hard to reduce the effects of drugs and gangs in their community. These people, at least the ones who vote and serve on juries, strive to keep their home from becoming the next county with the highest crime rate.

"Mr. Gil, please resume the witness stand," says Judge Cohen.

Lloyd braces himself at his seat before standing up confidently, buttoning his blazer, and walking casually up to the witness stand followed by two deputies.

The jurors' eyes remained fixed on him.

"You're under the same oath you took this morning. Go ahead and proceed, Mr. Moore," says Judge Cohen.

Prosecutor Jack Moore stands up and lays in directly with questions about Lloyd's dominant defense.

"Sir, how long have you been involved in BDSM?"

"For a long time," Lloyd replies, trying to mask his nervousness.

"How long?" questions Jack again.

"Years before Janice's death," answers Lloyd deceptively.

"How many times had you done this asphyxiation technique?"

"Dozens."

"Did you ever do it with your wife, Janice?" he asks.

"No, she wasn't into it. It was a different kind of relationship I had with her. She wasn't into any of that stuff," Lloyd says genuinely, before breaking down in quiet sniffles.

"I'm sorry, it's just that I miss my wife terribly. I turned to this subculture to deal with her death," continues Lloyd believably.

He locks eyes with Annabelle's husband Tim for a brief moment before Tim shifts his eyes downward.

Lloyd has practiced hard for this moment, hoping the jury sympathizes with him over the loss of Janice. And it seems to be working. One of the jurors reaches for a Kleenex.

"I thought you said you were into it years before Janice's death?" questions Jack suspiciously.

"Well, I was curious about it, reading about it, trying it as an amateur before I met Janice. But it wasn't until Janice died that I sought it out seriously. Look, I did not kill Janice Gil. I..." starts Lloyd before he's cut off by Jack Moore.

"OBJECTION! The defendant is being non-responsive," says Jack aggressively.

Judge Cohen turns to Lloyd.

"Mr. Gil, please wait for the next question," the judge says.

"Resume your questioning," says the judge, motioning to Jack.

"So I'm assuming you're familiar with all the terms, the toys, the limits, the safety of it all?" questions Jack rhetorically.

"Well, I thought I was. But it went too far with Annabelle," he says.

"Tell me this, sir. You're familiar with BDSM. Can you tell me what it stands for?" asks Jack.

"Submission, domination," Lloyd replies.

"What else? What's the B and the M?" snaps Jack.

Lloyd hesitates, searching his mind for all the things he's memorized about this culture. Richard had warned him that he better make himself an expert in this field if they were going to use this defense.

"Bondage, sadism, masochism. All that. It's an acronym for all of it," says Lloyd confidently.

"Very well. Wouldn't you agree that safety is one of the foundations of BDSM? You would have entered into an agreement or negotiation with your victim about what was going to transpire, wouldn't you?" asks Jack.

"We did. It just got out of hand. She was a tiny woman and she liked her neck snapped. She was enjoying it. I hate saying that, but it was something she asked me to do. Other women also asked for it. It's just that something went wrong with her," he says ridiculously.

"During the attempted assault of Veronica, the woman you met at The Coffee Grind, hadn't she warned you that Selena was going to come back from walking her dog?" asks Jack disbelievingly.

"No, she didn't mention anything about it," says Lloyd, before beginning to break down again. "I wasn't trying to do anything with Veronica. I was so startled when Selena walked in, because we were about to get intimate. I didn't know what to do. I was so afraid, I just went into a state of shock. I blacked out. It all happened so fast. But I wasn't planning on assaulting her," says Lloyd, burying his face in his hands.

Annabelle's husband Tim stands up abruptly and heads to leave the courtroom, shifting his glare between Richard and Lloyd until he pushes his way through the double doors.

"Let's go ahead and adjourn for the day. We are not in session tomorrow because of the court holiday. We will resume Monday morning. Members of the jury, all previous orders remain in place. Do not discuss the case until you retire to deliberations. Please be outside the courtroom at eight-thirty sharp Monday morning," says Judge Cohen, before leaving the bench.

58

INCAPACITATION

The courtroom is as packed this morning as it was last week when Lloyd was testifying.

Judge Cohen turns to Jack.

"Will you be presenting any rebuttal witnesses, Mr. Moore?"

"Yes, the people call Dr. Don Ariza."

For the next hour, Jack brilliantly directs the examination of Dr. Ariza, a forensic pathologist, who sits attentively in his black suit at the witness stand, with a portfolio of notes and his electronic tablet in front of him.

He's a Harvard Medical School graduate, who has practiced medicine for nine years and has conducted forensic examinations and autopsies the last five.

He belongs to every professional medical association one could think of. His resume is as impressive in the medical world as Richard's is in the legal field. Of over the one thousand autopsies he has conducted, he has testified a handful of times.

Jack focuses his question to the autopsies in this case.

"You testified that based on the injuries to the vaginal area of Annabelle Phillips, it appeared she was incapable of resistance. Is that your testimony?"

"Yes, it is."

"How can you be certain of that?"

"Mr. Gil would not have been able to inflict the level of traumatic injuries to her vaginal area, if she was conscious. We would expect her to fight him off to some extent and her injuries would have been far less substantial.

"It was likely he incapacitated her first, then assaulted her; so rough sex-play is really not what's going on here. Or if it was, it went beyond that at some point. It could have started that way, but the additional severe injuries sustained were definitely inflicted after she was incapacitated."

"How were the initial injuries incapacitating?"

"The incapacitation likely came from the mechanism of asphyxia."

"Do you mean choking her into an unconscious state?"

"Precisely."

"Is it consistent with your findings, that after rendering her unconscious, he would have inflicted traumatic injuries to her abdominal and vaginal area?"

"Absolutely."

"What injuries were observed to her vaginal area?"

"She had blunt impact trauma to the vaginal wall and the area she was carrying the baby, lacerations, abrasions and internal bleeding in the vaginal cavity."

"Could you tell the cause of the injuries?"

"The trauma likely came from the force of a foreign object. It could have been anything, a flashlight, a phone receiver, a can, a candlestick.

"What was the ultimate cause of death in Mrs. Phillips?"

"Multiple severe blunt impact injuries with lacerations of vagina and uterus where the baby was, along with intraperitoneal hemorrhage."

"How certain are you of this opinion, that Mrs. Phillips initially was incapacitated?"

"Very certain. It is with a strong medical certainty that the severe nature of the injuries strongly suggest she was incapacitated."

"Did you take into consideration the defendant's testimony, that in fact Mrs. Phillips consensually engaged in this rough sex-play, both asphyxia and intercourse?"

"I did."

"Could her injuries support that they were consenting parties in both the asphyxia and the vaginal and uterus trauma?" asks Jack.

"No. These injuries are not the result of BDSM power plays. And I say that with confidence.

"Those type of sessions would have been carried out in a planned manner. They are about mental discipline and training someone to control their mind. The injuries would have been far less substantial. BDSM is not about killing or unleashing the type of homicidal rage present in this case."

"What if he was inexperienced?" asks Jack.

"Sure it's *possible*, but not in this case. I'm certain Mrs. Phillips was incapacitated before Mr. Gil started unleashing his rage against her and violating her. I'm confident of that."

"And Mrs. Gil?"

"Her case is entirely different. There was no vaginal injury, just a blunt force trauma impact to the back of her head causing significant hemmoraging. That is why she and Baby Gil died. Two entirely different manners of death."

"No further questions of this witness."

59

CIRCUS RING

Courtroom trials can so quickly turn into a big circus ring, especially when the media is involved, egos of high-powered defense attorneys and prosecutors clash, and a dominatrix is about to testify. The courtroom seems even more packed now as everyone settles into their seats after the short break following Dr. Ariza's testimony.

Demitra did not spare anything to the imagination of the jury, the audience, or Judge Cohen. Wearing black fishnet stockings, a plaid miniskirt, knee-high, black, leather boots, and a leather corset top, she walks through the double doors of the courtroom and removes her sunglasses.

She saunters past the jury box up to the witness stand, perfectly balancing herself on her high, stiletto-heeled boots.

She looks impeccable. Her long blonde hair falls over her breasts. Red lipstick brightens her full lips. Lloyd, overwhelmed and turned on by her presence, remembers back to their night together.

Jack directs her examination.

"How long have you been a dominatrix?" he asks.

"It's been fifteen years. I started out in escort services then I moved to BDSM," replies Demitra.

"Why was that?" asks Jack curiously.

"It's safer. There's no sex involved. It's more morally acceptable in my mind," she says.

"You and Lloyd never discussed having sex, did you?"

"We did not discuss that. I wouldn't have allowed that," she says.

"Why not?"

"I'm a dominatrix. I control what happens. All the time," she says.

"What if a man wants to have sex?" he asks.

"My work is about mental discipline. To train oneself. To control one's mind. I'm the domme and the client is the sub. It's not his choice, it's mine. That's what they pay for, me to dominate them and tell them what to do, not the other way around," she asserts.

"Would you say Lloyd was receptive to following your rules during your conversation?" he asks.

"Yes. He was in agreement to comply with my rules. But he had some of his own too."

"As in...?"

"Having me wear a maternity top. He was rather manipulating. He had this way about him and got me to go along with it."

"Why go along with it?"

"BDSM is like playing with fire. It could be fun, for healing or pleasure and release. I try to accommodate my clients' requests. But, like playing with fire, you have to be careful," she says.

"How do you make it safe?" he asks.

"I always have the safety of the sub at the top of my mind. The sub's mental health and level of comfort is always the most important thing. That's why there's things like safe words. Words that you agree on beforehand that will be used to stop the session," she explains.

"What was your safe word?" he asks.

"Red," she replies.

"Who picked that?" he asks.

"That would have been Lloyd. The safe word I always offer up is 'Bunny,'" she says.

"Bunny?" asks Jack, curiously.

"That was the word my sister and I used. I've kept it ever since. It was just for things we'd do as kids, hair pulling, digging nails into each other, dominating one another," says Demitra.

"So Lloyd agreed to use the 'red' safe word with you?" asks Jack.

"He did."

"And you agreed to stop if he used this word?" Jack asks.

"Immediately. I play by my own rules," she says.

"When you first discussed using the safe word, did he appear to know what you were talking about?" he asks.

"Yes, he did. I didn't have to explain what that was or anything. It was just a matter of deciding what word we would pick," she replies.

"So if a woman yelled for help, said to stop, or used a safe word, is the domme supposed to listen?" he asks.

"Always. No exception. If you're asking, in the true world of BDSM, he would have known to stop and should have stopped," she says.

"Was Lloyd the submissive or the dominant during your session?"

"The sub. He wanted to switch, but I declined. I was always in control," says Demitra.

"What made you go to the police?" asks Jack.

"My sister had been working with the police. They were trying to get some solid evidence on him, get him to say something about the murders or something. But Mr. Gil started avoiding her. So that's when she reached out to me.

"She was pretty desperate. And confused. She wanted to help Lloyd get better, so we discussed helping him submit, break his cycle of rage. But she was also hoping I'd get him to say something about the murders; something we could take back to Investigator Kaplan. And that happened when he brought up the maternity top and I was able to get the bead clerk's earrings from my sister and turn them over to police."

"Just for the record, tell the jury who your sister is."

"Eva Flores."

"Are you close to her?"

"Yes. Through all this, we reconnected. We've had difficult lives. When she got in touch with me, I felt things might be different. And they have been."

"Were you ever hesitant to do what she was asking? To get close to a killer?"

"Not at the time. I'd do whatever for Eva. She's my sister. We had that kind of relationship growing up. And I knew it was important to her. She was just trying to do the right thing. But it wound up putting her in danger."

"Where is she now?"

"She's in South America.   She discovered she was pregnant so she left, afraid he'd do the same to her as he did to Annabelle and Janice."

Lloyd's heart rate speeds up. Thoughts race through his mind. He visualizes the scar on her pelvis and the discussion he had with her about her hysterectomy.

The entire courtroom begins to fill with loud whispers.

Richard walks over to Lloyd.

"Did you know that?" he asks, sternly.

"No idea. She couldn't have kids. That's what she told me," Lloyd whispers back.

Richard moves to the podium, asking matter-of-factly, "I thought she couldn't get pregnant."

"She thought so too. Told me she had a hysterectomy, but the current doctor discovered it was only a partial."

"I have no further questions."

60

CONCRETE EVIDENCE

Lloyd sits completely disheveled at the attorney-inmate meeting table at the jail in an orange jumpsuit, still feeling beat up and exhausted from finding out yesterday about Eva being pregnant. He sits and waits for Richard to arrive.

Lloyd buries his head in his hands and rests his elbows on the metal table. He closes his eyes and thinks hard about why Richard may have sounded so eager over the phone this morning about meeting today.

Before Lloyd can come up with one plausible explanation, Richard, dressed impeccably, walks towards him and sits down.

Lloyd looks up and finally after studying eachother for a while, says, "How is it looking?"

"The prosecution is scheduled to rest their rebuttal soon. Look, there's something else we need to talk about. There's been a huge development in your case," says Richard informatively.

"I don't have a lot of information on this. And I'm not going to be able to answer all your questions. I'm going to give you this information and I want you to process it for a day. Then I want to meet again. Tomorrow. And discuss how it impacts your potential defense."

"I don't know what this is about. But the way you are coming at me and treating me..." says Lloyd, defensively.

"Don't question my intentions or my style. I'm your attorney, Lloyd. I've told you from the start, I'm not concerned whether you committed these crimes or not. I don't need to know. But there are times when information about a crime is revealed. And when it helps us, we need to run with it. Just like when it hurts us, we need to deal with it."

Lloyd stays quiet and waits for Richard to continue.

"First, I'd like to talk to you about the charge against you for the murder of Janice," Richard says formally.

"Okay," replies Lloyd curiously.

Richard pauses, looks around the room, then back at Lloyd.

"It's going to be dropped," he finally says.

Lloyd focuses on Richard for a few moments, trying to figure out whether he's being truthful.

But after Richard locks eyes with him without flinching, Lloyd rests into a steady grin and reclines back.

"Don't look so smug," says Richard. "You're still facing the other murder for Annabelle, but you're no longer eligible for the death penalty," he continues.

"What is going on, Richard?"

"There's another man that is in custody right now for Janice's murder. He confessed to it," says Richard excitedly. "I'm sorry, Lloyd. I know you've been at the center of all this. I'm sorry this happened, but there's another man who's admitted to killing your wife. I spoke to the prosecutor this morning and that charge is going to be dropped. The jury will be instructed to not consider it.

"This can be a really good thing for you, Lloyd. This works perfectly with our defense. You've always claimed you didn't murder Janice and this information will bolster your credibility tremendously. We couldn't have asked for anything better. And the timing of it all... it's perfect," Richard says.

Lloyd stirs in his stool, shifting his eyes around the visiting room, then towards his hands, which are repeatedly contracting from a flexed position to a clenched one as he looks around, ready to fight anyone in sight.

Richard stays quiet, waiting for Lloyd's eyes to meet his and calm down.

Lloyd finally settles back into his body and waits for Richard to explain more.

I don't want to get into the details of it," says Richard calmingly.

"What the hell? You don't want to get into the details of it. That's my wife," says Lloyd possessively.

"I've been accused this whole time of killing her. I've spent months with everyone looking at me like I'm a killer, a murderer," he continues.

"What do you know about that? Where's my apology? I've told you all along I didn't kill her. I told police. No one believed me. I got charged with it anyway. I got my ass kicked in jail. I almost lost an eye. How do you want me to respond to this?" says Lloyd angrily.

"Look, I don't want to focus on this. We can't. We have to use this to our advantage in our defense. I know you feel wronged, Lloyd. We can file a civil lawsuit for all this. But *later*, this is all later. We need to focus on the remaining charge. I don't want you to lose sight of the trial that's going on right now. We have one objective: to get you acquitted or at a minimum, convicted on a lesser.

"This blows the credibility of the police and the prosecution. This is huge! Do you understand what I'm trying to say?" asks Richard rationally.

Lloyd takes a deep breath in before releasing it.

"You said from the start they were trying to pin her murder on me. I'm not surprised," says Lloyd logically.

"*Exactly.*"

"Who the hell killed my wife?" barks Lloyd unsettlingly.

Richard studies him, wondering how he will handle the information or whether he should withhold it.

"Tell me Richard, right now," Lloyd demands. "Or I swear, I will..."

"Ok. Ok," says Richard, cutting him off.

The two stare at eachother for several moments before Richard breaks the silence.

"Lloyd, it's Selena's dad, Tim. He admitted to killing Janice."

A swishing sound begins to swell Lloyd's head.

"It's looking like a revenge thing over Annabelle being killed. Police never found her killer. He pointed them at you, but no one took him serious so..."

The swishing sound in Lloyd's head overtakes Richard's words as he stares down at the metal table and pounds his clenched fist into it repeatedly. He doesn't stop until the Correction Deputy holds his arm back and a siren begins to blare.

61

QUESTION

After several weeks of Lloyd's trial, everyone now awaits the verdicts. The jury has been deliberating for a day and they've presented the first question to Judge Cohen. So he requested both the defense and prosecution to come to his courtroom, where they sit now.

Lloyd brushes shoulders with Richard in the courtroom, which is packed with people on both sides of the audience.

"Remain seated, come to order, court is now in session," yells the deputy.

Judge Cohen sits down and opens up a piece of paper, and reads the jury note to himself, before looking up and sharing it.

"Question: Do we all have to agree there is reasonable doubt for first degree murder, before considering second degree?"

The court reporter looks up nervously at Prosecutor Jack Moore and Marty, who is sitting behind him. Then her eyes shift over towards Richard, who is leaning over to Lloyd.

"Lloyd, this question is great for us."

"I know. I know. That's what I figured," replies Lloyd.

"Counsel, do you have any recommendations as to how you would like me to respond to this question?" asks Judge Cohen sternly, while looking at Richard first and then shifting his eyes to Jack.

"My requested response would be a simple 'no,'" says Richard swiftly.

Prosecutor Moore takes a moment, looks down at his printed papers with case law, and looks back up.

"My requested response would be, 'each juror must make a decision on their own. You must not be pressured either way to vote guilty or not guilty on each of the counts. You can take any length of time to consider your decision carefully," offers Jack desperately.

Richard speaks up again. "There's no need for this, Your Honor. The jurors have already been instructed on that. What we have here is the prosecutor, who is upset at the possibility that they are considering a lesser count or an acquittal on the murder. He's trying to penalize them. He could just request that they be polled at the end," persuades Richard.

Judge Cohen remains quiet, looking at both attorneys. He writes for a minute while the courtroom waits in anticipation. He finally looks up.

"Less is more," starts Judge Cohen. "Mr. Hill has a point. And frankly, I don't want to confuse them. It appears that they are trying to reach their decision, and I don't want to get them off track. However, I do want them to make individual decisions that they're comfortable standing by, so what I am inclined to do at this point is to tell them that they can consider the charges and lesser-related offenses in any order they choose, but all verdicts must be unanimous," says Judge Cohen decisively.

"Is there any further argument from either side?"

Silence fills the room, before the entire courtroom is adjourned. Two deputies remain, keeping an eye on Lloyd and Richard, who can't help but allow their mouths to burst into smiles at one another.

62

VERDICTS

When juries reach verdicts in high profile cases, word spreads quickly. Two days of deliberation was not a long period after a three week trial. And especially for one that started as a capital case.

While sitting in the courtroom, Lloyd fears the possibility of spending the rest of his life in prison. Prosecutor Moore worries at the possibility of letting a dangerous killer out on the streets. Marty is afraid of what Lloyd will do to Eva if he's set free. Richard is uneasy about his firm's reputation if Lloyd is convicted.

No one remembers the mini victories of the trial. Only outcomes and verdicts matter.

The jury files into the courtroom, one after the other, from their deliberation room. Richard and Lloyd stand at their counsel table. The jurors look neither towards them nor Jack, intentionally avoiding eye contact.

Prosecutor Moore stands with his hands behind his back. Marty stands in the same posture in the audience. The entire courtroom feels like a quiet funeral procession. The journalist who has been covering the case from the start sits in the back row. The courtroom is filled.

Annabelle's family looks the most anxious. Her mom wads the side of her skirt into her hand, crunching and releasing it.

"Remain seated, come to order, court is now in session," yells the deputy.

"We're on the record in People versus Lloyd Gil. The jury has resumed all their respective seats. Counsel for both sides are present, and Mr. Gil is present next to his counsel. Ladies and gentlemen of the jury, it's been brought to my attention that you have reached verdicts. Is that correct?" asks Judge Cohen.

"Yes," says a large man in the front row, holding up a yellow manila envelope. As he stands, his large stomach covered by a plaid blue shirt tucked into his jeans, protrudes over his belt buckle.

"Are you the foreperson, juror number nine?" Judge Cohen asks.

"Yes, Your Honor," he replies confidently.

The courtroom deputy moves from his posted position behind a desk towards the foreperson, takes the envelope, then swiftly walks up towards Judge Cohen, passing it to him.

The judge removes the verdict forms quickly and studies each one, before handing them to his clerk.

"Would you please read the verdicts, Madame Clerk?" he states.

Richard moves closer to Lloyd and reminds him to not react dramatically for the verdict. "The jury will be watching your every move. Compose yourself," he reminds Lloyd.

"People versus Lloyd Gil," starts the clerk, getting everyone's attention. "Verdict. We the jury in the above-entitled action find the defendant guilty of murder in the second degree of Victim Annabelle Phillips.

"Ladies and gentleman of the jury, is this your verdict?" she says, polling each and every juror, who answers in the affirmative.

Before she gets to the last juror, the entire courtroom is buzzing in a low-pitched chaos. Crying sounds come from the back of the courtroom where Annabelle's family is sitting.

The clerk moves to the next form, reading the guilty verdict for the criminal threat against Nurse Marie.

The verdicts will land him a sentence of fifteen years to life with the possibility of parole.

After the courtroom quiets down, Judge Cohen turns to Lloyd.

"Mr. Gil, you are ordered to remain in the custody of the Sheriff's Department. Sentencing is set for one month from today at eight-thirty in the morning, right here. This courtroom is adjourned."

63

CAGED

Lloyd rests his back into his pillow on the lower bunk bed of his six by eight foot state prison cell and starts writing.

Dear Loretta,

Since I received my life sentence last month, I know that you are probably upset at me over the case. I'm beginning to learn what is at the root of all this. I think I've carried out hatred and anger towards certain people who have that perfect kind of life I never had. Especially when they're bringing kids into this world.

My therapist told me that some of this may have to do with you and how I was subjected to abuse when you were carrying me.

Domestic Violence In Utero — a pregnant woman who endures abuse, which carries risks including the fetus experiencing fear, anxiety and stress, possibly well into adulthood.

YOU subjected me to this. Why didn't you leave my dad earlier? Why did you allow this? You never got me help for any of it. You never helped me understand it. Instead, when I was a teen and starting to have rage, you abandoned me. You rejected me.

Acceptance is a need. We all have a natural human desire to be a part of society, to fit in, to experience love, to grow into productive people. The healthy adult is taught to not let anybody reject them because they know they deserve acceptance.

Loretta, I want you to tell everyone I was a loving kid. I was a problem kid, but I had the biggest heart. You know everyone would agree.

THE SUBURBAN SEDUCCIÓN

I still remember when I stole your gold necklace and took it to school and gave it to my teacher Mrs. Garrett. I was only six years old. She refused it and rejected me—told me she couldn't accept it. I assaulted her and she told the principal. Yes, I pulled her hair and pushed her so hard, she fell and had to go to the nurse's office. They thought she might miscarry her baby.

I still remember putting a handful of her hair into my pocket to feel the rush of goodness that I prevailed. How dare you reject my good intentions, Mrs. Garrett. From that day on, it was evident that anyone pregnant or who rejected me would pay.

I still remember our pregnant neighbor Ericka. I attacked her and never understood why I was doing that either. I was only seventeen.

Like Dr. Blanchart said at the time, I didn't know how to control my urges and anger against pregnant women. She never understood why I was so angry, cuz you never told her about the abuse when you were pregnant. Maybe you didn't want to lose me, *but you had no idea how to protect me. You couldn't even protect yourself.*

You didn't follow Dr. Blanchart's recommendation to spend more time with me and go to counseling together and go to the movies together. Instead, you kicked me out and moved in Richard and his father. They were strangers. You substituted the books in MY bookshelf with hoity-toity books to impress your lawyer lover. Are you ashamed that you picked a shark over your own son? Why weren't you honest with Dr. Blanchart about your own shortcomings in motherhood?

Because of it all, I carried a rage I never understood up through my adulthood until I met Janice. She comforted me and put my demons at bay. And now she's gone. She too has abandoned me.

I need your full acceptance, visits, letters, money, support, while I'm in this cage. Write letters to the Governor to pardon me. Get my conviction appealed. You owe it to me. Pay for doctors to help me.

THE SUBURBAN SEDUCCIÓN

I wasn't conceived a killer, murderer, sociopath, psychopath. I was a salesman, husband, and almost a father, but a man who has lost faith in humanity.

No one grows up and wants to be a killer. It stands against everything I could have become. I've fought my urges for so long, even after I murdered Annabelle. I only wanted to live with my wife, behind our picket fence in a healthy relationship, traveling as a software executive. I tried to do the right thing. But the demons that started with YOU—became bigger.

Practice ACCEPTANCE for your own faults. My doctor says he wants to help me and heal my brain for all the damage that has been done. He says this is NOT me and I'm a better person. But for me to do this and move forward, I need you to accept your part in all this.

You should have spent the time figuring out what was wrong with me. Dr. McDonald says he can work with me. I need your help.

Yours truly,

White Picket Fence Killer aka YOUR son

P.S Tell Eva she can't hide forever.

64

VISIT

Lloyd makes his way in a single file line with other inmates from his housing unit to the visiting area of the State Prison.

Since being housed here for the last two months following his sentence, he has lost twenty pounds and has been fighting a cold, which has crept into his lungs and is on the verge of turning into a pneumonia.

Every weekend, he is allowed visits from family or friends so long as he requests they visit him and the prison clears it. None of this matters, since Lloyd has neither, except for today.

Lloyd stops at a desk leading into the visiting area. He submits to a pat down search, showing the correction deputy a gold chain he is wearing, the only type of jewelry he is allowed.

The deputy spells out the rules to Lloyd. Visits can last up to three hours and take place in a large, high school gym size room with meeting tables. A small play area sits to the side of the room against the wall, where kids come and play while the inmates spend time with their loved ones.

He can give one kiss and hug at the beginning and end of the visit, but otherwise no physical contact is allowed. He's already reluctant about his visit, so decided he wouldn't be making any physical contact during it.

The deputy documents on a roster Lloyd's clothing and chain and directs him into the visiting area. He walks into the room towards a metal table, sits, and waits. After the last inmate settles into his chair, the visitors walk into the room.

Lloyd's mom walks towards him, but he ignores her attempt to hug him.

"Hi, Lloyd," she says softly, resting into her side of the table.

Lloyd says nothing. The cool metal bench sends a chill through his blue, state-issued jumpsuit.

"Are you feeling okay? You look thin," she comments.

"I'm fine. I'm fine," says Lloyd.

"Are you eating?"

"Yes, they feed us really well here. Full, well-balanced meals. It's not so bad here," says Lloyd.

"Are you in special housing?" she asks.

"Yes, special housing," he says quickly, looking away.

"Look, what do you want?" he asks bluntly.

She takes a deep breath, exhaling loudly and shifting on her metal bench.

"I came here for a couple reasons," she starts. "First, to see how you're doing, Lloyd," she continues genuinely.

"I SAID I'M FINE!" he screams back at her defiantly.

A correction deputy standing and monitoring from a desk at the front of the room walks over to Lloyd, telling him to keep it down and show some respect or the visit will be terminated.

Lloyd glares at him, before facing back towards his mom, holding his head down.

"Lloyd, did you get the books I sent?" she asks.

"I haven't looked at them," he says.

"Well, I'd like you to. They were recommended to me by my pastor. They're self-help books," she says.

"I don't need them. Look, if you're here to preach to me, this visit is over," says Lloyd annoyed.

"I want you to get better. It seems like you want that too. Your anger has turned into hate in your heart. That's obvious from your letter. And hate kills.

"You don't even seem like you care about why you're here," she says, preaching to him.

"I'm in here for life. What does any of this matter? You and Richard didn't help. Why should I think you're trying to help me now?"

"Richard did help you, Lloyd. He saved you from the death penalty and got you a lighter sentence. A second degree conviction. What do you mean, we never helped you?"

"He did nothing. Someone else killed Janice. That's why I didn't get death. What the hell do you want? Is that what you came here for? To tell me to get help? You never wanted to help before. Why now?" he challenges. "You're the one who needs help," he continues defiantly.

"Lloyd, they're going to end this visit if you continue this way," she says.

"Are you done?" he asks sarcastically.

"I came for another reason."

Lloyd looks directly at her, curious.

"Will you consider showing the police where you dumped Annabelle's belongings? There was a locket she always carried with her. In her purse. It was a family heirloom. Her mom asked me the favor. I told her I'd ask you," she says.

"That's what you came for?" he says sarcastically.

"Can you consider it? It's the least we can do for her family," she says.

"Why do you give a shit about that woman?" he says angrily. "Her son-in-law killed Janice."

"Lloyd," she says patronizingly. "This is her mother we're talking about. I don't understand why you can't even care about her mother. She had nothing to do with this. You of all people should care, having lost Janice and all. You'd grasp onto anything to get close to her, even a locket. You'd want closure. Wouldn't you, Lloyd?" she asks, confusedly.

He says nothing in response.

"Are you done? If that's all you came for, I have nothing left to say," says Lloyd uncaringly.

"That's all, Lloyd," she replies, defeated.

"Can you put some money on my books?" he asks selfishly.

"I will, once you seriously consider what I've asked you," she says assertively.

He looks directly at her, holding her stare, before getting up to leave the visiting area.

65

ATTORNEY INMATE

Lloyd makes his way in a single file line from the prison kitchen, through the yard, and back to his housing unit. Lloyd prepares himself mentally for his legal consultation with a legally savvy inmate from his housing unit whom he befriended last week after his mom's visit.

Lloyd's housing unit is for special needs prisoners, including sex offenders, gang dropouts, and snitches. They are all at risk for being attacked by the average inmate, so to avoid lawsuits and liability, the state prison houses them away from the rest of the inmates.

Black inmates group together in one section of the line, white inmates file behind one another in another section, and Hispanics do the same. Everyone, segregated by race and their own choice, uses this as a way to survive.

Lloyd met "Legal," who is serving fifteen years to life in prison for stabbing a rival gang member. He is on year eighteen, having just been denied a parole release date.

Legal is known as a "lifer" because of his life sentence, but it's a myth. Life sentences are not necessarily for life. He became eligible after serving fifteen years of prison time to appear before a parole board to see if he had behaved in prison, engaged in self-help, and was suitable for release. Three years ago, Legal was determined to still be a danger to the community after it was discovered he had a cell phone in his bunk, which is against prison rules.

Legal's family had paid a correction deputy nine hundred dollars to smuggle it to him.

So the parole board told Legal to go for a few more years disciplinary free and he would have a good chance of getting out. His next hearing was coming up in two months, and Legal has been on his best behavior awaiting the date.

Legal knows everything there is to know about new laws and habeas corpus petitions, which are written directly by the prisoner to appellate courts to overturn decisions made by lower courts. He has a good track record in winning and his attorney rates reflect it.

He charges five hundred dollars to write a standard ten-page motion and his clients, other inmates, pay it.

Legal is about to meet with Lloyd for the second time since last week to strategize an appeal for his case.

Lloyd walks up to a metal table in the middle of the day room. Double person cells big enough for two bunk beds and a walking space line the top and bottom levels of the huge housing unit.

The correction deputy standing in the middle of the floor near a tall, stationary desk tells Lloyd that Legal said he'd be right back; he had to get his legal pad and a pen out of his cell.

Lloyd, sitting at Legal's table, begins writing notes down on his pad.

He goes through topics of discussion, bullet-pointing each of the topics: the pros and cons of divulging the whereabouts of Annabelle's purse and locket and appealing his murder conviction.

Legal walks up to the table and sits down across from Lloyd.   Tattoos cover both of his arms in sleeves of inked patterns, designs, and words. Letters across his forehead and replacing his eyebrows used to intimidate Lloyd, but now he's used to the idea that Legal is a gang member dropout. He had to leave his gang behind to have a chance of being granted a parole date.

Legal removes the empty, liter soda bottle from the table and places it under his chair.   The bottle is a reminder to other inmates that the table belongs to him so he can conduct his daily business.   No one is allowed to sit there except for Legal and those who have an appointment with him.   It's an unwritten rule that even the correction deputies seem to enforce when new, unsuspecting inmates move into the housing unit and have no clue about the unspoken rules, like this one.

Legal and Lloyd shake hands and within less than a minute, Legal gets right to the point.

"I brought some really good information today. Let's not forget; I'm your attorney right now, so anything we talk about is confidential.   Do you remember the privilege we discussed last time?" Legal asks.

"I do," replies Lloyd.

"Good. So I read all your trial transcripts. Man! Your defense... I've seen that defense used before. And a lot of times it doesn't work. The jury doesn't buy it. They don't get the whole dominatrix angle, but the way you presented it, it worked... like magic. Your attorney was good. Your brother, right?" asks Legal.

"*Step*brother," says Lloyd.

"And your testimony... damn!" says Legal.

"Pretty good, huh?" replies Lloyd.

"You're lucky, man. Real lucky."

"It doesn't seem so lucky."

"Well, it bought you a second degree murder. That's better than the death penalty."

Lloyd grunts.

"So what I found out since our last meeting is *pretty* interesting."

"I knew you'd come up with something," says Lloyd.

"The number one reason cases are reversed is for bad jury instructions."

"Okay."

"I'm a firm believer that the devil is in the details. I read through all your trial transcripts and looked for *any* error, specifically with things like jury instructions or expert testimony. These are the areas cases get reversed the most, so that's why I focus on them.

"There are a couple areas I'd like to attack. First, the way Demitra came into the picture is suspect. She came to you when Eva was working with police. Are you sure police weren't behind that?" asks Legal.

"She testified that it was all Eva's idea."

"I know. I read that in the transcripts. But c'mon, Lloyd. You don't think for a second that police didn't suggest that to her?"

"Hmmm."

"Regardless, I say we raise this as an issue. We'll make it look like entrapment, dirty police work. You were already lawyered up at the time. They shouldn't have been sticking informants on you to do their job."

"Right."

"Look, this isn't going to be the issue that'll get your case reversed. I'll put money on that. But it will upset the court and get them ready to reverse on the other issue we're going to raise. It's all about strategy. The court has been reversing cases for BS police tactics a lot recently."

Lloyd smirks, half-believing Legal's advice.

"So what's the real issue we've got a shot at?"

"I'm waiting on a little more research. But I'm focusing in on the expert testimony. I got another case reversed out of Judge Cohen's courtroom the same way. He's smart. But he doesn't know all the rules when it comes to experts. That's always been his weakness.

"Sometimes the judges are bad on jury instructions, voir dire, or other things. But Cohen's thing is the expert testimony. Give me one more week and I'll know if we have enough to fight this. It's looking *really* good so far."

"Man, are you serious? It's something that could work?"

"Look, I don't want to get your hopes up. We'll have it in a pleading next week if it's strong enough. It's looking good though."

"Thank you," yells Lloyd gloriously, raising his hands to the ceiling.

"Anything else, client?"

"Yeah," Lloyd says, taking a deep breath before continuing.

"What do you think about me showing police where I dumped Annabelle's stuff they never found?" Lloyd asks hesitantly.

"Why you wanna do that?" asks Legal.

"Mom's asking," replies Lloyd.

"It's not a bad idea. But you should wait 'til it's worth it; like you're getting something really big out of it. You've still got an appeal and habeas. You gotta wait at least 'til you exhaust your appeals. And I'd even wait 'til the stakes are higher," Legal says.

"How are they gonna get any higher? I'm already serving life," asks Lloyd.

"You never know, man. Maybe you pick up another case and you can use it to negotiate. Maybe you ask them to pay you for the information."

"Your mom came to you, requesting you to show where Annabelle's stuff is?" asks Legal.

"Yeah, she came to visit. She's pushing it. Says Annabelle's mom wants some locket. They wanna know where I dumped her purse," says Lloyd.

"Yeah, I've seen that before," says Legal, letting out a sigh. "It 'aint ever over for the family, man. And you should never assume it is. That family will be at every parole hearing you ever have, trust me. Making sure you 'aint *ever* getting out of here. That will become their purpose in life.

"But, if you start making things right now... Well let me ask you this. Do you want to tell them?" asks Legal.

"I really don't want anything to do with it. I've just been thinking about it," says Lloyd.

"It ain't worth it, in my opinion. At least, not right now. Unless she's offering you something big-time, like inheritance, something worth it. Wait 'til she comes at you with something bigger," says Legal.

Lloyd stays quiet.

"You got anything else on your mind?" he asks.

"What the hell do I gotta do to survive in here?" asks Lloyd, beginning to look nervous.

"Man, keep your head down and keep moving. Get involved in some help programs. There's a lot here. You might get another chance someday. I've seen some crazy things come out of here. Fix yourself. Read. Take up AA. There's a lot of us in it. You gotta get it straight up here," says Legal, pointing at his temple area.

"It's gonna be tough. You have a chance to make a difference in here, more than you know. You need to show you can be rehabilitated, you're getting your shit straight, when you get the chance to and resources to.

"You hear what I'm saying, man? Life in prison don't gotta be that bad. There's gonna be a date where you're going to have to go into a little room and convince the parole board that you've changed. Spend every day getting ready for that day. That's the day you'll really be fighting for your life. Start thinking about that now.

"I've learned the hard way and wasted *a lot* of time behind bars before getting straight. I've watched men go crazy in here, commit suicide, seen a lot of depression. I've been there. It don't have to be that way, especially with you. Does any of this make sense?" asks Legal.

"I hear you. But I'm different. A doctor wants to help me," says Lloyd.

"They all say that shit. Shrinks. Medical quacks wanna feed you medicine that will screw you up. Forget that shit.

You hold the key to unlock these bars. It's all up here," says Legal, pointing to his head.

Lloyd focuses on Legal, holding onto every word, and believing in himself for the first time.

"And right here," says Lloyd, pointing to his heart.

66

REVENGE

It doesn't take long for news to circulate the courthouse, the defense bar, and the prosecutor's office. Through text messages, social media, and word of mouth, news about Lloyd's case spreads like wild fire.

This also happens with inmates. They don't have the luxury of technology, so it takes a bit longer, but kites, letters passed around the jail, word of mouth, and phone calls all do the same job.

Today is Lloyd's resentencing and it's been three weeks since his verdicts were overturned by the Circuit Court. The entire jail seems to know of Lloyd's good fortune. And Lloyd realizes it, too. It took him a while to realize how lucky he was. But it finally began to sink in after talking to jail deputies, Richard, and other prison inmates.

An inmate like Lloyd Gil is bait for the inmates. Not only has he murdered an innocent woman, he murdered her unborn baby, and now his verdicts have been compromised.

The Circuit Court ruled that Dr. Ariza's testimony went too far and tainted the jury. He should have never been allowed to testify that the level of the victim's injuries proved she was incapacitated. It was for the jury to decide whether the injuries were "sex play" gone too far or a murderous rage inflicted after Lloyd incapacitated her.

It didn't seem fair to anyone on the prosecution team, but none of this mattered. The higher courts affirmed the decision and Lloyd was about to become a free man.

There are codes of ethics even among the incarcerated, and Lloyd had broken all of them. Assaulting and killing an innocent and pregnant woman deserved a hefty sentence, even in the eyes of the guilty.

Everyone, even the media, knew that Lloyd was responsible for the murder. It was obvious to everyone that Lloyd was the White Picket Fence Killer and everyone feared what would become of their county once he was released. But nothing could be done.

Debra Miller, the appointed head prosecutor, personally combed through the case law to see if there was anything that could be done to keep Lloyd behind bars longer. She found nothing.

Everyone was frustrated. But Lloyd didn't care about any of this. He could only focus on getting in and out of court today in one piece. He was in survival mode. The hearing was a formality so he could be formally released by Judge Cohen. The victim's family members and the attorneys will have a chance to speak, but regardless of what they say, he'll still be set free.

Lloyd stands smugly in the elevator, approaching the sallie port room next to Judge Cohen's courtroom.

The elevator door opens and before he is able to step out, Annabelle's husband, Tim, dressed in a bright orange jumpsuit, lunges towards Lloyd.

Lloyd has no chance to defend himself. Within seconds, he has Lloyd on the ground and is pounding his fist into Lloyd's face while clenching his t-shirt and upper neck portion of his jumpsuit.

Tim stops after punching him ten times and begins yelling at him.

"TELL ME! TELL ME, YOU ASSHOLE! DID SHE DO THAT? DID ANNABELLE REALLY DO THAT WITH YOU? YOUR SEX PLAY?" Tim yells, uncontrollably.

"SCREW YOU! YOU MURDERED MY WIFE!" yells Lloyd, trying to get up before being punched again.

"IS THIS PART OF YOUR SICK SEX SHIT?" Tim says, squeezing Lloyd by the throat with his hands.

"GET OFF ME!" yells Lloyd, trying to catch his breath while struggling hard.

Two jail deputies stand there, doing nothing. One finally tells Tim, "Let the system handle him."

"WERE YOU SLEEPING WITH HER? WERE YOU SLEEPING WITH HER?" Tim demands, before removing a razor blade from his pocket, wrapped in tape.

"Let justice take care of him," the deputy continues, a bit louder this time.

But Tim proceeds to stab Lloyd, before deputies try to pull him back.

While resisting, Tim yells, "I've waited eleven years for justice. You killed my wife and you're getting away with it! So I'm gonna kill you! Who else is gonna stop you?"

Lloyd lies in his blood, as it begins to pool around him.

67

SEARCH

It's not often that a prosecutor tries to strike a deal with a killer, but the pressure to keep tabs on Lloyd after he's released, has been mounting.

Marty, Jack Moore, and Richard walk into Lloyd's hospital room where he's been for a few days recovering from the stabbing. They surround Lloyd, watching him.

Lloyd sits in his hospital bed, falling in and out of consciousness. His prognosis is uncertain. Although groggy, he can hear most things happening around him, at least when he is awake and the pain medicine is not too strong.

Although Tim had not hit any vital organs stabbing Lloyd, he had lost so much blood that he had to undergo several blood transfusions. And his breathing had been cut off from being choked by Tim. Lloyd's face is swelled up. He is hardly recognizable.

After a couple minutes, Richard speaks up.

"I don't think he could consensually agree to anything right now. He's really in no condition. What is it you guys want to offer him?" asks Richard.

"If he tells us where Annabelle's purse is and the rest of her belongings, we will provide him with protection when he's released. You can see the world he's gonna face when he's on the outside. People will want to get at him. He needs protection," says Marty.

"It's true," agrees Jack.

"Well, that's awfully nice of you," says Richard sarcastically. "You guys couldn't even offer protection to Eva. Why should we think you're gonna be able to provide that to him?" says Richard, challenging them.

"Look. Does he want to worry about watching his back for the rest of his life, wondering if he's ever going to get killed? Look behind his back whenever he turns around or he's out on the streets? Cuz you know someone will get him. But if he gives us the information, the location where the stuff is, he never has to worry about that ever again," says Prosecutor Jack Moore.

"Well, I guess that's one less thing he'll have to worry about," says Richard. "Why do you want to do him a favor anyway?" he asks suspiciously.

"It was actually your mom's idea. She's been in contact with our office," says Marty, laughing.

"My mom?" questions Richard. "What's she doing contacting you?" he asks, concerned.

"She reached out shortly after the verdicts. Actually sending her condolences to the victims' families. She seemed really distraught over it. Told us about her difficulties with Lloyd when he was growing up, said it was her worst fear. She mentioned her and her late husband's commitment to your firm. And how she believes in the justice system, but felt it didn't turn out the way it was supposed to. Plus, you know this, but monitoring him helps us politically. We don't want him killing again and neither do you, Richard. That's bad PR for your firm," says Marty.

"My mom never told me she was in contact with you," says Richard.

"I think she's feeling a bit responsible, to the families of the victims. Like she could have done something differently. I've told her she did the best. She raised him the best she could. That none of this is her fault," says Richard.

Lloyd stirs in his bed.

"You're right, Richard. But what about the bail? She posted the bail. Had he not been out, those other assaults wouldn't have happened - Eva, Veronica, the bead store clerk. She feels bad about that too. She's really afraid what he's capable of, being released now. Maybe even hunting down Eva too, since she's pregnant now. That's why we want to talk to your boy. To find Annabelle's stuff. Your mom is on her way here. She wanted to be part of this conversation," says Jack .

"It's none of her business. Look, he's due to be released. You had your shot at him and things turned out the way they did. I'm not going to sit here and pretend like it will help him to have you guys trailing him the rest of his life, waiting for him to slip up.

"The jury bought the defense; it was sex play that got out of hand. You guys have tarnished his name in the paper. I think Mom's buying into it. Like she's beginning to believe that she could have done something. Intervened probably. But that's assuming there was something to intervene in. He was convicted of second degree. It was sex play gone bad. It wasn't premeditated. It wasn't planned," says Richard, upset.

"Don't play up the sex thing. That was b.s. and you know it. None of that happened. But good job on fooling the jury. Your boy's prints came back on the media letter that the jury never got to hear about. He claimed in that letter he killed. He never mentioned any sex play. Stop fooling yourself," says Marty defiantly.

A nurse in light pink scrubs walks in and checks the monitors attached to Lloyd with tubes and that are beeping loudly.

"When is he due to wake up?" asks Richard.

"Shortly. And Mrs. Hill is here. Were you expecting her?" the nurse asks Marty.

"Yes, can you send her in," replies Marty.

68

CLOSURE

Shortly after arriving, Lloyd's mother requests that everyone clear the room, except for Richard, Lloyd, and herself. The nursing staff, Jack, and Marty follow her demand. The deputy sheriff remains at the door, keeping an eye on Lloyd's ankle and hand, which are handcuffed to the bed rails.

Mrs. Hill, who is visibly frail, settles into a chair next to Lloyd's bed. The handles of her cloth book bag drape over her lap.

She has let the grey overwhelm her previously blonde hair bob. And now she covers it with a shabby knitted cap.

Her once smooth and freshly made-up face has been replaced with visible wrinkles and dry patches. Her dry and cracked lips look painful.

Richard watches her, feeling hopeless and wondering what of all this is her fault. What part is Lloyd's fault and what part is his? While Richard was growing up, she always treated him like her own biological son. She treated his father with such respect and loyalty. And Richard was grateful for that. What had gone wrong with Lloyd, he wonders.

Richard begins to speak to her, in an upsetting tone, but then silences himself when she looks at him with tears filled in her eyes.

Mrs. Hill holds Lloyd's hand and bows her head, mumbling some words to anyone who could hear.

The three sit in silence, until Richard finally speaks up.

"Mom, what is all this about?" he says.

She remains silent.

Lloyd's eyelids flutter until he is able to hold them up, looking at Richard first, then his mom, then back to Richard.

"Lloyd, can you hear us?" asks Mrs. Hill loudly.

Lloyd opens his eyes slowly. Richard stands up to close the hospital room door, assuring the deputy everything will be okay.

"Listen to me, both of you," says Mrs. Hill. "Lloyd, from what I understand, you will probably be released as soon as you're better. I do not support the Circuit Court's ruling. To look at these poor people, especially Annabelle's mother suffer is heartbreaking to me. I can't stay quiet any longer. If you kill again, I don't know what I'll do. I can't handle another murder, Lloyd. You need help. You assaulted that young woman when you were young. That was the reason I kicked you out. Every book you had and carried to get close to these young women, including Annabelle, was one of mine. You can't hold your resentment towards me," she says desperately.

"Mom. Calm down. Wait a minute. Lloyd was found guilty on second degree. The murder wasn't planned. And the entire case was overturned. He's an innocent man. You need to honor that. Accept it, mother," says Richard defensively.

"We need to stick together in this," he continues.

"Sticking together enables him, Richard. Don't talk to me about sticking together," she snaps back defiantly.

"Mom!" yells Richard. "Calm down. Lloyd's in no condition for this right now," he says sternly.

Lloyd shifts his eyes to Richard, for the first time appreciating his step-brother.

"Fine. Fine," says Mrs. Hill, backing down.

"What is this? What are you asking Lloyd to do concerning Annabelle's family?" asks Richard.

"This poor woman. Her poor mother. The locket she gave to her daughter has never been found. Have you seen her mother? She is hurting. I ran into her at Hal's. She's worked hard her entire life, then loses her daughter that way," she says, upset.

Lloyd stares at his mom, angrily.

"She just wants to find her purse. It has the locket. She just wants closure, Lloyd. Tell them where you hid her purse. And they'll get you the protection you need. You're going to be killed when you're out there. You need the police's help," she pleads.

"Mom, you can't trust law enforcement. It would be setting Lloyd up for disaster if they are monitoring him," says Richard distrustingly.

"They're going to protect him, not hurt him. This will protect our firm, the integrity of our firm and our reputation," she protests. "Tell them, Lloyd. Tell them. Do this for me," she pleads.

"I have no reason to do anything for you. You didn't do anything for me when you kicked me out," Lloyd says, struggling and breathing deeply.

"Lloyd. Mom put up bail for you. That helped your case in ways you won't understand. The community believed you were innocent with your family standing behind you. You can't say Mom did nothing for you," says Richard.

Lloyd looks away from them both.

"Lloyd, I know you hold that resentment against me. Let it go. Let it go. Stop carrying it with you," she says, protesting.

Lloyd looks back at her with distrust.

"Lloyd, I'm sorry. I'm sorry I did that. I did the best I could at that time, with everything that was going on. Your father abused me until I was finally able to leave," she says.

Lloyd looks away again, interlocking his fingers and thinking.

"You think I should be locked up forever, that I'm a monster," he says, muffled.

Everyone stays quiet.

"Say it. You guys think I deserved the death penalty; that I'm a rabid dog," whispers Lloyd, glaring at his mother.

Quiet fills the room.

"Just think about it, Lloyd. No one is saying anything. If the murder was an accident, it was an accident. I'm just telling you as your attorney, consider it. Consider doing this deal. Lead them to her belongings if you remember where you hid them and we can either accept the police's help or not. At least it gives you an option if you decide you need it once you're released," says Richard nonchalantly.

"This conversation is over," says Lloyd assertively.

69

SENTENCING

Lloyd's release has been delayed for a month, allowing him to recover from the injuries Tim caused. But now, it is the time and place for a release hearing. Despite sitting in a packed courtroom next to Richard in his wheelchair, still weak, it gets Lloyd no sympathy even from his mom who is sitting on the prosecution side.

The media had exposed all the evidence in Annabelle's murder that was never presented to the jury. The community was alarmed that he couldn't be retried for the murder. But as Jack Moore and his office combed through all case law, they were left with no recourse.

"Remain seated, come to order, court is now in session," barks the courtroom deputy.

Judge Cohen takes the bench in his black robe.

"We are here for resentencing in the case of People versus Lloyd Gil. Everyone in this courtroom must understand that the law requires me to release Mr. Gil. His verdicts were overturned. I am not here to discuss the Circuit Court's opinion. My job is to apply that ruling here today.

"To give the public some comfort, I have been made aware that Mr. Gil has agreed to cooperate with police in recovering his victim's belongings and has agreed to be monitored by law enforcement upon release. He was neither required to do this, but has elected to on his own will. I think this is one positive indication of his efforts toward rehabilitation.

"None of this makes up for any of the atrocities he inflicted upon our community, but will nonetheless perhaps ensure no further killings will result after his release.

"Will the victim's family members be giving statements today?" asks Judge Cohen.

"Yes, we're requesting to start with Cybil Phillips, Annabelle's mother. She would like to give a statement," says Prosecutor Jack Moore.

"Objection. My client's conviction on Annabelle's murder was reversed. That charge is now moot. She has no right to speak on a matter that is not before you, Your Honor," says Richard aggressively.

Jack Moore has to say nothing, before Judge Cohen dismisses Richard's argument and states that indeed she came to the entire trial, had to listen to the gruesome evidence, and although Lloyd's conviction was overturned, she was nonetheless affected by his actions with regard to Annabelle's murder.

Annabelle's mother comes forward to the podium and begins as strongly as possible for the mother of a murdered victim to.

Lloyd locks eyes with Selena for a moment. He instantly feels her emptiness and sadness, emotions new to him. He turns to face forward before the heaviness of his head causes his chin to slump into his neck involuntarily. It stays there for the rest of the sentencing.

"My name is Cybil Phillips. I am the mother of Annabelle. My daughter was a young, vibrant woman when she was murdered, a wife and mother to my only grandchild Selena. Not only did this evil man take my daughter, he did it in front of a child. Who knows what he would have done to her if he noticed her there.

"Now I've lost my son-in-law. He's waited for justice for Annabelle and then it was taken away. And it hasn't happened for any of us. He's facing charges for destroying this defendant's life, also, taking his wife's and his child's life. He went to Mr. Gil's home looking for him, to take care of business. But instead was met by Janice unexpectedly. He reacted and then went into shock. There's no excuse for his behavior or what he did after the fact to hide his mess.

"But I'm not so sure the defendant here, Lloyd Gil, is even capable of fully experiencing pain and the loss of his own wife or understanding how it came about.

"I'm not going to make excuses for Tim and his choices, but Mr. Gil put into effect a chain of events which pushed Tim, an otherwise gentle man, to the point of human evil. He snapped. He wanted Mr. Gil to pay for the pain that he inflicted on him.

"Tim wasn't going to stand by and watch someone be convicted of something he never did. So he came forward, admitting his guilt. Like a man.

"But this man, this man," she says, beginning to cry and pointing at Lloyd. "He killed Annabelle in front of Selena, who was only a young child at the time.

"Annabelle did nothing to deserve that. She had only befriended Mr. Gil and trusted him. Then, worst of all, he built a defense, one to suggest that Annabelle would have engaged in this sex play with him. That is ridiculous. She was neither the kind of woman to partake in that, nor would she have been enticed to. She was a Christian woman with strong morals, the way I raised her. It's insulting and degrading.

"A part of me wishes that Tim had killed this man when he had the chance to. And I feel horrible for even having those thoughts. Our family has lost hope in the criminal justice system. I rest my faith in the Lord and hope that he will work justice.

"Please do not release this man into our society. He will kill again. I know the verdicts were overturned, but please use your powers under the law to keep him behind bars. I pray that the Lord will fix him because he seems to have no remorse for what he has done to my family.

"Thank you for allowing me to speak. My grandaughter Selena wishes to speak next."

Lloyd goes numb, hearing only a swishing underwater sound for the rest of the sentencing.

70

AGREEMENT

Lloyd has a sense of nervousness he wasn't expecting when returning to the Canyon Base Lake scene. Even though they encouraged this after yesterday's release hearing, everyone in the car with Lloyd right now is disgusted by the whole crime scene visit, including Marty, Prosecutor Jack Moore, Richard, and his mom. Everyone in the car trailing behind them, holding Annabelle's mother and a victim advocate from the Prosecutor's Office, is anxious and afraid.

Part of the closure for a victim's family is sometimes for them to bear witness to the horrific crime details. It could mean looking at autopsy photos during a trial or seeing the victim's body at the coroner's office. It might be retrieving items off the clothing their loved one was wearing the night they were murdered. Sometimes it entails revisiting the crime scene and seeing for themselves where the murder took place.

Lloyd is set to be released officially in one week from custody. After discussing it at length with Richard, Lloyd agreed to show everyone where Annabelle's purse is and in return, receive a settlement from the police department for $100,000 for civil liberties violations for wrongful incarceration for Janice's murder. He agreed to be monitored by police for one year, registering his address and whereabouts with the local police department.

Five minutes away from Canyon Base Lake, Marty turns to Lloyd, who is sitting next to him in the disabled equipped van. The correction deputy pulls down the street leading to the lake.

"So you met her at Hal's, Lloyd. Take it from there."

"She wanted some computer equipment installed, so over the next couple weeks, we worked on the design, bought the different items. Eventually, we were working on it at her place," says Lloyd casually.

"And..." says Marty, waiting for Lloyd to finish.

Lloyd hesitates.

"Lloyd, part of the deal is that you tell us the details of the crime. Her family wants to know everything. That's part of the deal," says Jack Moore.

"He's right, Lloyd. It's part of the agreement," says Richard, pulling the four-page document they all signed before coming out to the lake.

"I didn't spend the last two days hashing over the verbiage on this contract for nothing. You spill the details of the murder, starting with meeting her at Hal's and ending with dumping her belongings over here. Be honest, Lloyd. Be honest," says Richard encouraging him.

Lloyd glares at him.

"It's okay, Lloyd. We're not going to judge you," says his mom, reassuringly.

"You're doing the right thing, man," says Prosecutor Jack Moore.

"I took her to the computer store right here at the Landing. We had been wanting to find a certain monitor for her system. By then, we had been putting it together for a few days and that was the last thing left to find," says Lloyd.

"The store was out of the monitor we were looking for, so we wound back up at her place.

"I remember when we started to walk back home, she told me that she was pregnant.

"It set me off. For reasons I didn't understand. I heard this swishing sound in my head. I felt like I was underwater, being suffocated. I just thought I was feeling lightheaded. I thought it was the sound of the lake. Something in the lake.

"Once we got inside her house, I felt calm, like my anxiety had gone away. But then it started up again, when I heard the girl starting to wake up. That's when it happened."

"Why, Lloyd? Why would you do that?" asks his mom.

Lloyd looks down, ashamed and stays silent.

"What happened next?" asks Marty, hurriedly, as the correction deputy pulls into the parking lot of the Landing area, a dock filled with shops and a boat store.

"I went into a rage. That's why," says Lloyd, glaring at his mother.

"And I never entirely understood it. But the doctor is saying it's about you, when you were pregnant with me..." says Lloyd, before Marty cuts him off.

"Lloyd, talk to me," redirects Marty.

"What happened after that?"

"I killed her and this relief came over me, but I could hear her daughter in the other room. I had to get out of there. So I wrapped up her body in a rug that was there. And I left with her body."

"Why'd you take her purse?"

"I wanted to make it look like a burglary. I threw some things off the coffee table, to make it look like a struggle. And I just left, with her body."

"Didn't you think about the girl?" asks Mrs. Hill.

"I don't know. Maybe I did. Maybe that's why I took the body. Then again, maybe I didn't. No one ever protected me, you didn't protect me. Why should I protect a kid like that. It meant nothing to me. I hate that I say that now, but that's how I felt at the time."

"What'd you do with her purse?" asks Marty.

"Buried it, over there," says Lloyd, pointing out a dirt area near the trees.

"I came over here the next day and buried her stuff, her clothes, her purse, everything I took from her house."

Everyone stays quiet.

"Lloyd, I'll need you to do a couple things once we park. First, I'll need you to show me where her belongings are. Next, I'll need you to not speak or answer any questions unless I ask you. I don't want you looking or speaking to Annabelle's mother at all. If she asks you a question, you'll be directed whether or not to answer it," says Marty.

"I'm not talking to anyone," says Lloyd, putting his head down, hanging it low.

The driver turns the car ignition off and begins to lower the wheelchair restraints down, so Lloyd could be released.

71

VNOK PAIN

Watching a VNOK's—victim's next of kin—pain, reliving the moments of their loved one's death can be one of the most emotionally disturbing moments for someone watching. At least for a person with a heart, like Mrs. Hill.

Prosecutor Jack Moore walks side by side with Cybil, Annabelle's mom. He explains what Lloyd told them about meeting Annabelle in the diner. Her mom would regret Annabelle having taken the waitressing job at Hal's Diner for extra money, especially when she was pregnant; as though not working there in the diner would have saved her life. Cybil would live with the guilt and the shame for not financially supporting her, anything to bring her back. None of her guilt made any sense, but to Cybil, she was convinced she could have saved her daughter's life, but failed.

The reality was that if it wasn't Annabelle, it would have been another pregnant suburban woman that Lloyd would have killed. Maybe someone else's wife, mother, or daughter. Annabelle was just a convenient target.

Cybil questions Marty if it was something sexual he was looking for. He presses on why Annabelle would have gone with Lloyd. What was it about Lloyd that attracted her to his company and allow him in her home. It was so out of character for her. Cybil had always taught her to be cautious about strangers.

"What is it that this man did or said? How did he get her to drop her guard down? It's not like her. It's not like her," she protests loudly.

Marty tries to calm her. "She trusted him, she wanted to trust him," he says.

Cybil directs her anger at Mrs. Hill.

"You raised this animal. Why didn't you do something about him? He's been like this since he was a child. And you couldn't control him? Look at all the lives he's destroyed. He's destroyed not only my family and all of the children in our family, but many families. Generations. You should have raised him better, gotten him help. You covered for him. You paid for him to have this lawyer, to get him off. You are behind all this, all of this," Cybil yells awkwardly, throwing her hands up, motioning to the lake and the forest area surrounding it.

The correction deputies surround the group closely following Lloyd. The collection technicians follow behind them.

"Let's keep moving," yells Marty, motioning for everyone to keep walking. He turns to Mrs. Hill, asking if she would push Lloyd in the wheelchair, to which he is shackled.

Marty makes his way over to Cybil, putting his hand on her shoulder, trying to console her with words for a couple minutes before returning back to Lloyd.

"So I think you said right about here, is that right? You came and dumped her belongings? We need the exact area, the best you can remember," says Marty assertively.

Lloyd directs his mom to push him in different directions, scanning the ground for a distinct kind of shrub or tree he recognizes to jar his memory.

The coolness of the air along with the cypress trees blocking any of the sun trying to shine down sends chills down Lloyd's arms. He wasn't expecting or dressed for the cold February temperature. His cough begins to set in steadily, but no one seems to care enough to console him, except his mom.

"Let's get this done. Where's the place you buried her stuff?" asks Lloyd's mom, sniffling from the cool air setting into her nasal cavity.

"Somewhere over here. I remember these trees," says Lloyd, pointing to the base of one of the cypress trees.

"I see part of something that looks like plastic," says Jack Moore.

Marty directs the forensic team to begin digging in the area indicated by Lloyd.

Slowly, they remove small shovels from their backpacks along with plastic bags.

Within ten minutes, a metal toolbox wrapped in a tarp sealed with duct tape and bungie cords has been opened and the first piece of Annabelle's clothing has been laid out on the tarp. It's her plaid shirt with her diner name tag, "Annabelle."

Cybil begins weeping uncontrollably, falling into Marty's arms. Marty tries to console her while the rest of her daughter's belongings are strewn out on the plastic. Her purse, her ID, cash, cigarettes, keys, and finally the rope and duct tape are laid out.

The last item removed from the box is a metal flashlight.

With each new item that surfaces, the reaction becomes harsher as though it breaks Cybil's heart over and over again.

"Why? Why? Why?" she repeats over and over again.

She stops after the twentieth time, when no one answers her.

72

LOSS

No one can truly understand the pain of a mother who has lost her child than one who has experienced the same. Mrs. Hill stands in the group looking in silence and disbelief at all of Annabelle's belongings strewn across the plastic. Annabelle's mother weeps on her knees, wanting to touch the items, but not being allowed to by the technicians because of their evidentiary value.

Everyone Lloyd has made contact with seems to have lost something. Richard, who stands with his arms crossed next to Lloyd, watches the technicians photograph all the items. Richard lost his wife's respect through his career choice to take on Lloyd's case. Some look at Lloyd's family and see a family having stuck together to fight for one of their own. But even Lloyd saw the reality of why Richard sacrificed for him—to build the reputation of Hill &

Associates. It was to make it as a top capital defender, the kind that news outlets pay for interviews, officials invite to speak at capital punishment symposiums, and organizations recruit to write anti-death penalty legislation.

To Richard, he expected it to be another notch on his belt, in his legal career. But at the end, it plunged him into a darkness and emptiness; the kind he had stereotyped his criminal defendants as having, the kind Lloyd had.

Cybil weeps silently. Annabelle's murder left behind a devastated family and generations of impact, similar to a tornado who wreaks havoc on entire towns, states, wiping through and destroying everything for decades to come. That's what murder does.

Marty stands near the technicians and wipes a tear from his eye before it trickles down his face. Marty had lost respect from his department, having never fully investigated a lead that was right in front of him this whole time. It was an embarrassment.

Even Judge Cohen had lost something on account of Lloyd. He lost the respect of the bench. His federal appointment was looking grim ever since the jury in The White Picket Fence Killer case had been reversed for an error he could have prevented.

Prosecutor Jack Moore stands near the shoveled dirt, which had been set aside by the forensic techs. Jack had lost respect at the Prosecutor's Office. His colleagues, who once looked up to him as being the top prosecutor of the county, now questioned the trial tactics he decided to use and the manner he directed the witness' examination. They questioned whether he was aggressive enough in trying to keep out Lloyd's defenses.

Lloyd was barely beginning to experience hurt, pain, remorse, and empathy. He had resorted to violence to gratify himself for reasons he was barely beginning to understand. Lloyd was starting to acknowledge his own defects and pent-up rage, knowing he would continue on the path he was on —a killer—if he didn't fix himself, whether in or out of custody.

Mrs. Hill stands behind Lloyd's wheelchair, with her hand resting on it. She, aside from the VNOKs, was the person affected the most. Even though she spoke with pastors, psychologists and friends, she couldn't shake the guilt she carried for having brought this monster into the world. She regretted having allowed herself to be abused by his father, staying with a man who had kicked her in the stomach so hard while pregnant with Lloyd, trying to abort him. She knew this in utero violence was what started a world of hate and rage growing inside Lloyd, all to be unleashed in the worst possible way.

Mrs. Hill carried the shame and guilt doubly, for Lloyd who had little, and herself. The pressure was like a pregnant woman, sharing all her energy, nutrients, and life with her child trying to compensate over and over again. Mrs. Hill wasn't eating for two, exercising for two or hydrating for two. In the killing context, she was crying for two, experiencing shame for two, and feeling remorseful for two.

She searched for answers. What could she do? Every time she was yelled at, such as by Annabelle's mom, sent hate mail, or read an article in the paper, it aged her over and over again. Her frailty was killing her.

There is no one who could understand more than what it was to lose someone than Mrs. Hill. She had lost Lloyd when he was eighteen years old, when she was forced to rid him from her life. It was something she would never forgive herself for, even though there was nothing to forgive herself for. It was a necessity. She never grasped the idea that even family has choices of who to help or not to help, even when it's one of their own in need.

Mrs. Hill had a loving husband, stepson, and thriving law practice she was helping her family with. All this required and deserved her attention. Some feel that you can never give up on a child, that if you brought them into this world, that they are forever your responsibility. This is how Mrs. Hill felt all these years, wondering whatever happened to Lloyd, then watching him go through his trial and beat the system. The responsibility to the world weighs heavily on the mind of a killer's mom; as much as it weighs on the mind of a victim's mother, who feels the guilt of not protecting her child from the dangers of the world.

Once the forensic techs finish photographing Annabelle's items, Marty looks up at Lloyd.

"The locket's not in the purse. Take us to where you tossed it," Marty says sternly.

73

RETRIBUTION

Marty pushes Lloyd's wheelchair through the forest area surrounding the lake. Smells of thyme and lavender fill the air. Spring is on the horizon in Tuckford County. The coolness of the air combined with the herbal scents give a crispness to the air. It's something no one is paying attention to except for Marty and Jack Moore.

Becoming desensitized to repeated crime scenes is what allows them to do their job, continue looking for and at decomposed or murdered bodies and photos of them. Fifteen years ago, the two would not have noticed the same things they can today, but the humanity of justice and the reality of their jobs set in from time to time. The human mind creates coping skills to make crime scene visits or field casings bearable.

"Lloyd, do you have any recollection where you threw the locket?" asks Marty.

"In the lake. But like I said, it was dark that night when I came back," says Lloyd matter-of-factly.

"Well, just try to remember back to that night," says Marty encouragingly.

"How deep is this lake? Is it possible to have the whole thing drained, so we don't have to deal with this," yells Cybil angrily.

"I just want to get a general idea so I know where to send the divers down the next time we're doing a search," says Marty.

"The lake's at least thirty feet deep in some areas," replies Prosecutor Jack Moore.

Around the entire lake, small landing docks extending from the land to the water stretch out. Some are roped with boats attached, while others are empty. Some butt up against small trails leading to homes, most seemingly vacation homes unoccupied.

"It was definitely off of one of these docks. I don't think it was very far from where I buried her stuff," he says, looking back about fifty yards closer to the items where the forensic department was still standing.

"I think there was some orange paint on a wood post connected to the dock," recalls Lloyd.

"Why don't we split up?" says Marty. "Go ahead and take a look at the docks we passed. For some orange paint," he continues. "We'll continue this way," he says, pointing to the remaining docks in front of them.

He, Mrs. Hill, and Lloyd continue up the way, stopping at each dock, looking for the orange paint.

"I want to say it was somewhere around here. I remember looking up and seeing the landing area. I was about in the middle of the landing area when I threw it in the water," Lloyd says, pointing to the landing area filled with shops.

"Maybe it will help to give you a visual," says Marty, rolling Lloyd's wheelchair to the end of one of the docks.

The three look out across the lake towards the landing. The wind starts to pick up, cooling their ears and numbing their noses.

Marty's cell phone begins to ring. It is Jack Moore, who is huddled with the rest of the group, close to one of the docks.

"Hey, Jack," says Marty.

"I can't hear you that well, you're breaking up," Marty continues, moving his phone away from his ear to view the level of reception on the screen.

"Stand here, please," directs Marty, motioning to Mrs. Hill to hold Lloyd's wheelchair handles before moving off the narrow dock.

"Go ahead, can you hear me?" asks Marty, talking into the phone at Jack, hoping for better reception by moving.

Mrs. Hill stands tall at the end of the dock with Lloyd in silence. They both look out into the lake.

"Why Lloyd? Why?" Mrs. Hill asks, quietly. "Why all this?" she continues disgustedly.

Lloyd turns back at his mom and gives her a look of disdain.

"It's all because of you. You turned me into this. You know that. This is all your fault," says Lloyd eerily, his dry lips pursing and his forehead stressing as his eyes squint.

"You couldn't be stopped, Lloyd. Everyone tried to help you. Demitra tried to help you learn how to submit. I can't believe I brought you into this world. You've carried this resentment with you for too long now. You've been sent to doctors, to prison, and even the system has given you a chance to change. I meant what I wrote in that Open Letter to the newspaper. Are you a rabid dog that needs to be put down? A cancer? Or can you be rehabilitated? Do you even feel anything?" says Mrs. Hill desperately.

"You did this. You're the reason I'm this way. That's what the doctor said," says Lloyd angrily.

Silence fills the air. The air sends chills against everyone's skin. Seconds seem like minutes.

Mrs. Hill begins to cry quietly. Lloyd feels her reaction for the first time, experiencing something he has never felt for her before and a slight sense of guilt for making her cry.

"I'm trying mom. I'm trying. I'm trying to understand why this happened and what's going on inside of me. I look back at all this and it's bothering me that I'm responsible for all of this."

She looks at Lloyd, wondering whether to trust what he's saying.

"Why did you toss the locket?"

"I saw it in the purse. I wanted to make it look like a robbery, like someone took it."

"You left the cash Lloyd. You could have taken that. I know what was inside that locket and I know you know too."

Marty's back faces Mrs. Hill and Lloyd as he speaks with Jack.

The forensic team huddles around a dock on the opposite side of the lake, waiting for Marty's direction.

A loud splash breaks the silence.

Marty runs up to Mrs. Hill, who is shaking, watching Lloyd and his wheelchair plummet deep into the lake.

74

HUMANITY OF JUSTICE

Sometimes we encounter a rabid dog in the criminal justice system, who neither can be stopped nor wants to be. Other times, even the most disturbed individuals can be rehabilitated, over time and with help. They can discover the root of their homicidal tendencies and repair their past and their future. They can reprogram their minds, their lives and their destinies. When they can't, we like to believe we have a system in place that deals with these people. But sometimes our system is not equipped to deal with them because they don't want to be helped or they are incapable of being helped. It is these that natural causes, a force greater, a will or human justice sometimes takes over. It is neither right nor wrong. It is the humanity of justice. It's the reality of justice.

A man takes the life of another for various reasons. Sometimes it is because of unsettled issues, rage, anger, drugs, alcohol, mental illness, a fear of abandonment, a rejection, that go back to deep-seated issues from childhood, family life, a psychiatric problem, or an anti-social personality disorder. A culmination of factors affect people. And everyone has the capacity to exercise a strong will and determination to change who they are and become who they want to be and keep their demons at bay.

But there are others who choose not to, and who are incapable of being helped. These are the dogs who abuse people, take out their problems on others, ignore the help of our mental health system and who choose instead to blame the world.

Some believe that until they are caged for life or sent to an afterlife, they will remain rabid dogs, disrupting generations of lives of innocent law abiding people.

Is Lloyd Gil one of these people? Some say, "yes," and believe the criminal justice system was ill-equipped to handle him. These are the same people who will root for the vigilantes to take care of him and hope his ill-fated karma will fester on him the rest of this life. Others say, "no," and believe he could be rehabilitated having now learned how his rage started, in utero.

Lloyd, now a free man five months after his release, opens his diary and begins writing:

"If anyone is in Christ, he is a new creation; the old has gone, the new has come."

2 Corinthians 5:17

He lifts his pen from the page of his diary, recaps it, and places his hand on Annabelle's gravestone. He looks at the gold locket, which is sitting in a small shadow box attached to her gravestone.   It looks shinier than it did after he recovered it while plummeting to the depths of the lake before making it up for air.

The multiple baby pictures representing generations of Annabelle's family cut perfectly to fit inside the locket were still in tact.

He opens his own new gold locket, adorned with a bright color photo of a newborn baby boy.   Lloyd turns it over and reads the words inscribed, "Let there be redemption. Love, Eva & Lloyd, Jr."

THE END

ABOUT THE AUTHOR

Debra Mares, the granddaughter of a Mexican migrant farm worker and factory seamstress, was born and raised in Los Angeles, is the first to graduate college in her family, and grew up dancing Ballet Folklorico and salsa. Debra followed a calling at eleven years old to be an attorney and voice for women, and appreciates international travel and culture. She holds a bachelor's degree in Political Science from UCLA and law degree from Loyola Law School, where she was an editor on the *Entertainment Law Review* and competed on the *Scott Moot Court Honors Board* and *Hispanic National Bar Association Moot Court Team*, where she placed her team second nationally and was recognized as top orator.

Debra has been a county prosecutor in Riverside, California since 2004 where she has prosecuted homicide cases and handled parole hearings for convicted murderers in the prison system. She is the co-founder and Executive Director of a life-skills and mentorship organization for at-risk youth in Riverside County. In 2012, Debra released Volume 1 of her debut legal thriller series, *The Mamacita Murders*. To follow her, visit www.DebraMaresNovels.com.

www.ingramcontent.com/pod-product-compliance
Lightning Source LLC
Chambersburg PA
CBHW031246170626
46807CB00001B/10